Praise for the
Shaker Mysteries by
DEBORAH WOODWORTH

"A complete and very charming portrait of a world,
its ways, and the beliefs of its people,
and an excellent mystery to draw you along."
Anne Perry

"Bits of Shaker lore add a fresh slant to a historical
novel that also offers a neat plot. But it is Rose
herself—intelligent, compassionate, and very strong—
whom readers will especially want to see again."
Star Tribune (Minneapolis, St. Paul)

"A marvelous heroine with wisdom and charm to
spare. Woodworth writes with grace and intelligence."
Carolyn Hart

"Readers are treated to a vivid look into a fascinating
culture while enjoying a first-rate mystery."
Publishers Weekly

"I look forward to the next episode of Sister Rose!"
Molly Weston, *Meritorious Mysteries*

Other Shaker Mysteries by
Deborah Woodworth

DEATH OF A WINTER SHAKER
A DEADLY SHAKER SPRING
SINS OF A SHAKER SUMMER
A SIMPLE SHAKER MURDER

DEBORAH WOODWORTH

KILLING GIFTS

— A —

SHAKER MYSTERY

AVON BOOKS
An Imprint of HarperCollins*Publishers*

AVON BOOKS
An Imprint of HarperCollins*Publishers*
10 East 53rd Street
New York, New York 10022-5299

Copyright © 2001 by Deborah Woodworth
ISBN: 0-380-80426-3
www.avonbooks.com

First Avon Books paperback printing: February 2001

Avon Trademark Reg. U.S. Pat. Off. and in Other Countries, Marca Registrada, Hecho en U.S.A.
HarperCollins® is a trademark of HarperCollins Publishers Inc.

Printed in the U.S.A.

10 9 8 7 6 5 4 3 2 1

For Norm, again and forever

ACKNOWLEDGMENTS

I am deeply grateful to many people who patiently gave of their time and their expertise to help me put together this story. Todd A. Burdick, Director of Interpretation and Education at Hancock Shaker Village, was invaluable for his knowledge of historical detail about the Hancock Shakers. Any errors are, of course, mine alone. For their memories and knowledge of train travel in the 1930s, many thanks to James R. Woodworth, David Schiferl, Mike Stousland, and Peter Dahoda. And, as always, I appreciate the insightful editorial comments provided by Tom Rucker; Becky Bohan; Norm Schiferl; my agent, Barbara Gislason; and my editor, Patricia Lande Grader.

AUTHOR'S NOTE

In the late 1930s, Hancock Shaker Village, in Massachusetts, was still open, though in decline. The community contained fewer than twenty-five members, only two of whom were brothers, as well as a few girls being raised by the sisters. Many buildings had been abandoned, including the lovely Round Stone Barn and the Meetinghouse. The Hancock Shakers lived a quiet life, their membership dwindling until the village closed in 1960. Hancock Shaker Village has been restored as a not-for-profit educational organization, open year round, where visitors may see how the Shakers lived during the nineteenth century.

Brother Ricardo lived in the village at the time of this story, and Fannie Estabrook was eldress of Hancock throughout the 1930s and until the village's demise. However, the following tale and Fannie's and Ricardo's parts in it are fiction.

Deborah Woodworth
May 1, 2000

JULIA MASTERS TWIRLED A HONEY-GOLD CURL AROUND HER finger and pushed out her lower lip in a pout that might have been alluring to someone other than her companion.

"I'm cold," Julia said. "I want my wrap."

"It's unseasonably warm."

"We're in for snow, and you know it." Julia's voice quivered with petulance.

"Then you should have dressed more warmly."

Julia paced the length of the unheated Summerhouse, hugging her bare arms. "Oh, stop being so mean," she said. "This is my very best dancing dress."

"So you said."

"Well, I wouldn't even have this one if it weren't for Cousin Vera in Boston. She hasn't passed me down one for winter yet—not something up-to-date. Anyway, why did I have to dress up just to meet in this stupid old Summerhouse? I'm not one of the sisters, you know."

"Indeed, you are not."

"Then why are we here?"

"I told you," her companion said with growing impatience. "I'm taking you dancing. You'll have so many invitations you'll be glad to be wearing something so pretty and light."

"You've never taken me dancing before." Julia tilted her

head and smiled, as she had earlier to her mirror. She knew her smile was fetching. Few men had ever been able to resist her. But her companion was immune to her soft shoulders and the sweet, inviting scent of the rosewater she'd swiped from the Shaker store to dab behind her ears.

The midwinter sun had drawn in the last of its rays and given the moon its turn. The silent cold enveloped Julia. Freezing and alone was an all-too-familiar state, and one she'd vowed never to feel again.

"This is silly and boring," Julia said. "If we're going dancing, then let's go. I still can't see why we had to meet here, of all places."

"It isn't silly. I wanted a quiet place. Sit down, Julia. I've brought something for you—an opportunity, shall we say? You'll understand when you see it."

"A present!" Julia spun toward the cracked wood table in the center of the Summerhouse. Her pink satin evening gown shimmered like a seashell in the moonlight as she clasped her hands together in childlike excitement. Two lengths of shiny fabric hung down her back to her waist; one of them had flipped forward over her breast, and she smoothed it back over her bare shoulder with a manicured finger.

"Sit down and be patient like a lady."

With an irritated sigh, Julia shivered and slid into a ladder-back chair. Her companion placed a package on the table in front of her, just out of reach. Julia eagerly stretched out her arm.

"What is it? I hope it's a necklace or a bracelet. Something really bright and sparkly." Julia's stiff fingers fumbled at the wrapping, a piece of calico tied with a ribbon. With a jewel or two, even if they were fake, she knew she could catch the eye of somebody important. Maybe she could get out of this boring town, go somewhere exciting, like Boston, or even New York.

Julia had managed to claw open the wrapping to find a

wooden box, one of those roundish Shaker ones. It would make a good jewelry case. She paused, savoring the thrill. She hadn't received a gift that wasn't a hand-me-down since the Christmas of '29, just after the crash. It might be years before she got another.

"I wanted you to understand."

Julia reached for the lid and lifted it.

"I wanted you to know, Julia—just a moment before . . . It's important. I wanted you to understand what you have done. Why you must pay." The voice now came from behind her. Julia did not turn around. She stared at the contents of the box, her painted eyebrows knit together and her scarlet lips parted.

"I wish I could see your face now," whispered her companion. "It would help somehow. But this way will have to suffice."

For most of the world's people, snowfalls ceased to be enchanting as soon as Christmas had passed. January and February were months to endure, especially in the Northeast, where gray skies dumped regular deposits on rolling hills and mountains and winter-weary villages.

The Shakers of Hancock, Massachusetts, however, not being of the world, watched with growing anticipation as the dreary midwinter days passed, bringing them closer to their treasured holiday—Mother Ann's Birthday. Their beloved foundress had been born on February 29, and since it wasn't currently a leap year, the celebration was planned for the first of March, less than two weeks away.

Preparations consumed the energy of the small band of remaining Shakers, which was why no one had so much as glanced toward the Summerhouse for days—despite its proximity to the large Brick Dwelling House where they lived, ate, and worshiped. After all, the sisters had scrubbed the small building months earlier, once the weather had turnèd too cold for afternoon tea. So there'd been no reason to go near it. No one had even noticed that the door was slightly ajar. As Eldress Fannie Estabrook explained to the Pittsfield police, no one had the slightest idea how long the body had been in there. It had probably happened at night, though, Fannie speculated, when the residents of the dwelling house were fast asleep after a long day of work.

Fannie knew the identity of the unfortunate young woman, as did all the sisters. Her name was Julia Masters, and she'd often helped out in the Fancy Goods Store, selling Shaker products to the world. No one could even guess why she'd been found dressed for a summer night on the town, her long dark blond hair piled on her head in disheveled curls, a style more reminiscent of the turn of the century than the late 1930s.

The quiet village of Hancock had never experienced a murder inside its boundaries, and the pacifist Shakers, unlike their worldly neighbors, went to great lengths to avoid having to view the body. Nevertheless, word got around. Julia's shell-pink silk-satin gown raised a few eyebrows among the Believers and some snickers among the hired help. Within hours, everyone had heard exactly how Julia looked when she was discovered by one of the hired men, Otis Friddle, on his way to work at the Barn Complex.

Her dress was a few years out of style, but by all accounts quite glamorous. The bias-cut bodice and narrow skirt hugged Julia's slender body as if it had been sewn around her. The same shiny pink fabric gathered into straps, which fastened at her shoulders and then flared into pieces that hung down her bare back like two narrow capes. It looked like one of the lengths of fabric had been used to strangle her. Her arms were bare, the skin translucent. With no body warmth to melt it, snow swirled around her frozen feet, shod in light dancing shoes, and settled as a thin dust above the narrow leather straps circling her ankles. Julia had been found slumped against the straight slats of an old Shaker chair, but her arms lay on the table in front of her, stretched forward.

"You will come right away, won't you, Rose?" pleaded Eldress Fannie. "Say you will. We are beside ourselves. Well, we all just . . ." The telephone line crackled and swallowed her next words. In an effort to hear better, Rose Callahan, eldress of the North Homage Shaker village, edged the telephone receiver under her thin white indoor cap and a thick layer of curly red hair.

"Slow down, Fannie. I can barely understand you." The longer Rose served as eldress, the more commanding her voice became. "Did you say that one of the sisters has died? I am with you in spirit, you know that, but—"

"*Not* one of the sisters," Fannie said, her voice quickening with frustration. "A young woman from Pittsfield. She helped out in the store sometimes, during busy seasons. Julia, her name was. A pleasant girl, friendly. Maybe too friendly, if you believe the rumors, but that's no reason to kill her, surely."

"Someone killed her?" Rose realized she was shouting to be heard, but she knew she was alone in the Ministry House, which she shared with Elder Wilhelm Lundel. Not content to let the brethren work on their own, Wilhelm had gone to the Medicinal Herb Shop to "help," though his knowledge was minimal.

"I'm afraid so," Fannie said, "and in our Summerhouse, too. I doubt I'll ever again wish to sip tea and watch a sunset from that dear little building. One of our own novitiates is under suspicion by the police, but we can't believe it. So you must come help us, Rose. You've . . . well, you've done this sort of thing before—remember you wrote to me about that dreadful situation last year with the poor man who was found hanged in your orchard?"

Rose sighed. She shouldn't have written that letter. It was a moment of hubris, for which she was about to be punished.

"And you *are* one of us," Fannie continued. "You will understand."

Rose hesitated only a moment. She didn't relish the idea of a midwinter dash across country. She'd never experienced February in Massachusetts, nor had she ever yearned to do so. She hated to miss Mother Ann's Birthday with her own village, and the first signs of spring in northern Kentucky. But Fannie was right—Rose would likely approach the crisis with deeper understanding and a more open mind than would anyone from the world.

"Of course I will come and help out," Rose said. "I'll pack immediately."

TWO

"HERE I AM!" A DIMINUTIVE FIGURE WRAPPED IN A CREAM wool coat swept like a snow swirl into the Ministry House library, where Rose had just hung up the telephone after Eldress Fannie's plea for her to travel to Massachusetts. Gennie Malone, Rose's former protégée, stood before her, eager auburn curls snaking out from under a rust felt hat with a narrow curled brim.

"Gennie!" Rose hugged the much smaller woman. "It's lovely to see you, but . . ." She held Gennie at arm's length. "You have that desperate look I remember from the times I'd assign you to help out in the kitchen."

"With Sister Elsa," Gennie said. "Very astute of you, Rose."

"Sit," Rose commanded. She lifted a ladder-back chair from its wall pegs and settled it close to her own desk chair. Gennie, who was not yet twenty, flopped down and heaved an exaggerated sigh.

"Tell me."

"It's Grady," Gennie said in the affectionate, irritated tone she reserved for her fiancé, Grady O'Neal, acting sheriff of Languor County. "Ever since Sheriff Brock resigned, Grady has spent every minute working, or thinking about work, or planning how to keep the job of sheriff."

"And you are feeling lonely?" Rose tried not to sound

7

hopeful. She now and then let herself wish for Gennie's return to North Homage, as a Believer. They could work side by side, she and Gennie, as they used to. Maybe Andrew, their trustee, would be willing to turn over the culinary herb industry to Gennie. Gennie loved herbs so, and she'd make a wonderful second trustee. *Sister Gennie . . . the name sounds so natural, as if it had been created especially for—*

"Grady wants me to marry him right away." Gennie pulled off her hat and ran her fingers through her tousled bob, which bounced around her face.

No mere hat can flatten those curls. Rose released her fond picture of "Sister Gennie" covered from head to toe in modest Shaker clothing.

"Where would he find time for a wedding?" Rose asked.

"I'm supposed to plan it," Gennie said. "Grady's so busy, he insists the only way we'll be able to see each other is if we're married. Besides . . ." Gennie's gaze left Rose's face and wandered over the neatly shelved books lining the wall. "He wants to start . . ." Gennie bit her lower lip.

"To start a family?" Rose asked.

Gennie nodded.

"You know, Gennie, I do understand what happens when you get married. I don't choose to participate, but if you do, it certainly won't affect our friendship." Rose shifted her position to recapture Gennie's gaze. "And I promise I won't perish of shock. I believe that some are called to celibacy, and some are not."

Gennie relaxed with a chuckle. "I suspect *I'm* more easily shocked than you are. Or maybe I just feel guilty for choosing the world over a celibate life of faith. I keep wondering if I made the right decision."

Rose kept her hopes under control this time. "You're just feeling confused right now because of Grady's pressure to marry. Remember, you can always insist you're not ready yet. Grady may be eager for a family, but you are still quite young."

Gennie's pretty face scrunched into an unhappy frown. "I do want to marry him," she said, "but—oh, I wish I could think more clearly." Her expression brightened. "Everything was so much simpler when I lived here with you and Agatha and the sisters. Could I . . . could I come back and stay awhile? Business is slow at the flower shop right now, so I'm not needed there. Couldn't I come and stay just a week or two, through Mother Ann's Birthday? I know you can always use more hands right now, with the celebration coming up. I'd even be willing to work in the kitchen—well, some of the time, anyway. I used to enjoy helping to make Mother Ann's Birthday Cake."

Rose fixed her with a raised eyebrow. "As I recall, you used to lick all the bowls. No wonder you liked the assignment."

"Elsa told on me, didn't she?" Elsa was almost everyone's least favorite sister, because of her frequent mean-spirited remarks, her un-Shaker–like ambition, and her habit of watching the other sisters for any breach of conduct, which she would promptly report to Elder Wilhelm.

Rose smiled. "I told the kitchen sisters to *let* you lick the bowls. You didn't get sweets very often, and I knew you loved them."

Gennie leaned forward with a beseeching look that Rose found hard to resist. "You've always understood me, Rose, even when I didn't understand myself. I could always talk to you. That's why I just know I can work out this wedding dilemma if only you'll let me stay here awhile and talk it all over with you, like I used to."

"Certainly, you can stay here as long as you wish, my dear, but you see, I won't be here." Rose quickly explained about Eldress Fannie's plea for her to come straight to Hancock.

Gennie's confused and bereft expression transformed into

glee. "How perfect! I'll come with you. When do we leave? Tomorrow?"

"But, Gennie, I don't think—"

"Don't you see, Rose? This couldn't be better. We can help each other!" The gold flecks in Gennie's brown eyes glittered with excitement, and Rose knew her well enough to assume that it was not the occurrence of violent death that gave her such a thrill. Well, not entirely anyway—Gennie did have a most worldly yen for adventure.

"This is a long journey, Gennie, and there may be danger at the other end."

"I've never been stronger and healthier. Oh please, Rose, please let me go with you. I've been saving money from my job at the flower shop, so I can pay my own way, and we can keep each other company and plan our strategy, and—"

"What about Grady? What will he say?"

"Grady can't tell me what to do." Gennie's small chin tightened. "Please, Rose, let me come with you. I've barely even been out of Kentucky!"

Rose wilted against the hard wood of her chair back. "I'll think about it. Call me on the telephone me this evening, and I'll let you know my decision."

"Wonderful!" Gennie bounced out of her chair, grabbed her hat and coat, gave Rose a quick hug, and headed for the library door. She crossed the threshold, then poked her head back inside. "I'll go home and start packing. Just in case."

Rose permitted herself a tired sigh and pushed an errant fluff of red hair back under her thin indoor cap. She'd spent an hour on the telephone, gathering information about the train trip to Hancock. She'd made the trip before, but never in midwinter and never with little hope of a ride to the railway station. Somehow she'd have to get to the Union Terminal in Cincinnati, and with Mother Ann's Birthday so close, it was doubtful that one of the brethren could be spared to drive her. With the country in such a slump, railway service from Languor, the nearest town, had been cut to a minimum. If she had to take the train to Cincinnati, it could add a day to her trip. Why had she ever agreed to do this? Surely there were competent police in Massachusetts.

Rose straightened the pages of notes scattered over the Ministry library desk. She'd make sense of them later, after her evening meal. She almost preferred the muddle of times and dates in front of her to the prospect of eating in the small Ministry dining room with Elder Wilhelm Lundel. The meal was sure to be a battle. Wilhelm would forget, as he often did, that they were now equal—elder and eldress—spiritual leaders of their community. He would forbid her to go off to Hancock and especially to get involved in another murder investigation. On the other hand, this time he couldn't threaten to have her removed as eldress, since Hancock was just down the road from Mount Lebanon, the Lead Society, in New York. The Ministry surely knew of Fannie's cry for help.

The bell summoning Believers to the evening meal rang at the same time as the telephone. Rose hesitated only a moment. A phone conversation with almost anyone was preferable to supper with Wilhelm. Eventually she'd have to inform him of her travel plans, but she was more than willing to put off their talk for a bit longer. She picked up the receiver.

A call was coming through from the Sheriff's Office. She should have known. By now Gennie would have told Grady about the trip to Massachusetts, no doubt expressing confidence that Rose would let her come along. Grady was a kind, honest young man, but overprotective where Gennie was concerned. He was only slowly learning that, for all her gentle sweetness, Gennie was a determined young woman.

"Rose? You aren't seriously thinking of taking Gennie all the way to Massachusetts, are you?"

"Well, I—"

"It's the middle of winter, for heaven's sakes. That's a dangerous trip. I can't have her traipsing around the countryside being accosted by who knows what on the railway. She's just a young girl!"

Apparently, Grady didn't consider the trip dangerous for Rose. She decided it best not to point out that if Gennie was such a "young girl," she had no business getting married. "I haven't yet told Gennie she could come along, Grady. I said I'd let her know later."

"Rose, it's outrageous to even consider taking her. I can't allow—"

"Gennie wants very much to come, and I am indeed seriously considering letting her. In fact, I'd enjoy having her." Grady was beginning to irritate her.

"Yes, but from what Gennie said, this isn't just a pleasure trip. You're going there to look into a murder, aren't you? I don't personally know the local police in Pittsfield, but I'm sure they can handle the investigation. I guess I can understand why the Hancock Shakers would want you there to keep an eye on things, but I can't see why Gennie should go. She'll just start investigating on her own and get herself into dangerous situations. She's done it before, but I've always been around to—"

"Rescue her? Grady, you can't possibly always be around, and Gennie is an adventurous young woman. I should hope it is one of the reasons you love her."

Grady mumbled something Rose was grateful not to be able to hear.

"Gennie is smart and resourceful," Rose said. "She'll be a great help to me." Until that moment, she hadn't realized she'd made up her mind. Well, Grady had only himself to blame; he needed to learn that Gennie could take care of herself.

Static over the telephone line covered what was no doubt

a huge sigh. "You're both unbelievably stubborn, you know that, don't you?" Grady's voice conveyed defeat. "When must you leave?"

"Tomorrow, if possible."

"All right, but I won't have Gennie sitting up all night in a coach. I'll take care of arranging the accommodations."

"Grady, you know full well that our Gennie is independent-minded, and she might not want you arranging everything for her."

"Nevertheless, leave the tickets to me. Furthermore, I'll be driving you myself to Cincinnati, to the terminal. I'll call this evening to let you know what time I'll be picking you up tomorrow."

Rose opened her mouth and closed it again. Grady could be imperious, but he had just solved her worst problem, besides confronting Wilhelm—transportation to the station.

"Rose?" Grady's normally firm voice quavered slightly. "Is Gennie . . . I mean, does she want to get away from me? Do you think she doesn't want to marry me?"

"Just give her time, Grady. Let her have her wings, and she will probably fly back to you." Rose was not unsympathetic—in her past, she had felt the joy and the painful uncertainty of worldly love. But she was very grateful to have chosen the path of celibacy; it was less befuddling.

"Far be it from me to interfere with thy calling," said Elder Wilhelm, one bushy white eyebrow arched in disdain. His insistence on using archaic language only increased the effect. "Though I can't imagine why the death of a shop girl should be of any concern to thee. It isn't as if she'd been a Shaker or even a novitiate."

Wilhelm had finished his evening meal during Rose's telephone conversation with Grady, and now the elder blocked the entrance to the Ministry dining room with his stocky, broad-shouldered body. Wilhelm wore his usual loose, brown work clothes patterned after those of the nine-teenth-century brethren. His thick white hair was cut just to the nape of his neck, and he was clean-shaven, as decreed by the era he so admired, a century earlier, when the Believers were strong in number and highly expressive in their faith. He held his flat-topped, wide-brimmed work hat at his chest, to demonstrate his intention to go back to work as soon as he'd finished this unimportant conversation.

Rose wished Wilhelm would move away from the dining room door. She was hungry, and she could still smell the baked ham and pumpkin bread Lydia, the Ministry's kitchen sister, had brought from the Center Family kitchen and re-heated for them.

Wilhelm regarded her with cold blue eyes. Somehow he conveyed impatience while rooted in place.

"The tragedy occurred on village property," Rose said. "The woman who was killed worked with the Hancock sisters in their Fancy Goods Store."

Wilhelm snorted in derision, implying it was to be expected that murder would result from such a foolish pursuit as selling fancy goods to the world.

"She was found in the Summerhouse by a farm worker hired by the village, and one of their novitiates is under suspicion. The situation could hardly be of *more* concern to the Hancock Believers—and therefore to me!"

Rose forced herself to stand her ground, while Wilhelm drew air into his barrel chest as if preparing to belt out a homily.

"Our brothers and sisters at Hancock need a firmer hand at the helm," he said. "Fannie is pure of heart, I am sure, but she is still merely . . ." Wilhelm's gaze turned heavenward.

"Merely a woman?" Rose completed his sentence in a dangerous whisper. "Like Mother Ann was merely a woman?"

Wilhelm shrugged his massive shoulders. "We both know

full well what has been happening to our Society. We grow weaker as we lose strong, young brethren. At North Homage, we at least have a community that is still productive, but in the East, the Society is mostly women these days. Women leading women. What place is there for brothers anymore? Why live as a Believer if thy life is to be governed by women?" For once, Wilhelm's wind-roughened face showed sadness, rather than anger and scorn. "Moreover," he added, "the theology left us by Mother Ann gave men and women equal footing; it did not place women above men."

For a moment, Rose was silenced. For her, the fading number of brethren in the Society had meant more difficulties for everyday life, but she had not thought about how it must feel to be one of those brethren. She found herself feeling a touch of sympathy for Wilhelm, and it surprised her. Then he gave her a faint smile, an expression Rose had come to dread.

"It doesn't surprise me that Hancock is scurrying for help; they have no elder to take control and deal effectively with the world. I suppose the best poor Fannie could think of was to send for thee." He pushed past Rose, and she decided to let him have the last word.

"By the way," Wilhelm said, behind her. "I sent thy portion of the evening meal back with Lydia for distribution to the poor, since thy schedule does not permit thee to appear at serving time."

With a heavy heart and an empty stomach, Rose walked through the Ministry dining room, past her untouched white place setting, and opened the door to the small kitchen. Lydia had gone already and taken the remains of the meal with her. Wilhelm's few dishes and utensils had been washed and left to drain dry. Rose opened the door of the small refrigerator and found it empty. In the pantry she found a small crust of brown bread, wrapped in a cloth, and an opened jar of raspberry jam. It would have to do. She carried her meager meal into the dining room and sat at her place. She was glad at least to be alone with her thoughts.

The winter sun had nearly set, and the darkening dining room windows seemed to chill the cozy room. Rose savored the chewy bread with its sweet topping, but it wasn't enough to lighten her sense of dread. Wilhelm had been right about the serious decline of men in the few remaining Shaker villages. She thought about Hancock. She had visited briefly, and she remembered that it had dwindled to mostly sisters. According to Fannie, in the past few months, the village had been blessed with the arrival of a goodly number of novitiates, potential Believers. Several of these hopefuls were men, and one of them was now suspected of murder. Rose knew that Believers would never, ever condone killing, even if it was sanctified by war. They would never knowingly hide a killer. Still, would it not be deeply important to Hancock that these men remain free to sign the Covenant?

Rose had the full support, the fervent pleas, of the eldress of the Hancock Society. What if Rose was unable to prove the suspected novitiate innocent of the crime? What if she had to be the one to turn him over to the police? Yet Rose could not quell her most chilling fear—that if she did not lend her aid, a murderer might be free to destroy life once again.

THREE

THE LOW-HANGING SUN BRIEFLY ESCAPED THE CLOUDS AND
bronzed the winter countryside as Grady O'Neal's brown
Buick followed a rutted back road that led out of North
Homage and north to Cincinnati. A weary Rose sat in the
backseat, throwing her arms across the luggage each time
the car bounced over a hole or veered to avoid a rock. Gennie sat in the front seat, gazing with simmering excitement
at the countryside as if she'd never seen it before. She was
too thrilled even to chatter, for which Rose was grateful.

Grady simmered with something darker—worry, perhaps.
"I made a call last night to Pittsfield," he said, raising his
voice so Rose could hear him over the noise of the motor.
Rose noticed the tight cords in the back of his young neck
and his quick sideways glance at Gennie.

"Why?" asked Gennie.

"You said you didn't know anyone in Pittsfield," Rose said
at the same time. Both their voices snapped with suspicion.

"Well, I couldn't let you two go out there and walk into
who-knows-what without trying to make sure you'd be safe.
I figured you'd both be angry, but that's—well, that's just the
way I am."

"Interfering?" Gennie asked.

Grady's shoulders twitched and his knuckles whitened on
the steering wheel.

Rose held her breath, waiting for an argument to begin. She hoped Grady would keep his attention on the road. Gennie and Grady were young, in love, and had grown up only miles from each other, yet they came from such different backgrounds. Orphaned at ten years old, Gennie had been raised and educated by the Shakers. She had been taught and shown that men and women were equal in God's eyes and, therefore, she would expect Grady to treat her as a partner. Grady had grown up in the world. The only son in a wealthy, tobacco-farming family, he'd attended college, served as deputy and now as sheriff, and he was used to having influence.

When Rose saw them together, it reminded her of trying to blend cold butter into milk; no matter how much she chased and mashed those little bits of butter, they remained separate unless she heated the mixture. Grady and Gennie's love for each other, when it prevailed, smoothed their differences. The rest of the time, they couldn't agree on much of anything.

Rose was tempted to indulge once again in her "Sister Gennie" reverie, but Grady surprised her. After a few moments of tense silence, he flexed his shoulders and spoke in a low voice. Without a thought that his words might not be meant for her hearing, Rose leaned forward.

"Gen," he said, "I know you think I'm bossy, and maybe I am, a bit, but it's because I'm worried. I just want to protect you."

"I'll be with Rose."

"I know, and I know you've both handled danger before. Maybe that's what worries me. You encourage each other."

"We both want the truth, Grady. It's what Rose taught me. Agatha, too. Your people brought you up to protect folks who are weaker or poorer than you, so you became a sheriff. The Shakers taught me to be honest and to abhor the killing of one human being by another." Gennie's voice brightened.

"So you see, we want the same thing, both of us. I worry about you, too, but I don't ask you to stop being a sheriff because it's dangerous, do I?"

"No, but—"

"So I deserve the same consideration from you." Gennie gave a quick nod of satisfaction, as if she'd just deciphered an obscure coded message. She turned back to the car window. The road had smoothed as they neared Cincinnati, though signs of desperate poverty dotted the landscape. Tattered shacks clustered at the base of rolling hills, stark brown with winter. Come spring, not far off, a near-tropical lushness would blanket the hills and disguise some of the destitution.

Grady's silence gave Rose a chance to break in with the questions she'd been burning to ask. "Who did you call in Pittsfield, Grady? The police, I assume?"

"Yeah, I got the chief's name and just called him at home. At first he was pretty sore that you all were butting—"

Gennie's head whipped toward him.

"Sorry, I mean that you'd be investigating, too. But I think I convinced him you could be useful. I told him a bit about how you'd helped the Languor Sheriff's Office in the past, and especially how much understanding you can add about the Shakers and how they think."

"So you indicated we would be his eyes and ears in Hancock?" Rose asked.

"Well, more or less."

Rose sat back to think through the implications of the role in which Grady had placed them. It would be best not to advertise any connection with the police if she hoped to gain the trust of the folks she'd be questioning, most of whom were strangers to her.

"His name's O'Malley, and he seemed like a reasonable guy," Grady said with a nervous jerk of his head toward the

backseat. "I don't think he'll deliberately make things difficult for you. He even shared some information with me."

"What?" Rose wasn't hopeful that she'd learn anything
Eldress Fannie hadn't told her already.

"They have a suspect," Grady said.

"The young novitiate?"

"Yeah, Sewell Yates was his name. I've got some notes I'll
give you at the terminal. Seems he was pretty friendly with
the victim before he decided to become a Shaker, and some
folks in Pittsfield suspect they never really broke it off."

Old information, Rose thought. "They have no real evidence, though, do they?"

"Not much. Everybody they've interviewed at Hancock
says the suspect was still overfriendly with the girls, despite
wanting to become a Shaker and all. More than one witness
saw him flirting with a couple of the hired girls, including
the victim."

"That's hardly evidence," Gennie said. She'd learned a lot
about such things since meeting Grady. "Flirting with someone doesn't mean you're getting ready to kill her. Maybe
this Sewell is just a Winter Shaker and only *says* he wants to
sign the Covenant. I'm surprised the eldress hasn't tossed
him out by now."

Grady didn't answer as he swerved to avoid a skinny
jackrabbit that leaped out of a culvert, right in front of the
Buick.

"Grady," Rose said when she'd straightened up again,
"did Chief O'Malley have anything to say about the murder
itself? About the place where the body was found or the
girl's clothing? Fannie said she was dressed for a summer
dance."

Grady swerved again to avoid something Rose couldn't
see, and it was several moments before he spoke. "Yeah, he
did mention something about that," he said slowly. "He's got
a theory. He thinks the strangling was done somewhere else,

maybe in the suspect's bedroom, which was in the Shaker dwelling house next door. Then O'Malley thinks the killer carried the body out to the Summerhouse and left her there like that's where it happened."

"But why?" Rose asked.

"Well, his idea is that the killer wanted to confuse folks about the actual time of death by chilling the body. Maybe he wanted to establish an alibi or just make it tough for anyone else to establish one."

Could there possibly be a Shaker, or even a novitiate, so calculating as that? Rose sat back against the leather seats and pulled her long, wool cloak tightly around her.

The Cincinnati Union Terminal did not seem to awe Rose, but then she'd seen it before. Gennie, on the other hand, had been only once to Cincinnati, as a young girl, before her parents had died. It had been Christmastime, a few years before the stock market crash, and they'd gone to Cincinnati to see the glorious decorations and to shop. Gennie's years with the Shakers had certainly been happy and safe, but she yearned for some of that long-ago excitement. Union Terminal brought it back to her.

Gennie linked her arm through Grady's and flashed him a smile. "Do we have time to look around, even a little?"

Grady grinned and squeezed her arm. "I thought you might want to, so I brought us here half an hour ahead of schedule."

"You two explore to your heart's content," Rose said. "I'm going to splash some water on my face. I'll meet you at the ticket booth."

Gennie suspected Rose was giving them time to say goodbye and perhaps to settle their tiff before separating for who knew how long. She smiled her thanks to Rose, who picked up her small satchel and disappeared into the crowd. Gennie felt a brief pang of loneliness, then shrugged it off. She released Grady's arm and twirled slowly to take in the huge terminal. Tilting her head upward, she gazed at the high domed ceiling. The loneliness hit again as her own movements reminded her of the Shaker dancing worship, in slow motion.

This will never do, Gennie told herself sternly. With the Shakers, she had always felt loved, but an outsider all the same. She swept off her hat and shook out her curls, bringing herself back to the world, where she belonged. She turned to Grady, who watched her with warmth in his deep brown eyes. A lock of his hair, straight and brown and difficult, had fallen across his forehead, as it always did. Gennie reached up and smoothed it back in place. As soon as she removed her hand, it fell forward again, and they both laughed.

In an instant, Grady grabbed her by the shoulders and pulled her toward him. He kissed her on the tip of her nose, triggering another giggle, which he silenced with a kiss full on her mouth, right there in the Cincinnati Union Terminal, while scads of people brushed past them in all directions. Finally he loosened his embrace and held her at arm's length, smiling into her eyes. She had never felt so happy, not even with Rose and Agatha and all the other sisters.

Gennie gazed back at him, wishing to extend the moment, but something distracted her—something behind Grady but still within her field of vision. Movement swirled around them, travelers with places to go and little time to get there. Besides herself and Grady, only one other figure stood still. A tall, broad-shouldered man in a double-breasted navy-blue suit lounged against a post, smoking a cigarette. His blue hat was tilted so that the black ribbon band appeared where his left eye would have been. The right eye, however, looked directly at her.

She shivered and rubbed her upper arms. The man must have realized she'd caught him staring, and he shifted his gaze to the surrounding crowd. He dropped his half-smoked cigarette on the floor, stubbed it out with his heel, and strolled away.

"Anything wrong, Gen? Are you cold?" Grady slipped out of his wool overcoat and put it over her shoulders. She didn't protest. It was easier to acquiesce to a sudden chill than to admit that a rude stranger had spooked her for a moment. If Grady knew, he'd try again to keep her from leaving with Rose, and that was the last thing Gennie wanted to risk. She just hadn't traveled much, that was all. She'd gone from the gentle Shaker life to Languor, which might be the county seat, but was little more than a small town. She worked in a florist's shop with Grady's sister, lived in a boardinghouse for young women, and spent her off hours with Grady and his people. Gennie straightened her shoulders and lifted her small chin. She needed this trip, and nothing would stop her from taking it.

"I'm fine now," she said, handing Grady his overcoat. "Come on, let's look around. Isn't this the most beautiful place?"

"It's almost time to meet Rose," Grady said, without enthusiasm. "Let me just pick up a *Cincinnati Enquirer*, since we're here." They'd paused near a kiosk that sold newspapers, magazines, cigars, and cigarettes. "Pick a couple of magazines, Gen. It's a long train ride."

Though she thought she'd be perfectly happy watching the countryside breeze by, Gennie picked up the latest editions of the *Ladies Home Journal* and *The American Home*. Might as well find out what she could look forward to as a married woman. Since the age of ten until just over a year ago, she had been living in a community where men and women slept, ate, and worked separately, joining one another only for worship—and for Union Meetings, where they could chat while sitting several feet across from each other. She'd missed the training most girls got growing up in a worldly home. Sometimes, when she was talking with her new girlfriends, she felt about twelve years old. Other times she felt much older than she was.

Gennie stowed her purchases in her satchel as Grady paid the wizened old man sitting on a stool inside the kiosk. While she waited, she opened another magazine at random to an ad showing a woman in a figure-hugging dress with slightly puffed sleeves. The model lounged in a chair, smoking a Camel. A few pages later, several brides in close-fitting satin wedding gowns admired an ornate set of sterling silver dinnerware. This was too much for Gennie. The Shakers had taught her the value of simplicity, and the picture seemed cruel in times like these, when so many had so little. She flipped the magazine shut. As she returned it to its display shelf, a man hurried up to the kiosk and bumped Grady's shoulder in his haste. Grady dropped his change, and both men bent down to retrieve it. Their backs were to Gennie.

The man leaned toward Grady and mumbled something that must have been an apology, because Grady smiled, and said, "No harm down. Don't give it a thought." Gennie felt a rush of warmth. Grady was such a gentleman, so polite, even to clumsy strangers. The man nodded once and turned to go on his way. Gennie's chest tightened as she saw his face. He was the same man who'd had a leisurely smoke and watched Grady and her embrace.

Now was the time to tell Grady her fears, but still she resisted. All sorts of people lived in the world, and some of them were men with less than honorable intentions. This man might be one such. Perhaps he had listened to their conversation and knew that Grady would not accompany her on her journey. He might not know about Rose's existence. What if he had selected Gennie for some evil purpose of his own? Would she be worldly enough to handle him? *Well, I'll just have to be, that's all. I'm going on this trip, and that's that!* She decided not to mention the incidents to Rose, either. No point in causing her worry.

When they reached the ticket booth, they found Rose waiting on a wooden bench, one arm draped over the satchel next to her. She looked like a visitor from the previous century. Her long, loose dress and hooded cloak might have gone unnoticed, but the palm sugar-scoop bonnet over her thin, white indoor cap gave her away. The clothing of passersby ranged from smart to worn, but they all stared. Rose seemed oblivious. Gennie was willing to bet that the book on her lap was a copy of the *Testimonies of Mother Ann Lee*, the Shaker foundress. Rose hadn't been an eldress for very long—not much longer than Gennie had been out in the world. They both still had much to learn.

Grady collected their tickets and handed them over with clear reluctance. "I've gotten you berths together for overnight, so you won't have to sit up in coach."

"Grady, you didn't have to pay for my ticket," Rose said. "The Society can reimburse—"

"Nonsense. I can afford it, and I want the two of you to be as comfortable as possible. It's too bad you couldn't have delayed your trip until summer; I could have gotten you a roomette on one of those fancy new Pullmans."

"Yea, it was rude of the killer not to wait," Rose said quietly.

Gennie grinned and noticed that Grady, ever polite, pretended not to hear. He accompanied them to the tracks and hailed a redcap to stow Gennie's extra luggage in the baggage car.

"Remember, call me every other night, Gen," he said, and gave her a farewell kiss. "You will at least try to stay out of trouble, won't you?"

Gennie merely laughed and gave his hand a quick squeeze. She couldn't blame him for being worried; she supposed she would be, too, if he were going off to investigate a murder hundreds of miles away. It was good for him to find out what it felt like.

"She'll be fine, Grady," Rose said. "We are not going off into uncharted territory. Hancock is as quiet and gentle a village as North Homage." At Grady's raised eyebrows, she added, "Well, perhaps *more* quiet and gentle, in some ways—at least, under ordinary circumstances. With God's grace and Mother Ann's assistance, circumstances will be ordinary again in no time."

"Now tell me everything," Gennie said. "What's the plan? What part shall I play? Will you call me your assistant, or should I just wander in and ask to be a novitiate? What do you think? Oh, I have an idea—didn't you tell me the dead girl worked in the Fancy Goods Store? What if I ask for a job there? Then I could room in Hancock, couldn't I? That might be easier, because I could chat with all the other hired help, and I wouldn't have to pretend to be a Believer, although I could, of course, and that might be—"

"Gennie, slow down! We have lots of time before we reach Pittsfield," Rose said. They'd barely settled into a coach car, stowed their small satchels on the floor near their feet, and pulled away from the station. Not five minutes earlier, Gennie's face had been streaked with tears as she'd waved good-bye to Grady.

"Let me gather my thoughts for a bit, and then we'll talk." Rose patted Gennie's arm, then leaned her head back against the seat and closed her eyes.

Gennie couldn't help a small sigh. Rose seemed so calm about everything. She wasn't interested in watching the scenery or exploring the train or even planning their investigation. Well, it wouldn't hurt to explore by herself, would it? She stood and brushed the creases out of her new wool suit. Rose opened her eyes.

"I'm just going to look around the train," Gennie said, "so you can have some quiet."

Rose's eyes were closed again before Gennie had left her

window view and edged into the corridor. Gennie didn't yet have her train legs, and she stumbled as the car rounded a curve. She reached the door and hesitated. Though she'd taken several short train rides since entering the world, she'd never walked from car to car by herself. Grady had always been there to hold her elbow as they negotiated the unsteady passage.

She squared her small shoulders, pulled open the door, and stepped outside. She expected the roar of the wind past the speeding train, but it seemed louder than she'd remembered, now she was on her own. The shifting floor over the coupling just about sent her scurrying back inside the car behind her. Instead, she scolded herself. After all, she was the one who didn't want to be treated like a helpless baby. She hurried to the next car and congratulated herself on her bravery.

The thrill was beginning to fade after Gennie had traversed three more cars full of sleepy, bored passengers. She decided to try just one more. As soon as she entered the next car, she had that delicious naughty feeling she got each time she tried on a stylish gown, especially when the bodice was cut a shade low for Shaker comfort. She had found the club car. She stepped inside, wrinkling her nose at the acrid mixture of cigar and cigarette smoke. The few women in the car sat close to the door, reading or chatting. Despite the early hour, several men relaxed in stuffed easy chairs around small tables, sipping what looked to her now practiced eye to be whiskey.

Gennie was not the least bit shocked, and she was pleased with herself for this evidence of worldly sophistication. Fascinated by the scene before her, she took in every detail, from the worn but plush easy chairs to the waiter dressed in a crisp white jacket. Only slowly did she realize that every eye in the car had turned toward her. Some of the male gazes gleamed with appreciation. The women looked her up and down with grudging admiration for the new rust wool suit that hugged her slight frame and the small swirl of a hat perched amid her curls. Gennie knew these were well-off women; they envied her appearance, not her relative wealth. In fact, without Grady's help, she'd more likely be traveling in a boxcar. Gennie drew herself up with pride, as much as she could manage with a mere five feet of height.

She took a step into the club car, trying to look as if she belonged in such a place. A young man sitting near the middle of the car eyed her over his whiskey glass. He put down his drink, stood, and started toward her. Gennie's heart climbed up her throat. With a quick, nervous smile, she spun around and made for the exit. With more speed than grace, Gennie traversed the coupling and opened the door to the passenger car she'd recently left. She found herself inches from the sinister man she'd seen in the terminal. His eyes widened as if he recognized her and didn't expect to see her there. She noticed his eyes were bloodshot; perhaps the club car was his natural habitat. With a murmured "excuse me," she slid past him and hurried back toward the safety of Rose.

FOUR

DULCIE MASTERS LEANED HER FACE TOWARD THE SPICY warmth of the baked bean soup bubbling in the Hancock Shakers' biggest stovetop cauldron. Today she wasn't feeling so ill, but she always seemed to be cold. And hungry. Maybe the Ritz wasn't serving up baked bean soup to the rich, but the lumpy red-brown stuff looked mighty tasty to Dulcie—better by far than her suppers before she'd come to work for the Shakers, when she was lucky to have a potato. She'd gone without for so long that her wispy brown hair had started to fall out, but now it was growing back nice and fluffy again. She reached up and smoothed her hand over her head.

"Need me to chop any more onion for that soup?" Carlotta DiAngelo's hand hovered over a large, yellow onion. "Dulcie, you here today?"

"What?" Dulcie started and spun around.

"Onions?" Carlotta's thin, sharp-featured face tightened in irritation, like an impatient fox waiting for something interesting to chase.

Dulcie shook her head. "No, save it. Winter's got some time to go yet." It wouldn't do to run short of food; then the sisters might decide it was too risky to share their meals with the hired help. They might even let her go, her and Carlotta, and maybe even her fiancé, Theodore, and then there'd be nothing. Dulcie turned back to the soup to hide her pale, expressive face, in case it showed any evidence of her fears. Carlotta had known her since childhood, and she'd tease. It was her way.

"Well, then, what are we supposed to do next?" Carlotta had a nasal voice, which often grew into a whine, especially when she got bored. "You'd think they could've left us at least one sister in here. Why do we have to do everything ourselves?"

Dulcie gave the soup a good stir and took a deep, delicious breath, so she wouldn't get irritable, too. "I told you," she said, without turning around, "they're all fixing things up for Mother Ann's Birthday and for that eldress who's coming to visit."

"Just what we need—company. I suppose we'll have to wait on her, too."

Dulcie heard the clatter of crockery and guessed Carlotta was gathering soup bowls for the imminent arrival of the Believers, several novitiates, and the hired help for their noontime meal. The clattering stopped. Dulcie guessed Carlotta was about to speak—probably another complaint or maybe a bit of gossip.

"Why don't you get those bowls set up in the dining room?" Dulcie asked quickly. "They'll all be along soon, and it'd be good if we could show the sisters we can work in the kitchen without them."

"In a minute," Carlotta said. Several moments of silence followed, which Dulcie filled with vigorous stirring.

"Listen, Dulcie," Carlotta said. "Something's wrong, I can tell. I can always tell. It's Julia, ain't it? You can't let that bother you. I mean, it's not like you two was all that close, you know, despite you and her being sisters. She was wild. She got what she asked for."

"You don't know anything about anything!" Dulcie's normally gentle voice seemed to crash around the room and bounce off the copper-bottomed pots. Carlotta jerked as if it had shoved her backward.

"Look, I'm just trying to help. If you want to feel sorry for her, that's your business, but Julia never deserved nothing but what she got. You gotta get on with things and look on the bright side—she's not around to embarrass you anymore. Seems to me Theodore will be grateful not to have her for a sister-in-law."

To her chagrin, Dulcie was shaking, but not entirely from anger. She stumbled to the worktable and leaned over it, steadying herself with her hands flat on its nicked surface.

"Hey, you okay?" Carlotta asked, scraping a chair over to Dulcie. "Here, sit. Did you eat breakfast? I wondered about that. You disappeared right after we served, and you didn't come back to eat. What're you up to, anyway? Where do you sneak off to all the time?"

From the floor above them came the faint sound of feet scuffing across a wood floor, signaling the arrival of the Believers and their guests. Carlotta clicked her tongue and said, "I suppose those bowls of soup had better get served, or we'll hear about it. You're sure in no condition to do the carrying; you'd fall right over and take supper with you. I guess that leaves me." With a sigh of martyrdom, she clattered some bowls on a tray. "Dulcie, my girl, you stay right here, and I expect to hear all about what's wrong, soon as I finish," Carlotta said, as she piled some items in the dumbwaiter and headed upstairs to serve.

As soon as Carlotta's back had disappeared, Dulcie hurried up the stairs to the ground floor and left by a back entrance, forgetting to grab her frayed jacket from a wall peg.

Dulcie rounded the corner of the Brick Dwelling House and the wind sliced through her. She shivered and clasped her arms tightly around her upper arms. She wished she'd paused long enough to grab that old jacket of hers. Not that it would have helped much; the cloth had worn thin, and the patches at the elbow were working loose. Sister Abigail had given her the old wool Shaker dress she was wearing, and now she wished she'd gone ahead and used the white kerchief that the sisters used to crisscross over their bodices in the old days. At least it would have provided one more layer.

She hadn't really considered where to go, once she'd escaped the kitchen. They were running out of rosewater for their baking; maybe she'd visit the Fancy Goods Store. It always seemed warmer there—maybe because it was attached to the Trustees' Office, where lots of folks visited from the world. She could surely talk the sisters into contributing a bottle of rosewater from their supply. It wasn't as if they had many customers these days, though they were hoping that Mother Ann's Birthday might bring in a few more collectors to buy the special Shaker dolls and pincushions and so forth the sewing sisters were making. But, no, the sisters would be in the dining room, and Julia was no longer there to mind the shop over the noon hour, so it would be closed.

Dulcie stopped on the path. A convulsive shiver shook her as she looked around the deserted village and gulped back a sob. The emptiness felt like a punishment, all she could look forward to in her life. She'd done such an awful thing. Of course, it was Julia's fault as much as anyone else's. Shame caught like a bone in her throat. With Julia gone, there was no one she could talk to—not the sisters, kind as they were; not her so-called friend, Carlotta; not even Theodore. Especially not Theodore.

Her footsteps broke the silence as she stepped off the cleared path onto the crusty snow. All she wanted was to go back to the Brick Dwelling House, to her warm little room, in which the Shakers were letting her stay while she worked for them. She'd curl up into a ball on her narrow bed, and pull the soft wool coverlet over her head. She might get caught, though. Instead, she crunched through the snow toward the old Round Stone Barn. It wasn't used anymore. She could usually count on being alone there. Being alone terrified her but seemed only right, somehow. Maybe she'd stay there until she died of the cold. In her most frightening nightmares, she nearly always died of either hunger or the cold, so it was only fitting that she should miss supper and freeze alone in the barn. Maybe that would fix things again.

Clouds of deep gray easily overpowered the weak winter sun, turning noon to near dusk. The Round Stone Barn was built on a hill, with entrances by ramps to all three levels. Dulcie jogged stiffly toward the upper entrance, noting that hers were the first feet to make prints in the snow. If the village missed her too quickly, she supposed someone could follow her footsteps, but if the sky kept its promise, fresh snow would cover her tracks within hours.

She slipped inside the barn and let her eyes adjust to the dimmer light. At one time, hay had been delivered by horse and wagon to this level and then pitched down to the animals below. Dulcie had never seen the barn in those days. Now it was just a sad, old abandoned building, with wind whistling through the cracks between the stones. Bits of ancient hay had blown into corners and stuck there, and no hands could be spared to tidy it up.

Without purpose, Dulcie began walking around the circle, clutching herself more tightly each time she passed a crack in the wall. About halfway around, she saw an old blanket tossed against the outer wall, as if someone had made a futile attempt to heal the injured stone. She grabbed the blanket and pulled it around her shoulders, not minding the bits of hay that poked at her shoulders and back. Relief from the cold lightened her mood somewhat, and she started to walk again.

A few minutes later, she realized she was not alone. Someone must have entered at a lower level, so she'd missed seeing the footsteps in the snow. Voices drifted up to her—

angry, male voices. Carefully, she peered over the edge of the hayloft walkway. Exiting the stall just below her, she saw the tops of three heads—gray, gray-black, and blond. She recognized them all. The three men were novitiates, who had expressed a desire to become covenanted Believers and were living in the village, working side by side with the Shakers, as they explored the faith.

Sewell Yates, his gray-streaked dark head bent toward the ground, kicked absently at some old hay on the barn floor. He looked downhearted, and Dulcie felt sorry for him. He was such a mild-mannered fellow, always friendly to the women, from the sisters to the hired help. Theodore hated how friendly Sewell was to her and kept muttering about how he shouldn't be a novitiate if that's the way he was going to behave. But whenever she looked in those sad brown eyes, Dulcie felt her heart soften.

"This barn is a useless eyesore. We ought to get rid of it, just tear it down and start fresh." The harsh voice belonged to Johnny Jenkins, a tall, broad-shouldered man with wavy blond hair. Dulcie thought he was mean, but Julia had liked him a lot—probably because he was still legally married, and a Shaker novitiate to boot. Julia had always fancied herself a temptress. Dulcie shivered and pulled her scratchy blanket closer at the memory of Julia.

"We mustn't do that," Sewell said. The poor man sounded like he was pleading, Dulcie thought; you'd never know he was in charge of fixing the buildings, and Johnny was supposed to follow his orders.

"This barn is an architectural marvel. There's nothing else quite like it anywhere. It's our duty to preserve it," Sewell continued. "With some work, we can bring it back, I know we can."

"But will it ever be *useful* again?" asked the third man of the group, Aldon Stearn. He leaned back against a wooden pillar and crossed his arms. "Sometimes, Sewell, I wonder if you're suited for this life. You continue to value worldly things, like buildings, over the tenets of your faith." Though his words were cruel, his deep baritone sounded more disappointed than contemptuous.

Sewell tightened his shoulders and seemed to become even thinner.

"Our time would be better spent if we concentrated on saving the Meetinghouse," Aldon said. "That building, at least, is central to our faith. We are here to create a heaven on earth, not to preserve Hancock Village as a monument to a glorious past. None of that matters. What we do here, now, that's what matters. We must do what is right every minute of every day." His voice rose, clear and insistent, up to Dulcie. It mesmerized her. She'd heard some of the sisters say that Aldon needed to study humility more deeply, but whenever he spoke of the Shaker faith, she tingled. She could still hear the preacher's voice in him—the voice that had enthralled her all those years she'd attended his Congregationalist church in Pittsfield. At the same time, a sudden dread caught her like a blow in the chest, knocking the breath out of her.

Johnny snorted in derision. He paced in a circle, looking to Dulcie like one of those lions she'd once seen at the circus, with his blond curls burnished by a sudden appearance of the sun through the windows encircling the top of the barn. "You're both wasting time," he said. "If we want to keep this place going, we gotta move fast. We need money to create heaven on earth. All the talking in the world won't do it."

"Given the abysmal state of the world's economy, just what do you think will bring in all this . . . lucre?" Aldon asked.

The silent Sewell had returned to kicking the dirty floor, his head bent. Dulcie wanted to run right down there and tell him to speak up, but she could never do such a bold thing. After all, she never really spoke up for herself, did she? Another wave of shame brought a painful heat to her cold cheeks.

"We gotta think big," Johnny said, warming to his subject. "Put this place on the map. We could maybe stick concrete in the holes in these walls and turn the place into a restaurant—you know, serve good Shaker food for a fair price. We've still got all that kitchen equipment from when the village had lots of Believers. We could get it working again, move it in here—it would help heat the place. We've got lots of extra tables and chairs and dishes. Not everybody in the world is poor. We've had some folks come by wanting to collect Shaker furniture. I bet lots more would come to sit on Shaker ladder-back chairs and eat real Shaker food. Maybe we could get the whole Brethren's Workshop going again, make lots of furniture and sell it to collectors. Then we could—"

"Perhaps we could even make use of all our spare beds and turn the upper stories into a *brothel*," Aldon said. "We could hire more women from the world—like that shopgirl."

Dulcie gasped despite herself, as she used to when Aldon had shouted about sin during a sermon. She wasn't shocked by his reference to Julia, whose reputation was well-known. She edged closer to the drop-off. Aldon stood, stiff and straight, his hands balled into fists. Sewell shrank back, and Johnny, for once, was silent.

To Dulcie's surprise and pleasure, it was Sewell who broke the stunned silence. "I . . . I think we're forgetting," he said, "that this is a barn, and we have limited resources. It's a *good* barn, a special one." Emboldened, Sewell straightened and waved his arm upward to draw attention to the structure. All three heads looked up, and Dulcie pulled back out of sight.

"I believe," Sewell said, "that part of making a heaven on earth is preserving and using what we have, and we have this lovely barn. So that's what we're going to do." His words were bolder than his voice. He turned quickly and left, as if he feared he wouldn't be able to withstand any more argument.

Cold and hunger had replaced Dulcie's longing for oblivion with a stronger yearning for food and the warmth of her bed. She pushed through the snow, taking a circuitous route back to the Brick Dwelling House. She had just passed the south side of the Poultry House when she found herself face-to-face with the one man she wanted most to avoid—her fiancé, Theodore Geist. It was useless to walk away, so she offered him a feeble smile.

"Dulcie, how many times have I told you, you should stay indoors in weather like this. Where did you get that filthy cloak? Give it here and take my coat."

Dulcie realized she was still wearing the old blanket she'd found in the barn. She had no idea how to explain it, so she pulled it tighter around her shoulders and laughed. "Don't be silly," she said, with an attempt at lightness. "I wasn't feeling well, so I thought a bit of fresh air would fix me up. I'm heading right back to my room now."

She tried to push past him, but he grabbed her by the shoulders. He was far bigger and stronger, and she knew it was no use struggling. She stood immobile and stared at his muscular chest.

"I want you to stop letting these Shakers give you clothes," Theodore said. "First you start wearing that old Shaker dress that makes you look like a fat frump, and then they give you a ratty old cloak that shouldn't be given to a hobo. Why do you let them do this? You used to be fairly pretty, but now . . ." He looked her up and down, shaking his head.

Her cheeks burned with humiliation, and she wrenched out of his grip. "I'm tired, Theodore, just let me go back to my room."

Theodore grabbed her elbow and yanked her around. "What have I said about talking back to me?"

Dulcie wilted. She knew what would happen if she defied Theodore—and the truth was, she didn't want to do so. She just wanted him to take care of her. That was all she'd ever wanted, and it was the one thing she couldn't ask of him now.

"I'm sorry," she said. "I was being selfish, but I'm just so tired."

Theodore squeezed her elbow a little too hard. "All right, then, you go back and have a short nap. Later we'd better have a talk. The police are asking questions."

"They've already asked me a million questions," Dulcie said. "What can be left?"

"They've been asking everyone here about you and Julia, whether you had fights or anything, and how you were getting along before she died."

Dulcie's knees buckled, and Theodore's strong arms kept her from falling.

"Look, don't worry, okay? I told them you two got along fine, and nobody'd know better than me." Theodore gave her a shake. "I'm taking care of this, got it?"

"But Julia and me, we fought a lot," Dulcie said. "Especially at the end, but all the time we were growing up, too. Carlotta knows that."

A crunching sound from near the Poultry House made Theodore loosen his grip, and Dulcie pulled away.

"Is anything wrong, Dulcie?" Esther Jenkins, bundled in a heavy wool coat and high boots, crossed the snow toward them. A few feet away she stopped and glared at Theodore. "Dulcie is frail, Theodore. You know that. You shouldn't keep her out in this weather."

Dulcie did not appreciate the concern, nor did she care for Esther, who was always telling her what to do. Esther had a perfect oval face that always looked to Dulcie as if it belonged on one of those cameos that rich women wear. Even at her kindest, Esther sounded like she was directing the servants. You'd hardly know she was as poor as the rest of them, and even poorer once her husband, Johnny, up and joined the Shakers, leaving her with six little ones to feed. No wonder she'd shown up at the Hancock Fancy Goods Store one day, herding all six children, and said she wanted to be a novitiate.

Theodore put an arm around Dulcie's shoulders and directed her toward the Brick Dwelling House. To Dulcie's relief, he said nothing to challenge Esther. After all, Esther was a novitiate, and they couldn't afford to have Theodore lose his job. It would mean they couldn't get married, and it occurred to Dulcie that getting married soon would be the answer to her prayer. Then maybe she'd feel safe.

FIVE

AFTER A LONG AFTERNOON SPENT SITTING AND WATCHING
the countryside glide by, Rose and Gennie were more than
ready to head for the dining car. Their coach seats were
softer than the typical Shaker ladder-back chair, but neither
woman was used to being sedentary for more than a brief
spell. The porter had just come through, announcing first
call for dinner, but there was no need to hurry. As a Shaker,
Rose was accustomed to a timely supper, to save evening
time for work or worship or perhaps a Union Meeting. The
other passengers, however, were of the world and showed
little interest in early dining. Rose and Gennie had plenty of
time to refresh themselves in the women's washroom before
joining the short line waiting to be seated in the dining car.

Rose was glad to see Gennie excited again. She'd come
back from her exploration of the train looking shaken. When
Rose had asked if she'd had a scare, Gennie had said only
that crossing from one car to another had made her a bit
nervous. Then she had turned her face toward the window
and studied the scenery until her head drooped against the
back of her seat.

As they stood in line, Rose noticed that Gennie's eyes
darted among the other passengers, as if looking for someone.

"Gennie, are you certain nothing is wrong?" Rose asked.

"What? Oh, no, nothing at all." Gennie flashed a quick, confident smile. Rose sensed this wasn't the truth, but she didn't press. Gennie belonged to the world now. Pride had become more important to her, and it was no longer Rose's job to wean her from it. Rose supposed her own sadness over this state of affairs must be close to what a parent feels when a child grows up and seems to forget everything she was so carefully taught. *Perhaps this is a lesson for my own humility,* Rose chided herself as a dining car waiter escorted them to their table. *I can't teach everyone to be a Shaker!*

They sat side by side in silence, Gennie again by the window, until their soup course had been served. Though she was used to eating in silence, Rose longed to get Gennie talking. To be truthful, she felt intimidated by the nearness of a waiter, who stood at attention in front of their table, steadying himself against the wall of the dining car. Not by so much as the flicker of an eye had he betrayed any surprise at seeing Rose still in her long, loose Shaker dress and thin white cap. With his starched white jacket and his impassive face, he looked more like an ebony statue than a man, but Rose knew that if she signaled to him, he'd be there instantly. She noticed that the other diners ignored the waiters, stationed every few tables, as if they were not quite human. She could not. Shakers served one another, and they believed that all people, whatever their skin color, were equal in the eyes of God. While Rose believed fervently in such a way of life, it was making conversation awkward for her.

When it was time to remove their empty soup plates, Rose noticed that another waiter—younger and bigger—spoke briefly with their waiter, then exchanged places with him. As their new waiter swept away the soiled plates and carried them to the back of the car, Rose took advantage of his absence. She touched Gennie's arm lightly and said, "I hope you aren't regretting your desire to come along on this trip. I know it's far away from Grady, and from home, and—"

"Rose, I'm not scared, honest! Oh, I know I've been much quieter than I usually am, but I've just been thinking, that's all. Now, let's talk about how we're going to solve this crime. What's the plan?" She gazed at Rose with raised eyebrows over brown eyes that brimmed with confidence in Rose's ability to figure everything out.

"Well, I guess we can talk about that now, if you wish."

At that moment, the waiter returned carrying two plates of roast beef, potatoes, and crisp green beans. Rose was unused to so much food after so little work, and she was alarmed at the prospect of eating everything on her plate to avoid wasting it.

"Would you care for coffee now or later, miss?" The waiter asked, looking toward Gennie. Rose noticed that he did not make the same offer to her.

"After, thanks," Gennie said, with her most charming smile. The waiter nodded and withdrew to his position in front of their table.

"So what should I be?" Gennie asked. "A novitiate maybe? I think I could pull that off without too much trouble."

Rose shook her head and thought quickly. She wanted to keep Gennie out of danger as much as possible for both their sakes. If Gennie lived with the hired women in Hancock Village, Rose would spend half her time worrying about what sort of danger she might foolishly plunge into headlong. A boardinghouse in Pittsfield would be the safest place for her. "Nay, I'd rather you spent more of your time getting to know the hired workers," Rose said. "You know what it's like—we have to hire people for much of the work, especially the farming, because our brethren are too few and often too far advanced in years to do it all themselves. But then we've let the world into our lives, and sometimes we can't control what happens as a result. The hired workers won't talk to us, or sometimes they aren't as honest or they don't work as hard as a Shaker. Hancock has dwindled sadly; you'll see when you get there. They have had to hire an uncomfortable number of people from the world, who live and eat and work beside them. I need you to be my eyes and ears among those workers."

"Sounds like fun," Gennie said. "Just please, please don't ask me to work in the kitchen. You know how I hate that."

"No more than necessary, I promise. They have two girls already, and the kitchen is one place the sisters still work regularly. I think the Fancy Goods Store might be the best place for you."

Both women paused at the thought of Gennie stepping in for the dead girl.

"Did you ever meet her, Rose? Julia, I mean."

"I did, just briefly, when I visited Hancock last autumn. I was in the store one afternoon, speaking with Sister Abigail about how well some of the goods were selling—I've always wanted us to open a Fancy Goods Store in North Homage, you know—when this lively girl with blond curls came bursting in and began to chatter away. She must have talked for twenty minutes straight about her men friends and the dances they were taking her to. I remember she complained quite a lot about how few party dresses she had. She didn't seem to care that her audience was two Shaker sisters, who had no use for party dresses."

"Sounds boring," Gennie said. "I hope I don't start doing that."

Rose laughed. "I will be sure to tell you if you head in that direction. But, nay, she wasn't really boring, just . . ." Rose's pale forehead furrowed as she cast her mind back to that day. "In a way, she was charming. She wanted pleasure, excitement, the admiration of men."

"Was she one of those spoiled rich girls? I've seen a few of them since Grady and I got engaged. Just because their people didn't lose everything in '29, they think they're better than everyone else."

Gennie's anger was apparent in her voice, and Rose understood. Gennie's family had not been so lucky. Rose chewed a bite of her roast beef—really, it was nearly as tender as a Shaker recipe—to give Gennie a chance to calm down.

"Though I do not know for certain," Rose said, "I suspect Julia was just the opposite—a very poor girl, who'd had little gaiety in her life up to that time. She seemed starved, in a way, and starvation can sometimes lead one to grab more than one's share. I felt sorry for her." Rose took a sip of water. "I could see, though, that she would have been immensely appealing to men, especially men of a certain type."

Gennie's fork clattered on her plate, and Rose smiled. "Remember, Gennie," she said, "I am not such an innocent as all that. I have seen a great deal beyond my own village— sometimes more than I wanted to. The world can be very cruel to its children." Rose scooped up the last bite of mashed potato and forced herself to eat it. The waiter was instantly at her elbow to remove the empty plate. As he did so, his eyes met hers for a fraction of a second. She smiled at him, but he had already gone.

"So do you suspect that one of these 'men of a certain type' killed Julia?" Gennie asked. "A lovers' quarrel maybe?"

"It's possible," Rose said. "I'll know more when I've spent some time at Hancock. But it's an idea you might pursue more easily than I. Sister Fannie told me that most of the hired hands grew up in Pittsfield and have known each other for years. Try to get them talking about each other and about Julia."

"Yes, what a good idea!" Gennie almost bounced in her seat with excitement. "All I need is one good gossip to start with, and I'll be able to name all of Julia's gentlemen friends in no time."

Again the waiter appeared, as if he had dropped from the ceiling. He held two cups of steaming liquid. He placed one cup near Gennie's right hand and moved the milk and sugar next to it.

"But I didn't order anything," Rose said, as he placed the other cup before her.

"It's a sweet, warm lemonade, Sister. It'll help ward off the chill." He bowed slightly and returned to his impassive stance in front of their table.

Rose could now see that her beverage was pale in color. She raised it to her lips and breathed in the citrus fragrance. It triggered a stab of homesickness for her village, where some of her most peaceful hours had been spent sipping rose hip and lemon balm tea as she noted the day's activities in her journal. She prayed silently and fervently that the terrible event in Hancock would prove to be the tragic result of a lovers' quarrel and nothing to do with the Shakers, so she could return home in short order, maybe even by Mother Ann's Birthday—and with an easy mind.

Rose emerged from her reverie to find Gennie, her curly head at a speculative tilt, watching the waiter, who seemed not to notice. It was then that Rose realized—not only had he called her "Sister," but he knew that Shakers were not supposed to drink stimulants.

"Gennie, I wish you'd give up the idea that I'm a sheltered fuddy-duddy, rapidly approaching old age. I work from before sunup to well after sundown; I can easily climb a short ladder to the upper berth. Besides, this is your first rail journey—you should have the window." Rose was in the lead as she and Gennie made their way back to their Pullman car, which was being transformed into a sleeping car. They had walked the length of the train, up to the baggage car, to tire themselves out and work off the heavy dinner. They were more than ready for bed. When the Society paid her travel expenses, Rose always sat up in a coach car, so even a windowless upper berth was a luxury that embarrassed her.

"Well, all right," Gennie said. "I'll admit, I want to see what the world looks like, speeding by at night. I'm so excited, I'll never be able to sleep."

Conversation stopped as they pushed open the heavy door leading to the linkage connecting with the next car. The world whizzed past them as they crossed the unsteady metal flooring that covered the couplings between the coaches. The train noise seemed deafening to Rose, who was more used to the gentler sounds of hungry livestock and dancing feet on a smooth pine floor.

She pulled open the tight-fitting door to their Pullman sleeping car and held it for Gennie. The sudden quiet, as the door slammed shut, was a relief. They turned sideways to pass other passengers returning from the washrooms. Rose felt uncomfortable, being forced to walk so close to several men, but she was grateful that she could spend the night in a bed, instead of sleeping in a seat and awakening stiff and achy.

Gennie headed for the women's washroom, as Rose surveyed their accommodations. Their berths were located about halfway through the coach. Curtains hung across both upper and lower berths, and a short ladder lay ready for Rose to clamber up into her bed. As she hooked her foot on the first rung, Rose glanced toward the end of the car and noticed a porter still hanging curtains at the last set of seats. She recognized the impassive face and broad shoulders. It was their waiter. Times were tough for railroads, too. They cut their crews wherever possible, and whoever was lucky enough to remain would do the work of two.

The porter looked across at her and gave her a slight nod. He finished hanging the curtain and walked toward her. Curious, she waited. With a quick glance up and down the car, he stopped before her, clearly trying to keep some distance between them.

"Could I talk to you for a minute?" he asked.

"Of course. May I know your name?" she asked.

He seemed surprised by her question. "My name is Hezekiah, Sister."

"And mine is Rose, Hezekiah." She was relieved that he did not extend his hand. The handshake was so accepted in the world, and so awkward for her. "You called me 'Sister,' " she said. "Do you know about us?"

"I know that you are a Shaker by your dress," Hezekiah said. "I know you are good people. I wondered if you and the young miss might be traveling to Hancock?"

"Indeed, we are. Do you come from Pittsfield?"

For the first time, Hezekiah smiled, a gentle smile that revealed a row of strong, yellow teeth. "I was born in Mississippi and raised in Pittsfield, Sister. My folks wanted to get as far north as possible."

"I'm afraid I'm from North Homage village, in Kentucky."

"I meant no offense." Hezekiah glanced toward the end of the car as if afraid someone would overhear his faux pas and chastise him.

"And I take no offense, I assure you."

He lowered his eyes, perhaps sensing he was overstepping his bounds. "Begging your pardon, Sister, but I know the folks at Hancock, used to do farm work for them before I got this job with the Pullman Company. My folks used to talk about the Shakers, how they was so kind and generous. That's why I wanted to work for them. They treated me fine. It was Sister Fannie gave me the letter that got me this job, just a couple months ago." His spine straightened when he mentioned his job, and Rose understood his pride.

A portly man returning from the washroom pushed past them with a critical glance at Hezekiah. Rose knew they didn't have much time. She was immensely curious about why Hezekiah would risk losing his position to speak to her.

Hezekiah took one step toward her and lowered his voice. "Maybe it's not my place to say this, Sister, but I wanted to warn you. They just had a murder at Hancock, a pretty young lady, and I noticed the young miss with you, and, well, I guess I just thought you oughta know what you're getting into. The Hancock Shakers are good people, but there's a killer in their village. I wouldn't go near the place, if I was you."

"Hezekiah, I appreciate your concern, but I know about the murder," she said, "because Sister Fannie sent for me to help find out what happened. If you left recently, then perhaps you knew the other hired workers and the novitiates?"

"Yes. I knew 'em all."

"Then perhaps you might be willing to help me. I don't know those people. Could you tell me anything about them, anything you heard or noticed that might help me get to the bottom of this tragedy? It would be a great help to Sister Fannie and the others."

Hezekiah's dark, broad face pinched in concern and concentration, and his deep brown eyes studied the flowered carpeting. "Maybe I shouldn't say this, but seeing as how it's for Sister Fannie . . . Those novitiates, they just arrived in the last few months I was there. I know the Shakers need more folk to join them, but I didn't trust these new ones, not a one of them."

"Of all the novitiates, is there anyone you think could be capable of such a horrible crime?"

"Several of 'em, I'd say."

An older porter, a small light-skinned man with curly white hair, entered the coach and raised bushy white eyebrows at Hezekiah.

"I'm sorry, Sister, but I'd best get busy. I can't lose this job." He began to straighten the curtain over the upper berth, and Rose could see that his large hands were shaking.

"I understand, Hezekiah. If you think of anything, you'll tell me, won't you?"

"Yes, Sister." Hezekiah turned to leave, then paused and turned back to Rose. "There's three I'd watch, if I was you—Sewell, Aldon, and Johnny. They all work together. To my mind, they don't act much like Shakers. Especially Sewell—his manner's a bit too free with the ladies, to my way of thinking. It's more than that, though. Ever since those folks arrived, that whole village changed. It's like they brought along the devil. Seemed like everybody turned mean. Some of them was going out and about at night. I'd see 'em from my window or hear them over my room, making noises like . . ."

"Like what, Hezekiah? You can say anything to me."

"Well, Eldress Fannie used to say they wanted to live like the angels in a Heaven on earth, but by the time I left, it was like Hell sent up a pack of demons instead." He spun around and was gone.

Gennie snuggled into her berth and turned toward the windows. The converted seats didn't create a bed as soft as hers back in her boardinghouse room in Languor, but the enclosed area was warm and cozy. The rhythmic clickety-clack of the train wheels soothed her jumpy nerves. Sleep didn't come quickly, as it usually did for her.

She watched the hills and villages glide by in the moonlight, gradually becoming more snow-splotched. She thought through the day. So far, the journey had lived up to her excited imaginings, but it seemed that every time she relaxed and enjoyed herself, that odd man would show up. It had happened again in the diner. She and Rose had finished their fresh fruit dessert and their planning, and they'd stood up to leave. Since they'd sat facing the direction the train was going, it was the first time Gennie had looked in back of her. There he was. He sat at a small table at the end of the car, sipping coffee and looking straight at her. He'd averted his eyes immediately and pretended to stare out the window. Gennie was only slightly encouraged—at least he'd seemed to understand that he'd been too forward. But she still felt a chill go down her spine.

Gennie wasn't about to confide her fears to anyone, including Rose. After all, she told herself, Rose might think she'd become far too prideful about her appearance. Since leaving the Shakers, Gennie had enjoyed many a worldly man's appreciation for her small, slender figure and her mass of auburn curls. Perhaps that was why she hesitated to marry Grady as quickly as he wished—she'd begun to see she had choices. At this moment, though, she missed Grady with a ferocity that shook her, even as she relished the adventure before her.

She curled up in a ball and pulled her covers tightly over her shoulders. Warmth relaxed her limbs, bringing her closer to sleep. Her eyelids wanted to droop, but she opened them as she felt the train slow to a stop. Out her window she saw a dimly lit platform and a dirty, snow-crusted sign announcing a town she'd never heard of. A small stone station, badly in need of a cleaning, was nearly dark inside. Under a meager shelter stood a large man, hunched in a thick overcoat, waiting for the coach doors to open.

Gennie watched sleepily, glad she was warm and snug in bed. A burst of wind swirled the snow under the wood benches lined up against the station wall. A figure exited the train and walked toward her. He stopped to chat briefly with the large man. They parted, and the large man stepped up onto the train. The exiting passenger walked past Gennie's window, almost close enough for her to reach out and touch. The man was tall and broad-shouldered, and he kept his hands deep in the pockets of his overcoat. His dark hat was tilted over his forehead to stop the wind. Gennie didn't have to see his face to know it was the strange man who had set her nerves on edge since Cincinnati. He hurried through the station house door and slammed it behind him. Gennie held her breath. The train shivered, then started forward, but the man did not reappear. Gennie released her breath in a deep sigh. He would not be disturbing her again. She was asleep before the caboose had cleared the station.

SIX

"COME ON IN AND JOIN US, GENNIE. WE'RE JUST HAVING A glass of sherry together by the fire." Mrs. Alexander, proprietor of Mrs. Alexander's Boardinghouse for Young Women, where Rose had insisted that Gennie stay, gestured her into her parlor to join the other boarders. "I have some nice tea ready, if you'd rather not imbibe, though I must admit I never saw the harm in a tiny glass of sherry, and I'm so glad that silly law is gone, so I can have a little sip in the evening again." Mrs. Alexander looked as if she might often indulge in more than the occasional tiny glass, and as if this wasn't her first sip of the evening.

After the long train journey to Pittsfield, Massachusetts, Gennie was more than ready for something stronger than tea. She glanced at the small circle around the fireplace and noted that she was the only young woman in the Boardinghouse for Young Women. She wasn't surprised. Times were hard, and any paying boarder must be a godsend. Besides herself, there were only two. An elderly man appeared to be snoozing in an overstuffed chair, one hand holding his sherry glass balanced on his thin thigh. He opened a sleepy eye when Mrs. Alexander introduced him as Mr. Bing, a long-term resident, then he resumed his nap. The other boarder—a plump, bright-eyed, middle-aged woman— scooted to one side of a worn velvet loveseat to make room for Gennie. The woman smiled warmly, and Gennie found herself settling on the frayed, lumpy cushion and accepting a glass of sherry, neglecting to mention her age. It suited her purposes to be thought of as older. She introduced herself, thankful that she could use her real name; a false name would be sure to confuse her at some point.

"I'm Mrs. Butterfield," the woman next to her said, "but do call me Helen. Everyone does. Have a sip of your sherry, it'll warm your bones."

Gennie did as she was told. The sweet liquid burned her throat all the way down, but she suppressed a cough and pretended sherry was an everyday indulgence for her.

"Now, tell me all about yourself," Helen Butterfield said. "You have a sweet accent, rather Southern, I'd say. Where did you come from, and what is such a lovely young girl doing here all alone?"

Gennie put her glass on the table in front of her. She'd spent hours concocting her story, and it wouldn't do to let her mind get muddled. She reminded herself to keep it brief. It was more important to get information than to give it.

"Times are so hard back where I come from," she said. "I just thought I'd come East to see if I could find a job." She gave Helen her most ingenuous smile, then relaxed against the back of the loveseat and gazed around the room. She felt as if she'd been thrust decades back in time, the room was so littered with Victorian knickknacks. Next to her, a brocade-covered lampshade with a long fringe gave a rosy glow to her sherry glass. It brought back vague memories of her long-dead mother, who had loved pretty things. The light touch of a hand on her forearm brought her back to the present.

"You must be exhausted, poor dear," Helen said.

"She just came in today, you know," said Mrs. Alexander. "Probably had to sit up all night on the train, with heaven knows what sort of person snoring next to her."

Gennie smiled and didn't offer the information that she'd

slept peacefully in a berth, with Rose just above her. It would sound as if she had more resources than she'd led them to believe.

"Have you been here long?" Gennie asked Helen.

"Oh, no, dear, just arrived myself, though not from so far away as you, I suppose." Helen sipped her sherry and sighed with appreciation. With disconcerting suddenness, she turned her bright gaze back to Gennie. "Tell me, do you have family back—where did you say you were from? The South? Tennessee, perhaps?" She raised her eyebrows and paused. Gennie chose to taste her own sherry again, and said not a word.

"Your family must be quite worried about you, traveling all alone like this. You must let me look after you while you're settling in."

"That's most kind of you," Gennie said, "but I'm sure I'll be fine. This isn't Boston, after all."

"I should say not!" said Mrs. Alexander. "A young lady is quite safe here in Pittsfield. Why, we have Shakers nearby, after all."

A snore from the snoozing Mr. Bing distracted them long enough for Gennie to decide that now was as good a chance as any to begin her questioning, despite the intrusive presence of Mrs. Helen Butterfield.

"Oh, I've heard of the Shakers," Gennie said. "I've heard they are very generous and kind. Do you suppose I might get a job with the Shakers here? Do they need any extra hands, do you know?"

In the awkward silence that followed, Gennie turned her innocent gaze on each person in turn. Mr. Bing had opened his eyes partway and watched her with drowsy curiosity. Helen Butterfield's eyes were a shade too bright, and Mrs. Alexander was trying to hide her obvious excitement with a veneer of sadness.

"Oh dear," said Mrs. Alexander, "I suppose you'll hear

about it sooner or later, so I might as well tell you." She slid to the edge of her seat and leaned forward. "Hancock Village is what our Shakers call their home, and I've been there many a time, buying eggs and butter. Never had the least trouble with them, not since I've been living here, which is my whole sixty years. Well, no trouble until recently, that is."

Mr. Bing's head lolled back against his chair again, but the women all leaned in toward one another. Mrs. Alexander took a large gulp of sherry. "You see," she said, "there's been a murder in Hancock Village. A pretty young girl it was, no older than you," she said, nodding to Gennie, "though not so ladylike, of course."

Gennie feigned shock. "Do they know who did it?" she asked.

"Well, as I said, a lady, she wasn't," Mrs. Alexander said, raising her eyebrows.

"Celibates!" said Mr. Bing. He unfolded his long body from his seat, poured himself another sherry, and downed it in one gulp.

"I beg your pardon, Mr. Bing?" asked Gennie.

"Celibates," he repeated, "pure and simple. In more ways than one." He guffawed and poured another sherry. "It's unnatural, that's what it is. Leads to all kinds of evil doings." He drained his glass. "My father was celibate. See what it got him." He slid back into his chair and closed his eyes.

Gennie's mouth twitched. She tried to maintain her composure, but she lost the struggle when Helen caught her eye. Mrs. Alexander looked on in confusion as they laughed themselves to tears. Luckily, the sherry had sent Mr. Bing to sleep, and the unladylike behavior failed to rouse him.

"He was, you know," Mrs. Alexander said. The drawn skin of her cheeks had turned a dull red, but she poured herself another glass of sherry.

"Who was what?" asked Helen.

"Mr. Bing's father. He was a Shaker. An orphan, he was,

brought to the Shakers when he was just a baby." Mrs. Alexander sipped twice. "He left at twenty-one or so. Word around town was he'd had a . . . well, you know, something going with one of the young sisters. He never would say, though. He was a closemouthed sort of man." She drowned her regret in more sherry. "Not like the young ones nowadays."

"Has anyone left the Shakers recently?" Gennie asked.

Mrs. Alexander cackled, and a few drops of amber liquid sloshed on her hand. She seemed not to notice. "There's hardly anyone left to leave," she said. "and most of them older than me. I like the old sisters, though. It's those new ones . . . I s'pose the Shakers know what they're doing, and beggars can't be . . ." Her eyes blinked lazily and she frowned, apparently searching for her lost train of thought. "When I was a little tyke," she said, "my mother used to take me along to visit the sisters for tea. Ooh, what a big, lovely place it was in those days."

"These 'new ones,' " Gennie prodded. "Do you think they're just bread-and-butter Shakers?" When Mrs. Alexander squinted at her, Gennie realized she'd revealed more inside knowledge of the Shakers than she'd wanted to. "I mean, do you think they're just using the Shakers to get a bed and meals?"

"Oh, I wouldn't put it past that lot," Mrs. Alexander said. "Poor Honora." She shook her head sadly.

"I beg your pardon?" Gennie asked.

"Oh, you wouldn't know her, dear. Poor Honora had such a wonderful life once. She did love being a clergyman's wife, and she was very good at it, even though sometimes she had to look the other way when her husband's eyes started roving."

Gennie had no idea what to say, or even if Poor Honora had anything to do with Hancock Shaker Village.

"Is Honora a Shaker now?" Helen Butterfield asked.

"Oh, dear me, no. It's that husband of hers, Aldon. He's the one went to the Shakers. Poor Honora never got over it. The shame, you know. I mean, it's one thing if your husband chooses to keep company with other women, that happens, but when he chooses—well, you know, *celibacy*." Mrs. Alexander looked at her empty glass.

"Here, let me get you some more sherry," Gennie said. She grabbed the glass from Mrs. Alexander's shaky hand, but she made no move toward the decanter. She wanted all the information she could get before Mrs. Alexander drifted off to the same land as Mr. Bing. Gennie was vaguely aware that Helen had settled back and was listening quietly.

"Do you know them well—the new lot?" Gennie asked.

"I most certainly do. My late husband, bless his soul, used to own the greengrocer's in town, and those children were such a nuisance." She frowned at her own empty glass in Gennie's hand, then snuggled back in her armchair, apparently content to gossip.

"What children do you mean?" Gennie was losing hope that she'd get anything sensible from Mrs. Alexander, but it was worth a try.

"Oh, I don't remember all their names, it was so long ago. I can tell you, those children were nothing but little thieves, and they should be ashamed to set foot on Shaker land. Of course, they didn't come from good families, so I suppose they couldn't help themselves."

"Are you talking about the novitiates?" Gennie could hear the frustration in her own voice. What good was a gossip if she couldn't follow her own storyline?

Mrs. Alexander squinted again; the term "novitiate" clearly meant nothing to her.

"Are these the same folks . . . ?" But Gennie could see it was no use. Mrs. Alexander had slipped sideways against the side of her wing-backed chair. Her face had softened into blissful peace. She and Mr. Bing snored in harmony.

"Perhaps we should let them rest, my dear," Helen Butter-field said. "I'm sure you can find out more in the morning."

"I wasn't trying to find out anything."

"No, of course not." Helen patted her shoulder, which for some reason irritated Gennie.

"You haven't mentioned what your business here is," Gennie said.

"I guess we didn't get around to me." Helen gathered up the empty sherry glasses and arranged them on a tray. She laughed lightly. "Well, I'm a collector, my dear, that's all. I collect Shaker furniture and whatnot. In fact, I'm planning a trip out to Hancock bright and early tomorrow morning. I have an idea—why don't we go together? We can go right to the Fancy Goods Store, and you can get that job you said you were looking for. I'm quite sure they'll welcome you. Good night, now." She moved quickly for a large woman, and she was halfway up the staircase before Gennie could form her next question.

Rose tossed off her covers and shivered. Six A.M. seemed to arrive earlier in the East than it had in Kentucky, where it hadn't seemed so frigid outside of one's toasty bed linens. Her hands shook as she pulled on her wool work dress. Folks here must be tolerant of the cold, so they kept their buildings cooler than she was used to. Or perhaps Hancock had suffered even more than North Homage from this end-less Depression, and they were cutting expenses wherever possible. Rose guessed the washroom might be even colder, so she wrapped her long outdoor cloak around her.

When she returned, she quickly tidied her retiring room, praying silently as she did so. She had arrived late the night before, and she'd chosen sleep in a real bed—one that wasn't moving—over unpacking her satchel. She folded her few belongings into the drawers built into the wall. She shook out her spare work dress and a winter Sabbathday dress and hung them on hangers, which she hooked over pegs lining the wall.

Rose looked around her temporary home. She'd barely glanced at it before falling into bed. The room was so like hers back at North Homage, yet different in ways that Elder Wilhelm would never have tolerated. On one wall peg hung a framed photo, probably dating back several decades, of horses in a pasture. An empty vase on her simple pine desk was, she knew from her previous visit, filled with flowers during warmer weather.

Rose started at the sight of her own thin frame and her pale, freckled face looking back at her from a large mirror hanging from several wall pegs. In North Homage, only a small, and usually cloudy, mirror was allowed in each retiring room, so Believers would not be tempted to admire their own appearances. It was one of Rose's duties, as eldress, to tidy Elder Wilhelm's room and mend his clothing, so she knew that he shaved with only a small pocket mirror.

The bell rang for breakfast, and Rose reluctantly slipped off her cloak and rehung it on a peg hanger. She would not be leaving the building until after the meal, so she had no good excuse to take it along.

She closed her retiring room door and found herself alone in a wide hallway, punctuated by numerous doors. Weak winter sunlight from two large windows did its best to brighten the hallway, but it also reflected off a thin layer of dust along the edges of the floor. Rose was torn between sadness and an ingrained desire to clean. She knew that the sisters did their best, but they were so few now, and growing older. They couldn't sweep every corner, every day—not in buildings that once had housed at least two hundred and fifty hard-working Believers. So much of the work was hired out these days, and cleanliness didn't have the same meaning for folks from the world. Rose vowed that, if she could find the time, she would help out wherever she could. In fact, it would be a good way to get to know everyone involved in the tragedy.

The hallway was silent. Everyone else had gathered for breakfast, so Rose hurried down the women's staircase and entered a small room outside the dining room, where the other sisters were praying before their silent entrance. Several women from the world waited also, though they did not pray. At least they were quiet.

Rose located the eldress, Sister Fannie, a small, vibrant woman in her late sixties. At a signal from Fannie, the sisters filed into the dining room and took their seats. Fannie led Rose into an adjoining, much smaller dining room. Rose was pleased. When she had visited Hancock before, she and Fannie had always eaten with the others, rather than sequester themselves in the cheery Ministry dining room.

"Rose, I am so glad you are here," Fannie said, when they'd settled across from each other at the small trestle table. A kitchen sister brought them white serving dishes holding steamed brown bread, hotcakes, and a small amount of precious maple syrup.

"I know I said at least three times last evening how glad I was to see you, but you were half dead with exhaustion. It's a long trip to make, especially in winter, and it's hard to be away from your own Family so close to Mother Ann's Birthday, but I am so very relieved that you have come." Fannie pushed the serving plates closer to Rose. "You must be famished, as well. I know they fed you on the train, but it wasn't good Shaker food, after all."

Rose, for whom the train meals had been far too generous, said nothing. In fact, a Shaker breakfast looked delightful to her, especially the maple syrup, which they almost never had in Kentucky. She took a healthy serving of everything.

Fannie, on the other hand, fixed her empty plate with a frown. "I'm afraid things are not as they were when you visited last," she said finally. "And I feel responsible."

"Fannie, you mustn't blame yourself. You could not possibly have controlled the actions of someone depraved enough to kill another human being." Rose took the liberty of sliding a hotcake onto Fannie's plate. "First, eat something," she said, pouring a dollop of syrup on the hotcake. "Then tell me everything, and let me handle the situation from now on. You have your hands full already, getting ready for Mother Ann's Birthday."

Fannie managed a wan smile and a bite of hotcake. "I am *so* glad you are here, Rose. I know you'll get to the bottom of this horrible killing, but I do bear some responsibility. Now don't argue with me. Let me explain." She cut another bite and pushed it around with her fork. "As you well know, times have been very lean for us here. Oh, I know it has been the same for you, in the West, but somehow you've held on to more Believers. We are mostly sisters left, and we are no longer young."

Fannie stared out the large dining room window, where the weak morning sunlight brightened as it flashed off the snow. "Our faith is as strong as ever, but otherwise our heaven on earth is shrinking. We live almost entirely within these walls. We no longer use our Meetinghouse or our Schoolhouse. Our lovely Round Stone Barn is empty and cracked. We've had to sell a great deal of our land. To do any farming at all nowadays, we must hire men from the world. We hire women to help in the Fancy Goods Store and in the kitchen. We buy our goods from town, instead of supporting ourselves, as we used to. We tried to be more welcoming to the world, hoping to attract more Believers, but if anything, it seems to be backfiring."

Rose said nothing. On her last visit, she had seen everything Fannie described. North Homage was suffering, as well, but they'd been lucky enough to gather some fine, young Believers in recent years. Elder Wilhelm's insistence that they wear old-fashioned dress, hold dancing worship, and keep as separate from the world as possible might, Rose admitted, actually have something to do with their slight advantage. It wasn't a thought she cared to explore just then.

Fannie chewed slowly on a corner of her slice of brown bread. "In my eagerness to accept new Believers, I may have been too trusting."

Rose put down her fork. "Are you saying that you suspect one of your novitiates of being a killer?"

Fannie met her eyes. "I pray not, of course. But these novitiates are not like those I remember from times past. Certainly we had our share of Winter Shakers, and I could usually tell which they were in short order." She shook her head. "These new ones are . . . hard."

"Their natures, do you mean?"

Fannie nodded. "In part, it is pride. They seem unwilling to put aside their own petty desires, for the good of the Society. At times, they act as though driven by greed. I have spent untold hours laboring with them in confession, and they profess to understand, but then one of the hired hands will complain of being harshly treated by a novitiate, or one novitiate will come to me with stories putting one of the others in a bad light. Their hubris seems unconquerable. I had thought of sending them all back to the world."

"Yet you did not."

Fannie shook her head sadly. "I did not. I told myself they had been sent to us, that Holy Mother Wisdom wanted us to show them a better way. And I suppose . . ." Fannie poked at her remaining piece of hotcake until it turned to a sticky pulp. "I suppose I was feeling downhearted about our dwindling numbers, and these novitiates have brought such wonderful skills with them."

"And you hoped they would give you new life? There is no shame in that, Fannie. Some of the most devoted Believers had great wills to conquer before they could truly serve God and others."

Fannie looked unconvinced. Still shaking her head, she consumed the rest of her breakfast, as Rose had hoped she would, rather than throw it away.

"Tell me what you know about each of the novitiates—and the hired help, too," Rose said, once Fannie had crossed her cutlery over her plate and laid her cloth napkin on top. A pot brimming with spearmint tea had been steeping at her elbow, so she poured a cup for each of them and settled back against the curved slats of her chair.

Fannie held her cup close to her lips and breathed deeply before taking a sip. "You are right, of course. The sooner we get to work, the sooner this nightmare will be over. I'll begin with the hired help. I know very little about them, except that they all come from Pittsfield, and I believe they have known one another for many years." Fannie took another sip and frowned. "Now that I think of it, the novitiates all come from Pittsfield, as well, so everyone might know everyone."

"Don't worry," Rose said. "I'll sort it out."

"Of course. Well, Julia Masters, the girl who was killed, worked sometimes in the Fancy Goods Store. She was pretty and poor and, I'm afraid, not quite honest. Little items used to disappear whenever she worked."

"You didn't confront her about it?"

"I was planning to do so, of course. In fact, I was ready to let her go, but Sister Abigail is so kind-hearted, she asked me to give the girl another chance. She promised she would speak to Julia and watch her very carefully. You can find out quite a lot about Julia, I'm sure, by speaking with her sister, Dulcie. She helps out in the kitchen. Dulcie is a good worker, a very honest girl, though the kitchen sisters tell me she's been ill of late. She was destitute when she came to us. She probably wouldn't have enough to eat without this job, so we keep her on all the time, even when the sisters could easily handle the kitchen work themselves."

"How did Dulcie get along with her sister?"

"Oh, fine, probably. I don't really know. But I'm sure Dulcie had nothing to do with her sister's death."

"Why?"

"Well, I just can't believe that Dulcie . . . I mean, she's *such* a hard worker."

Rose realized she would get little useful information about possible suspects from Fannie, who saw mostly the good in people. She sipped her tea and allowed herself to pause as the minty liquid warmed her throat. "Tell me about the others," she said.

"Dulcie is engaged to be married to Theodore Geist, our hired farm manager. He would not perhaps be my first choice for Dulcie, but worldly love often leads one astray, I find."

"What do you dislike about him?"

"Well, not dislike precisely, it's just that he can be some-what overbearing. Mind you, he's a fine farm manager. He watches over the other hired farm workers and keeps the shirkers in line, but I've heard from some of the novitiates that he challenges their authority. Anyway, I'm sure he'll take good care of Dulcie."

"You are very fond of Dulcie, aren't you?"

A kitchen sister arrived to clear their table, and Fannie did not answer.

"I've told everyone why you are here," Fannie said, when the sister had left. "I've asked them all to cooperate with you. The novitiates, in particular, are frightened that the po-lice won't treat them fairly, so I hope they will see you as a friend."

"Unless one of them is the killer."

"I refuse to think such a terrible thought," Fannie said. "I'm sure you will find that the killer is an outsider, perhaps a vagrant or someone from Pittsfield with whom Julia kept company."

"You don't suspect any of the hired workers, either?"

"Of course not."

"Will the hired workers talk to me?" Rose asked.

"I've told them to be totally honest with you. They may hesitate at first, but I'm sure you'll win them over." Fannie filled their cups with the remains of the spearmint tea. The set of her chin made it clear she could not suspect anyone known to her of such a heinous act as murder.

"Now," Fannie said, "let's discuss something cheerier. We are having such a special celebration for Mother Ann's Birthday on the first of March."

"Special? In what way?" For Rose, Mother Ann's Birthday was special enough, just as it was usually celebrated. What could be better?

"Another of my foolish brainstorms, I'm afraid," Fannie said, pushing back her chair. "Such hard times all around—I thought that this year we'd have a big celebration and include our neighbors. We've been working for weeks, cooking candies and sewing special Shaker dolls to sell and to give to some of the poorer children, making sweetbreads and cakes, and so forth. We plan to make Mother Ann's Birthday Cake twenty times over, even if it means going without butter for months. That's why, you see, we've hired several extra people, including Carlotta, in the kitchen. She's a friend of Dulcie's."

Rose's head was beginning to swim with potential suspects, and they hadn't even discussed the individual novitiates.

"I suppose she knew Julia, as well?"

"Of course. I believe the three girls grew up together. I'm afraid I can't tell you much about Carlotta, though. I hired her on Dulcie's recommendation."

"Are Dulcie and Carlotta in the kitchen now, do you think? Perhaps we could just drop in, so I could get to know them at once." Rose swung her ladder-back chair upside down onto a couple of wall pegs and headed for the door back into the main dining room. There was no point in talking further about the hired help; she'd learn more by observing them herself. Besides, she was tired of idle sitting.

"Better yet," Rose said, as they headed toward the stairs, down to the basement kitchen. "Why don't you tell them I'd like to help out for a while, and I'll take it from there. Then you can get back to your duties, which must be nagging at you."

"Have I mentioned," Fannie asked, "how glad I am that you are here?"

SEVEN

GENNIE WAS UP EARLY, NEARLY AS EARLY AS WHEN SHE'D
lived with the Shakers, but her motive for doing so was less
than noble. She hoped to avoid Helen Butterfield's too-curious
interest in her comings and goings. Mrs. Alexander was still
sleeping off her countless glasses of sherry, so Gennie was
able to tiptoe into the kitchen, break off hunks of bread and
cheese for herself, and be out the door before hearing a
sound from any of the other rooms in the boardinghouse.

She eased the heavy front door shut behind her and stood
on the large, covered porch, nibbling her bread and cheese
and wondering what on earth to do next. She had to get to
Hancock Village, which she knew to be just a few miles
down the road from Pittsfield. How to get there was the
question.

The boardinghouse was located on a wide street lined
with large Victorian houses—palaces, they seemed to Gennie—which showed no signs of life. The predawn light gave
a grayish cast to the snow that covered everything in sight.
Her breath froze into puffs of white smoke, and her stylish
but thin wool coat, plenty warm enough for a Kentucky winter, felt no thicker than cotton flannel. She longed for a nice,
heavy Shaker Dorothy cloak with a deep hood.

I'm not doing any good just standing here, Gennie lec-
tured herself. Hanging on to the railing, she navigated the

icy steps and skidded toward the sidewalk. Her smooth-soled boots had been made for Kentucky, too. With a guilty lilt of pleasure, she decided that a shopping trip was called for. Grady had made sure she had plenty of money, so the only problem would be finding the time. Perhaps she could buy what she needed from the Shakers. The Fancy Goods Store must have cloaks, at least.

Heartened by these thoughts, Gennie pulled her coat tighter around her small body and headed in the direction of the railway station. When she and Rose had arrived the day before, Rose had somehow arranged for transportation to take Gennie to the boardinghouse, so the station must be where taxis and so forth gathered. It had seemed like a short trip. Surely she could get there by foot. It did occur to her to wonder how safe she was, walking all alone before dawn on strange city streets. Was Massachusetts as safe and friendly as Languor, Kentucky?

After six blocks, Gennie decided that either she'd gone off in the wrong direction, or she'd miscalculated the distance to the railway station. Her boots were soaked through, her hands and cheeks felt raw, and she thought she'd never be warm again. However, the sun had appeared on the horizon, and the snow had begun to sparkle. She'd reached a street with small shops, in which lights were flicking on. Her spirits lifted. Surely she'd soon be able to ask directions. Maybe she wouldn't even have to go as far as the station; maybe someone kind would offer her a ride.

As if in answer to her unspoken prayer, she heard the honk of a car horn, and a dirt-streaked, gray-and-black Model A coupe sloshed to a halt beside her. Behind the wheel sat Helen Butterfield. She wore a jaunty, brown-lacquered straw hat, which contrasted sharply with her thick fur coat. She waved and leaned over to open the passenger door. Unable to think of a reason not to, Gennie slid in beside her.

"Well, here you are, my dear. I knocked on your door this morning, thinking we might breakfast together, but when there was no answer, well, I must admit I got worried and peeked inside. Yes, I know, it was rude of me to do so, but I couldn't bear to think of you ill and unable to answer, so I went ahead and did the rude thing." Helen glanced sideways at her. "What on earth can you be doing out so early?"

I could ask you the same thing, Gennie thought, but was too polite to say. "Just exploring," she said. "I'm an early riser."

"I'll say," Helen said. "You must have been out walking before dawn."

Gennie said nothing.

"As I mentioned last evening, I'm heading on out to Hancock," Helen said. "Why not come along?"

God had a funny way of answering one's prayers, Gennie thought. All in all, she'd have preferred a taxi. She'd have to be more specific next time.

"That would be wonderful," Gennie said. "You said you collected Shaker things, didn't you? Isn't it a bit early to go rummaging through Hancock's extra furniture?"

"Oh, just thought I'd get an early start, you know. Yes, collecting, that's what I do; it's my passion. Who knows, somebody else might be looking for the same items I am, so the faster I get there, the more likely I'll be the one to get just what I want."

"What *do* you want?" Gennie was torn; she appreciated the ride and the warmth, but Helen Butterfield annoyed her.

"Oh, you know, some of those wonderful ladder-back chairs, for instance."

"Didn't the Shakers make lots of ladder-back chairs? Can they really be so rare?"

"You'd be surprised," Helen said. "Do you think you'll try for a job in the Fancy Goods Store?"

"Probably." Gennie turned her head away from Helen and

stared out the window at the frozen countryside as they sped along far too fast on the snowy road.

"Whoops!" Helen said cheerfully as they skidded over a clump of ice. She straightened the car with the ease of an expert and picked up speed again.

"We'll be there before you know it," Helen said. "I'll introduce you to Sister Abigail in the Fancy Goods Shop. I've been there before, so I know my way around. In fact, I'd be glad to give you a tour."

"I couldn't trouble you," Gennie said quickly. "I'm sure I'll find my way around in no time. I'm more interested in securing a job just now."

"Of course," Helen said. To Gennie's relief, she lapsed into silence until they reached the entrance to Hancock Village.

"Well, here we are," Helen said, as she pulled up beside an ornate, Victorian building.

"Are you sure?" Gennie asked.

"I know why you're startled," Helen said. "It doesn't look much like a Shaker building, does it? Late last century, the Hancock Shakers thought they'd renovate their Trustees' Office, which is what this building used to be."

Gennie gazed in surprise at the porch, the bay windows, and the narrow tower that reached above the roof. "Why would they do such a thing?" she asked.

"No idea. Maybe they wanted to blend in better—you know, so folks would be more comfortable and maybe want to become Shakers. Anyway, wait until you see the Fancy Goods Store. It's a collector's delight. Come along, they'll be open by now. They're up and about early." For a plump woman, Helen bounced out of the coupe with ease, then slammed the door. Gennie followed more slowly. She was still in shock. The buildings back in North Homage always kept their clean and simple lines, even when they were renovated.

Gennie followed Helen across the porch and through the front door. To her right, she caught a brief glimpse of a parlor that could have been in any house of the world. Helen entered a doorway to the left. Gennie found herself in an enchanting room crammed with Shaker memorabilia. The pegs encircling the room were all put to use holding everything from flat brooms to lovely Dorothy cloaks fashioned from bright red broadcloth and lined with silk. Colorful weavings hung over the ladder-back chairs, and baskets and curved wood boxes covered several round tables. A long countertop divided the room and also served to display candies and other small items, such as linen kerchiefs, fans, and bottles of rosewater.

Gennie was drawn toward the glass case on top of the counter. It looked as if it had been transported from a bakery, complete with frothy confections. She'd never seen such a display of small boxes of all shapes, lined with blue and red and violet satin. Scattered among the boxes she saw calico or satin-covered pincushions, some with shiny maple stands that could clamp to the side of a table. In the corners sat some Shaker dolls with funny, wrinkled heads. Gennie examined them more closely and realized the heads were made of dried apples. She couldn't remember the North Homage sisters ever making such dolls.

As if guarding the goodies beneath them, several Shaker dolls with porcelain heads—the kind Gennie remembered—were propped up on top of the glass case. The women clustered on the left, and the men on the right. All were dressed as if they had just returned from Sabbathday dancing worship, the sisters in loose butternut wool dresses and dark blue cloaks, the brethren in blue trousers and surcoats. Their painted china faces smiled complacently, as though worship had left them content.

"Lovely, isn't it?" Helen gave Gennie a little push into the room and guided her toward the counter, where an elderly sister sat in a rocking chair, barely visible behind a large jar of candied sweetflag root. "Let me introduce you to Sister Abigail."

"However did you make all these lovely things?" Gennie asked. "I thought there were so few . . . I mean . . ."

Sister Abigail grinned, creating rippling wrinkles around the corners of her mouth. "I know what you mean, child, and you are right. We are few now, but we wanted to make this a very special birthday for Mother Ann, so we've worked hard. And to be honest, we asked our brothers and sisters at Sabbathday Lake for help, and they sent us boxes of beautiful items from their own supply." Abigail wore a modified version of the old-fashioned Shaker dress that Gennie was used to; it was more fitted to the sister's spare frame, with a small shawl that buttoned over her bodice.

"So you know something about us Shakers?" Abigail asked.

"Yes, a bit." Gennie launched into her story—which she'd perfected since the night before—that she'd wanted to go out into the world and fend for herself, and she wanted to see what it was like to live in a totally different part of the country. The story sounded weak as she recited it, but Abigail seemed to sympathize.

"As it happens," she said, "we are in need of some help just now." She said nothing about Julia's death. "Can you count out change?"

"Of course. I finished school, and I've worked in a flower shop, so I even have some sales experience."

"Then welcome. Have you someplace to be now, or would you like to begin?"

"I'd like to begin."

Helen Butterfield had kept silent through the entire negotiation, and Gennie had almost forgotten her presence. Now Helen heaved herself out of a rocking chair in the corner. "What great luck," she said. "I'll be in and out every day to look at furniture and such, so I'll drive you to and from. This will be such fun!"

"Fun" wasn't the word that came to Gennie's mind. She'd have to be clever to do her sleuthing with Helen hanging over her shoulder. Though it was selfish and Rose would disapprove, Gennie said a silent prayer for the widow Mrs. Butterfield to become totally engrossed in her hunt for collectibles and to forget Gennie's existence. Helen, apparently unaffected by Gennie's prayer, sank back into the rocker with a sigh of contentment.

Gennie hid her aggravation with a bright smile as a tall, middle-aged woman entered the store. The woman's expression hardened as she stared at Gennie, who felt like slinking behind the counter.

"Honora, how nice of you to drop in," Sister Abigail said, with a friendliness that sounded forced. To Gennie's relief, Honora's harsh gaze shifted away from her, and she was able to study the woman without embarrassment. She recognized the name. From what she'd gathered during Mrs. Alexander's sherry-induced mumblings, the novitiate named Aldon had abandoned both his wife and his job as a minister to become a Believer. Honora was his wife's name, and this Honora certainly looked bitter enough to be an abandoned wife.

"We've finished more cloaks," Abigail said. "I know you were interested at one time. Shall I show you? We can always hem one to fit you."

"No, thank you." Honora's voice was deep and clipped, as if she resented the suggestion. She picked up a basket, frowned as if disappointed in its quality, and dropped it back on the table. Gennie was intrigued. Honora must once have been a lovely young woman. She had high cheekbones and full lips, and her thick brown hair, lightly streaked with gray, was pulled into a bun that rested on her neck. Her clothes were at least ten years old, Gennie guessed. Her dress had the shapeless look of a 1920s style, and Gennie could see the line in the fabric where the hem had been lowered. Matted fur trimmed the neck and wrists of her wool coat, and one elbow was close to needing a patch. Gennie doubted Honora could afford the twenty-six dollars for a Shaker cloak.

"I wish to speak to the eldress," Honora said. "Please call her here."

Abigail paused a few moments before responding. "I'm sure Fannie would be delighted to speak with you later in the day," she said. "Right now, I'm afraid she is busy with preparations for the celebration. You are planning to attend, aren't you? We'd love to have you."

"If the eldress refuses to speak with me, I will go directly to my husband."

Abigail stiffened. "I'm afraid that won't be possible. As you know, the brethren must keep apart."

"He isn't one of your so-called brethren, he is *my husband*, and I have a right to speak with him. What kind of people are you, anyway? You are keeping a wife from her husband. I should send the police out here. This can't be legal."

"I'm deeply sorry," Abigail said softly, "that Aldon's decision to become a Believer has caused you pain, Honora, but it is his decision to make, and I can't help but believe he was guided here. I pray that you will soften your heart toward him."

"Look at it this way," said Helen, from her rocking chair, "he hasn't left you for another woman. It took God to replace you." Helen beamed, as if she had offered the ultimate comfort. Gennie held her breath and watched, from her safe space behind the counter.

Her dark eyes crackling like fireworks, Honora turned on Helen. "Who are you, and what gives you the right to speak to me like that?" She looked Helen up and down. "You're obviously not one of *them*, you're too fat and lazy, so I suggest you keep your opinions to yourself." She turned toward the door, then suddenly swiveled around. Gennie couldn't help shrinking back as Honora marched to the counter, grabbed a handful of candied sweetflag, glared defiantly around the room, and left.

The store was silent for several minutes after Honora's dramatic exit. Gennie slid into a ladder-back chair and thought fondly of her nice, quiet mornings in the Languor Flower Shop, where the angriest customer she'd dealt with had complained that his roses had wilted before he could present them to his sweetheart.

"Does she visit often?" Gennie asked.

"Once or twice a week, I'm afraid," Abigail said. She released a long sigh. "She's very hungry, poor woman. Very hungry and very angry."

Rose busied herself scrubbing pans, everyone's least favorite task, and pondered the silence. Fannie had introduced her all around the kitchen, then left. Rose was the only Shaker sister in the room, and the two hired women seemed to feel too shy to talk around her. They avoided looking in her direction, so she took advantage of the situation to study them.

Both young women appeared to be about the same age, but there the similarity ended. Dulcie Masters, the dead girl's sister, was dressed in an old, loose Shaker work dress and she wore no apron, so her figure was completely hidden. Her face was round and pale. She moved quickly and seemed intent on her task. Though no indoor cap covered her pale brown hair, she looked and acted as if she were indeed a sister.

The woman named Carlotta DiAngelo was dark and thin, all sharp angles, with the hooded eyes of a hawk. Her gray cotton work dress fitted her snugly and fell to just below her knees, as if she'd grown up wearing it. Her movements were slow, bored. Clearly, she would rather be somewhere else.

Though both women wore light sweaters, neither seemed to notice the chill, which drove Rose to keep her hands in the warm, soapy water as long as possible. The kitchen was located in the basement of the Brick Dwelling House, and the several large ovens mostly went unused, so the temperature was much lower than Rose was used to back in North Homage's kitchen. Her wool work dress wasn't enough to keep her shoulders warm. She'd thought about working in her cloak, but it would be awkward.

The pans finished, Rose dried her hands and decided it was time to get the two women to talk. The faster she resolved this terrible situation, the faster she could get home to her own warm, cozy kitchen.

"Fannie mentioned that you two grew up together in Pittsfield," Rose said, as she swung a copper-bottomed pan onto a wall peg. She turned back around to find Dulcie staring wide-eyed at her as if she'd threatened them with expulsion into the cold.

"Why'd you want to talk to Fannie about us for?" Carlotta's expression had hardened into a mask of distrust. "We ain't important. We're just the hired help. Although you'd hardly know it to look at Dulcie." She grinned at Dulcie, whose cheeks reddened.

"We do not think less of you because you are not Shakers," Rose said.

Neither woman responded. Rose suspected they did not believe her. "Is there anything the sisters could do to make you feel more welcome here? I'd be glad to help."

Carlotta snorted softly, and Dulcie said only, "The sisters have been very kind." She lifted a flat broom from its peg and began sweeping up crumbs from under the worktable.

Rose had hoped to earn some trust to ease her questioning, but she saw her stay in Hancock stretching into weeks if she could not find a way to loosen the tongues of these people. Fannie had said that Carlotta was a bit of a gossip, but she certainly hid it well. Back in Kentucky, Rose could always count on a gossip to be a good source of information. Maybe people were different here, more closemouthed around strangers. Agatha wasn't there to urge her to be patient, and Rose was not one to sit on her hands. It was time to push ahead.

"Dulcie," she said, keeping her voice gentle and friendly, "I'm so sorry about your sister's sad death. You must be very upset. Were you close?"

Dulcie stopped in mid-sweep and looked as if she might crumple. But she said only "Thank you," and returned to her sweeping.

Rose tried again. "Carlotta, Fannie mentioned that you and Julia were the same age. Did you go to school together?"

Carlotta laughed. "If you can call fourth grade school," she said.

"You didn't go to the Shaker school?"

Carlotta shrugged her bony shoulders. "For a year. It was boring. I had better ways to spend my time." She snorted and tossed her straight dark hair, like a frustrated mare impatient for her feed. "Maybe things are different down where you come from, but around here, we have to work hard just to eat and stay warm. Julia and me, we didn't have rich families. We had to make do."

"You went to work young?" Rose asked.

Carlotta didn't respond.

"I suppose you had to work also, Dulcie?"

Again, Carlotta gave her characteristic snort. It was beginning to irritate Rose. "Dulcie? No, she's the baby sister. She got to go all the way through the Shaker school, got herself this job, and even got herself engaged, didn't you, Dulcie?" The bitterness in Carlotta's voice was unmistakable. She slopped a damp cloth onto the worktable as if it were responsible for her hard life.

"It's not my fault you and Julia were so wild," Dulcie

said. Her soft voice slid into a whine. "You didn't have to go
and—"

"You mind your own affairs, Miss Dulcie Goody Two-
Shoes," Carlotta said, "and I wouldn't be a bit surprised if
you're wilder than you let on." She tossed her cloth in the
sink and headed for the door. "You two can clean this place
up by yourselves."

Rose watched Carlotta's thin back disappear. It seemed
her questions had poked at a sore spot or two. It might be
worth tracking down some information about this so-called
wildness that Dulcie had attributed to both Carlotta and Julia. At this point, Rose was willing to look at anything that
might help explain the girl's death. She turned to ask Dulcie
for more information, but the young woman's cheeks had
lost all color, and her chest heaved under her loose bodice.
Before Rose realized what was happening, Dulcie's eyes
rolled upward, and she collapsed, crashing against a ladder-
back chair as she fell.

Rose ran to her and felt her pulse, which was slow and
weak. She had broken the delicate chair and scraped her
forehead on a cracked slat. An alarming amount of blood ran
down the side of her head. Rose grabbed a clean rag and
pressed it against the wound. She decided not to raise the
alarm just yet. The cut was small, surely too small to need a
stitch, and she knew that even slight head wounds bled profusely. This might be her only chance to probe Dulcie's secrets without prying ears around. She wished fervently that
she could call Josie, North Homage's Infirmary nurse,
whose discretion could be counted on.

In a few minutes, the bleeding stopped. Dulcie moaned
and opened her eyes. She squinted at Rose as if she couldn't
place her, then tried to scramble to her feet too quickly and
tumbled down again. This time, Rose was able to catch her
by her shoulders, which felt surprisingly thin.

"You've hurt yourself, but not too badly," Rose said, helping Dulcie to an undamaged chair. "But I'm very concerned about this fainting spell. Have you had any before now?"

Dulcie shook her head.

"Have you been feeling unwell?"

"Just a little. It's nothing to worry about." Dulcie tried to stand, and Rose pushed her back down.

"A fainting spell is indeed something to worry about," Rose said, using the firm tone she reserved for sisters who tried to avoid a much-needed confession. "You need to tell someone. If you are afraid to talk to Fannie or any of the Hancock sisters for fear of losing your job, then you'd better tell me. I can help you, and I give my word as a Believer that I will do my utmost to protect you." She pulled over another chair and sat directly across from Dulcie. "Let me help you," she said, more gently.

Tears spilled down Dulcie's cheeks and diluted the track of drying blood. She wiped away the tears and swallowed hard. Her red-rimmed eyes searched Rose's face with the hope and longing of a terrified child.

"If you tell," she said, "my life will be over."

Rose leaned toward her and took her cold hands. "If you don't let someone help you, this secret, whatever it is, might make you very ill."

Dulcie took a deep, ragged breath. "I'm not ill," she said. "I'm pregnant."

EIGHT

PART OF THE BRICK DWELLING HOUSE'S THIRD FLOOR
had been set aside to house the female hired help who
needed a place to live. Despite the sparse furnishings, for
most of the women these were the warmest, cleanest, and
most private rooms they had lived in for many years. After
Dulcie's startling revelation, Rose accompanied the young
woman back to her room to extract the whole story. Since
she'd become eldress, Rose had heard enough of the sisters' confessions to know that nothing could shock her—
and that the process could work miracles with a soul in
desperation. It mattered little that Dulcie was not a Shaker
sister.

Surrounded by her own belongings, Dulcie was calmer.
Rose glanced around the room, so familiar to her because it
was so similar to all other Shaker retiring rooms. Dulcie put
some effort into keeping it neat. The linens on the narrow
bed were as smooth as any Shaker hands could have made
them. The floor was swept, and a spare Shaker work dress
hung from a hanger hooked over a wall peg. However, Dulcie's worldly sensibilities showed in the decorations she had
placed wherever she could find a surface—a cluster of old
photographs in cracked frames; an empty red glass vase; a
bottle of cheap perfume; and an old Shaker box, in need of
refinishing.

Shyly, Dulcie offered Rose the one ladder-back chair, then sat on her bed. "It was kind of you to bring me back to my room," she said. "I'm feeling much better now, really I am. You don't need to stay."

"I was hoping we could talk awhile," Rose said.

Dulcie's puffy eyes roamed around her room, landing everywhere except on Rose. "I wish I could offer you some tea or something."

"That isn't necessary." Rose pulled her chair closer to the bed. "Dulcie, I think we should talk about what you told me just now in the kitchen."

Dulcie scooted farther back on her bed. "There's nothing you can do," she said. "It's my problem."

"Nay, it isn't just your problem," Rose said. "You are carrying a child, and if you do nothing to care for yourself, you and your child will both suffer."

Dulcie nervously twirled a ring with a small red stone around her finger.

"Is that your engagement ring?" Rose asked.

"It's a promise ring. Theodore gave it to me. He's saving for a real engagement ring."

Rose's question seemed to upset Dulcie even more. "I believe that I can help you," Rose said. "If you will let me. Have you been to a doctor?"

"I could never afford a doctor."

"The sisters would take you, and they would pay."

"No, they can't know. You don't understand. Oh, I shouldn't have told you anything. It was so stupid of me. Theodore is right about me." With an awkward movement that seemed to cause pain, she pulled her legs underneath her.

"Theodore is your fiancé, isn't he? Did he warn you not to reveal your condition to anyone?"

Dulcie said nothing.

"If he values the world's opinion over your health and the baby's future, if he won't take responsibility, then he is not worthy of you." The words came out harsher than Rose had intended.

"I know the Hancock Shakers well. I can promise you that Sister Fannie will help you through this, but you must confide in her. Or let me tell her. She and I will guard your privacy as long as possible, and you will have a place to live and be cared for during the birthing."

"No!" Dulcie flinched, as if the power of her own voice had frightened her. "You can't tell *anyone. Please.* Theodore would find out. He would never stand for it. He would leave me. I can't . . . I can't let that happen."

Rose's compassion was being sorely tested. She considered tucking Dulcie into her bed, then marching right over to Fannie and telling her everything. After all, the Believers considered it helpful to air sins to the entire community. Better to get this all out in the open. Better that she hadn't gotten involved in the first place, Rose thought. Her still evolving eldress instincts had gotten her into quagmires before. Yet on the other hand, both Dulcie and Theodore were connected with Julia, the dead girl, so Rose must inevitably involve herself with them.

"I'll tell you what," she said. "You won't be able to hide your condition forever, but I won't reveal it for as long as possible. Meanwhile, I myself will take you to a doctor." Wilhelm wouldn't like it, but she could have Andrew wire her sufficient funds to cover the expense of a doctor's visit and whatever medication might be necessary.

"But then the doctor would know," Dulcie objected. "He would tell Theodore and everyone else."

"Doctors don't do that. He will respect your privacy. If it will help you feel safer, I will take you to a doctor in another town. You *must* get medical care. You are obviously ill and in pain, and you are putting your baby in danger."

Dulcie was silent for several moments and then raised her eyes to Rose's face. "All right," she said, with a steadier voice. "I'll go with you to see a doctor. I know it may not seem like it, but I want my baby to have a good life."

Rose sighed with her whole body. She urged Dulcie to snuggle under her covers and rest. Feeling drained herself, Rose turned out the light and closed the retiring room door behind her. Her work had just become even more complicated. Regretfully, she rejected the notion of a nap and, instead, headed out into the cold to find Brother Ricardo, who oversaw the Brick Garage, so she could arrange to borrow an automobile as soon as possible.

After the excitement of Honora Stearn's visit, the Hancock Fancy Goods Store had settled into what was, for Gennie, frustrating boredom. Kitchen work was tedious, but at least cooking and cleaning up kept her busy. The flower shop she worked in was slow at times, but she could always immerse herself in arranging flowers and herbs. Here in the Fancy Goods Store, she had absolutely, totally nothing to do. Though it had only been a few hours, she felt as if she'd already sat for days, watching the door for any sign of an actual human being.

Sister Abigail spent her time in apparent bliss, rocking gently and knitting a red scarf at breakneck speed. She had asked nothing of Gennie, and she offered nothing in the way of conversation. Meanwhile, Gennie had wiped imaginary dust from every item in the store and rearranged the display of boxes. At Abigail's urging, she had sampled the candied sweetflag, savoring its sweet spiciness. Now she slumped against the curved slats of a ladder-back chair and lapsed into fond thoughts of Grady and longings to be with him.

Working in the store, she decided, would net her nothing except to keep her safely away from the excitement, which she suspected was Rose's intent all along. She should have insisted on pretending to be a novitiate. She'd be in the thick of things right now, working side by side with the murder suspects. The thought of what she was missing propelled her out of her chair so fast that it scraped the floor. Abigail started, gave her a puzzled look, then began to count her stitches.

"Sorry, I . . ." Gennie said, but Abigail was already engrossed in her knitting. With a sigh, Gennie turned to the window. A young man was approaching the store. He was dressed in simple brown work clothes, clearly Shaker in style, though not as old-fashioned as the clothing Wilhelm insisted they wear in North Homage. He must be one of the novitiates.

From what she could see, he was tall and thin and not at all bad-looking. She'd lived with the Shakers long enough to experience a twinge of guilt when she noticed an attractive man, but that didn't stop her. He swept some snow off the steps with his feet, then whipped off his hat as he crossed the porch toward the front door. Gennie caught sight of wavy black hair, streaked with silver.

By the time he came through the inner door leading to the Fancy Goods Store, Gennie had positioned herself behind the counter. She gave him a welcoming smile as he entered. He stopped just inside the door and returned her smile, holding her gaze with his own. There was something else in those liquid brown eyes, something compelling. Now she felt genuine guilt. However, she told herself that this intriguing man was a Shaker novitiate and just being friendly to the newly hired help. Nothing to worry about. But she rearranged her face into a more businesslike demeanor.

"Sewell, how nice of you to stop by," Abigail said, carefully pushing her knitting back on the needles and laying it on her rocking chair seat as she rose to greet him. "Let me introduce you to Miss Gennie Malone, who has come all the way up from the South to help us. Gennie, this is Sewell, soon to be one of the brethren, we hope." Such was the pride and warmth in her voice that Abigail might have been introducing her own son.

Sewell shifted his gaze back to Gennie, tilting his head with interest. Gennie felt her cheeks flush.

"All the way from the warm South, just to help us? We are honored," he said. He had a gentle voice, which reminded Gennie of her favorite crick, behind the herb fields at North Homage, after a spring rain. It was impossible to take offense at his teasing.

"Sewell has been such a godsend," Abigail said. "He has architectural training, you know, and he has been developing all sorts of wonderful plans for saving our poor old buildings."

Gennie noticed that Sewell continued to hold her eyes while Abigail extolled his virtues. "It's work that I enjoy," he said, with quiet modesty. "Did you know the Shakers in Kentucky?" he asked.

"I've heard good things about them."

"Ah. Then perhaps you are considering becoming a Believer?"

Gennie couldn't think of a quick answer to that, so she just shrugged.

"That was too personal a question, I'm sorry," Sewell said. "I only wondered because you've come such a long way just to be with Shakers." He shifted his gaze and his smile to Abigail.

"I've come with difficult news, Abigail," he said. "I may not be able to finish those oval boxes you wanted as quickly as I'd hoped. The police want to question me again this afternoon. I suspect they may arrest me for Julia's murder."

Abigail dropped onto her rocking chair with a thump, ignoring the pile of knitting beneath her. "They can't possibly think you had anything to do with that. Can they?" Her voice came out as a squeak.

Now that she was no longer the object of attention, Gennie

watched Sewell carefully. She was surprised at his open admission of his fears. She noted that he was more than thin; he was gaunt, his flesh drawn tightly over long, slight bones. In the light from the windows, his cheeks were hollow caverns beneath his cheekbones. Gennie felt an urge to feed him.

Before Sewell had a chance to answer, a thin young woman, dressed in worldly work clothes and carrying a basket full of fabric items, slipped in the door just behind him. She edged around and stood too close to him. He didn't move, but his eyes darted nervously. The young woman's grin and one arched eyebrow conveyed both flirtation and challenge, as if she were daring him to step out of bounds.

"Hello, Carlotta," he said. With a nod to Gennie and Abigail, he was out the door before Carlotta could formulate a response.

Carlotta turned her grin on Gennie. "Dreamy, isn't he?" she asked. "You must be the girl who's takin' Julia's place, now she's dead."

Gennie said nothing. As she remembered from Rose's description, Carlotta was a hired girl, a friend of Julia's, who worked in the kitchen, which probably explained her odd disposition. Kitchen work could make anyone cranky and rebellious.

"Are those the extra pincushions the sisters promised?" Abigail asked, with none of the warmth she'd lavished on Sewell.

"Yeah, and some of those ugly apple-head dolls."

"I'll take them, and you can get back to work."

"Sure," said Carlotta. "Also, Fannie said I should ask if you want Miss Gennie here to have a sandwich during the noon meal, like Julia used to sometimes, so you can go eat in the dining room with the others. Of course, after Julia, you may not want any more girls left alone in the shop."

"That'll be enough, Carlotta. No one can be sure it was Julia who took those items, so don't go spreading stories around. The poor girl is gone; leave her be." Abigail turned to Gennie. "Would you be willing to stay and eat here while I'm in the dining room? After I return, you can have an hour to yourself before coming back to work. Otherwise, we have to close the store during the noon hour."

"That would be fine," Gennie said, trying to keep her enthusiasm out of her voice. An hour on her own, to wander around the village. Then she could finally get some useful sleuthing done.

"I'll be along in about half an hour then," Carlotta said. "Wish I could stay for a chat, but the food won't cook itself."

Abigail and Gennie watched Carlotta negotiate the snowy walk toward the Brick Dwelling House. "I know that girl is a friend of Dulcie's," Abigail muttered, "but I'm glad she'll only be here through Mother Ann's Birthday. I doubt she does much work at all when no one is looking. It's so difficult these days, with so few of us. Right now we have nearly as much hired help as we do Believers, and none of them cares about work as we do. Not even Dulcie and Theodore, though they're the best of the lot."

Abigail shook her head and returned to her rocking chair to resume her knitting. She seemed to have forgotten Gennie's presence. "Imagine accusing Julia of theft, just because she worked here," Abigail muttered under her breath as she frowned at her stitches. "Why, it could have been anyone wandering in when there was just poor Julia to watch over everything. Probably just a child wanting a toy to play with. They have so little nowadays."

NINE

GENNIE DEVOURED HER CHEESE SANDWICH AND LINGERED over the pot of peppermint tea Carlotta had brought her from the kitchen. She was alone in the Fancy Goods Shop, since Sister Abigail had invited Mrs. Butterfield to join her in the dining room. Gennie was plotting the hour she'd have to herself, after Abigail's return. If she could escape Mrs. Butterfield and find other transportation back to the boarding-house, maybe she could extend her investigations after store hours.

Helen Butterfield was becoming a problem, but not one that couldn't be solved with a little cleverness, an alteration in Rose's plans for her, and maybe a tiny white lie. Gennie had decided to plead poverty and see if she could wangle a room in the Brick Dwelling House, where she knew other hired girls lived. Rose wouldn't like it and would probably worry endlessly about her, but Gennie was determined. She would surely go crazy if she could have only one hour of excitement a day. Right after her time off, she'd talk to Abigail about moving in that evening. She'd offer a cut in her wages. She didn't really need the money, after all; Grady had given her plenty.

Grady. She frowned at the soggy bits of peppermint leaf in the bottom of her cup. He'd find out about the plan as soon as she called him that evening, as she'd promised to do, and he wouldn't like it any better than Rose. On the other hand, if she were to spend one more night in the boardinghouse, she could sort of forget to mention to him that she was moving the next day. They'd agreed she would call every other day. That would give her two whole days living in Hancock before she had to deal with Grady, and maybe she'd have gotten Rose on her side by then. Honestly, those two. She loved them both deeply, but they just wouldn't let her grow up. She was nearly twenty, and she'd been out in the world for almost two years. It was time they understood that she was a modern woman. She could take care of herself.

With the noon meal finished, Rose put aside her worries about Dulcie and planned her afternoon. Arranging a car to take Dulcie to a doctor later in the afternoon had turned out to be easy. Brother Ricardo hadn't questioned her purpose or even asked whether she felt comfortable driving on snowy Massachusetts roads. Rose wasn't entirely confident of her ability and almost wished he had insisted upon driving her, though it would have made Dulcie anxious. On the other hand, a nice, private chat with the young woman could prove helpful.

With the noon meal just finished, Rose set out to see the place where Julia Masters had died—the Sisters' Summerhouse. Rose wrapped herself in her cloak and pulled a pair of galoshes over her shoes, so she could wander around in the snow without catching her death. She knew the Summerhouse was unheated, so she expected to suffer even inside.

As she walked around outside the small building, it struck her that the killer had been bold to the point of recklessness. The Summerhouse was so near the Brick Dwelling House. Though it was largely ignored during the winter months, the thought that someone had strangled Julia so close to the living quarters of all the Hancock Shakers chilled her far more than the snow drifting over the tops of her galoshes.

The body had been found at a small old table where the sisters often sat on warm summer evenings to share a pot of tea. The windows of the nearby dwelling house were usually kept closed during the winter, and the other buildings surrounding the Summerhouse would have been empty at night, so it was understandable that no one heard a scream or a struggle. However, it surprised her that no one could determine how long Julia had sat at the table, her dead hands seeming to reach for some unknown item. Fannie had said only that the village was so distracted by the plans for Mother Ann's Birthday celebration that no one had even glanced into the Summerhouse.

Rose tried the front door. It was unlocked, open to the world even after such a betrayal. She stepped inside. The building was tiny, especially compared with the huge Brick Dwelling House. Unlike many of the other buildings, it was still used. Yet, to Rose, it had the forlorn look of an abandoned home. It held one nicked old table and a ladder-back chair badly in need of repair and a new finish. Dust gathered in ridges across the floor. For Rose, the smell of death still lingered.

There wasn't much more to be learned from the lonely building; it raised more questions than it answered. How could a girl in a summer dancing gown be enticed to a nighttime rendezvous in such a place? Had Julia been positioned after death to look as if she were reaching for something? Food? A gift? Was she meeting with a blackmailer, who had something she wanted back? Surely a blackmailer would be unlikely to kill his source of illicit income. Was Julia the blackmailer, killed by her victim? Were her outstretched arms meant to symbolize a greedy, grasping nature?

A gust of wind from the open door swirled snow around her feet, and Rose shivered, more with horror than with cold. She believed, along with her brethren, that all killing was evil, but there was something especially malevolent about this murder. The frigid air in the Summerhouse befitted the cold-blooded nature of the act. This killer was surely no jilted lover, driven by anguish to destroy the thing he loved most. The murder must have been planned with precision, or it would never have happened.

Rose was more than ready to leave and begin her search for answers. She closed the door behind her and felt her soul lighten just to be out of the building. She wondered if the Hancock sisters might consider a cleansing ritual, to purify their Summerhouse before they used it again. A few years earlier, Rose would never have seen the value of such an old-fashioned service, but she'd found herself changing recently. Those century-old rituals, used so frequently during Mother Ann's Work, were now almost unknown. The dancing and the singing and the mimed actions bound Believers together and connected them to Heaven, their spiritual home. She'd come to see how valuable this could be—though perhaps she wouldn't admit it to Wilhelm just yet.

"Well, sweet Nellie, have you missed me?" A man the size and shape of a leprechaun slapped the rump of a Holstein, which mooed in response. "I thought you might, so I've come to visit you." The man's short, scrawny body curved backward as he stretched and yawned. "Time for a nap," he said. "Try not to make a racket, there's a good girl."

Rose's galoshes made little noise on the wood floor of the Barn Complex as she approached the sound of the hired man's voice. She caught sight of his head, covered with tight sandy curls, just before he slipped down to the hay-coated ground beside the passive animal, presumably to begin the promised nap. *This has to be Otis*, she thought. *No Shaker brother would be so lazy as to nap during work hours.*

Otis Friddle had, according to Fannie, found Julia's lifeless body as he'd headed past the Summerhouse on his way to the Barn Complex, which was east of the abandoned Round Stone Barn. It was astonishing that such a lazy man would even bother to look into the Summerhouse—but then, since he was walking the long way around, he was probably trying to slow down his journey to work.

"Are you Otis?" Rose asked loudly, as she peered into the stall.

His sandy head, with hay woven into the curls, popped up over the Holstein's black-and-white back. "Lord Almighty, you scared the life out of me! Sister, I mean. I mean, you startled me, Sister. Yep, that's me—Otis Friddle, rhymes with griddle."

Otis's head ducked down again and reappeared at Nellie's rump. He flashed a smile full of crooked, tobacco-stained teeth.

Rose had visited Hancock before, but hired folk came and went, and Otis had not been among the ones she'd met. Nor, she suspected, would he stay long.

"I believe Fannie explained that she asked me here to help solve the tragic death of Julia Masters."

"Ah, yes, I remember now. Your name's Violet, right?"

"Rose," she said. "Sister Rose."

"Right. Rose." He smiled again and backed up, as if he considered the conversation over.

"I was told I'd find you here," Rose said. She tried to sound friendly, though she was growing impatient. "I was also told that you were the one who discovered Julia's body." Otis had wizened, weather-worn features that made it difficult to determine his age. He could have been anywhere from thirty to fifty years old.

"Poor Julia. Yeah, I'm the one found her. Gave me a terrible shock, I don't mind telling you."

"Would you be willing to interrupt your work and talk with me about it?" Rose asked.

"Sure," Otis said. Her sarcasm was lost on him.

"I need to know everything you remember, no matter how inconsequential it might seem."

"I already talked to the police."

"I know, but Fannie has asked me to look into this, so I'd appreciate hearing your observations firsthand."

Otis ducked around the cow's rump and let himself out of the stall. "Glad to help, of course," he said. Rose suspected his willingness had much to do with avoiding work, but she had to admit he was also giving up his nap to talk to her.

"This floor's cold on the feet," Otis said.

Rose controlled her irritation as Otis sauntered through the long, chilly main section of the Barn complex looking for a place to sit. *If he'd move a little faster,* she thought, *maybe his feet wouldn't get so cold.* Rose sighed at her own impatience. She certainly did have a penchant for uncharitable thoughts, and a confession to the eldress might be a good idea.

Otis led her to some hay bales piled crookedly against the wall and climbed on top of one, crossing his legs underneath him. Rose was grateful he knew enough not to offer to help her up—though his motivation was more likely sheer laziness than good manners. Never mind, she just wanted to get on with the task at hand. Luckily, she was tall and strong, since she did some physical labor every day, as did all the able-bodied Believers in North Homage. She hoisted herself onto a hay bale next to Otis's.

"What time did you find Julia?" she asked.

Otis pulled out a piece of hay and began chewing on it. "Way before dawn," he said. "I was on my way to do the milking."

The sun rose about six-thirty this time of year, but it was likely that Otis was not quite as prompt as he'd implied.

"Did you see anyone else around? Anyone at all?"

"Nope, not a soul. Not after I got past the Barn Complex, that is."

"Who did you see near the barn?"

Otis scrunched up his face and multiplied his wrinkles. "Just the usual folk. Hired men."

"Who, exactly?"

"Well, Theodore, but he's our boss, so of course he'd be up and about. Then just as I was passing the barn, Theodore met up with Aldon and then Sewell, those two baby Shakers. They didn't see me."

Probably because you stayed out of sight to avoid getting hauled in to work, Rose thought. "If you were on your way to milk the cows, what took you to the area of the Summerhouse? Surely it was out of your way?"

Otis spit a hunk of pulverized hay on the stone floor, then selected another. "Had to pick something up at the Brethren's Workshop," he said.

"So you left the Brick Dwelling House, walked past the Barn Complex, then headed northwest to the Brethren's Workshop?"

Otis nodded and chewed.

Rose had an excellent geographical memory, and she could see the arrangement of Hancock Village in her mind. "I'm still puzzled," she said. "To return to the barn, you should have headed southeast, but instead you went west and rounded the Summerhouse. Why was that?"

Otis stiffened. "Didn't know I was going to get the third degree about it," he said. "I just wanted a walk, was all. It was snowing. I like snow."

Perhaps it was not out of the question for an Easterner to do such a thing, Rose reasoned, though it made little sense to her. The pleasures of wandering around in the snow escaped her.

"All right, so you walked past the Summerhouse and looked inside, where you saw—would you describe what you saw, in your own words?"

Otis chewed, spit, then began the ritual again. Rose felt her appetite dwindling.

"I looked in through the window and saw the table and the chair, with Julia in it. Damn shame. Pretty girl."

"Tell me everything you did after that." Rose was hoping to get him to say more than a sentence or two at a time. At this rate, the questioning would take all afternoon.

Otis shrugged. "I ran inside, of course, to see if I could help her. She was too far gone, though. Cold as ice. So I left and went to the big house and called for help."

"Did you move Julia?"

"Are you kidding? The whole thing was too spooky for me. I just wanted the hell out. There she was, leaning on the table with her arms out like she was reaching for food or something, and she was wearing that frilly dress with no sleeves. I thought maybe she'd had a spell and then froze to death, but I couldn't figure why she'd be there in the first place."

"Could you tell she'd been strangled?"

Otis looked sheepish. "Well, I guessed it, on account of that long piece of her dress was still wrapped around her neck. Didn't look decent, so I unwound it. The cops gave me hell for that."

"I can imagine," Rose said. If Julia had been strangled with her own dress, the killer could be either a man or a woman. It wouldn't take an inordinate amount of strength to strangle someone from behind with a long length of fabric.

"After you called for help, did you go back with the others to the Summerhouse?"

"Well, yeah, I did. I mean, I was spooked and all, but this is a pretty boring place most of the time. I didn't want to miss anything. Besides, I figured these Shakers would be too shocked to be worth much, so I went back inside with Sister Fannie. She was the only one brave enough to look. Besides Dulcie, of course."

"Dulcie? She saw her sister's body?"

"Yeah, she was there first, before me and Sister Fannie.

She must have run right over. She was Julia's sister, after all. When we got there, she was fussing over Julia's body like she was trying to figure out how she died. She even lifted up the skirt. Don't know why." Otis's face broadened in a ghoulish grin. "I didn't mind seeing Julia's legs one last time, I can tell you." He watched Rose closely, as if hoping for signs of embarrassment. She did not oblige.

"What happened next?"

"Nothing much. Sister Fannie chased us out and made one of those baby Shakers—Johnny Jenkins, it was—guard the door until the police arrived."

"Fannie said the police suspect that Sewell Yates had something to do with Julia's death. Do you have any idea why they might think such a thing?"

Otis's eyebrows lifted and turned his forehead into a maze of crevices. "No one told you about Sewell?" He chuckled. "That Sewell, if he ever makes it to grown-up Shaker, that might be enough to make me believe in miracles. Sewell's got an eye for the girls, he has. I've seen him flirt with every girl in this place, even the old biddies. Just can't help himself. He had his eye on Julia and Dulcie both. Can't blame him. They're both pretty things, though Dulcie's looking more and more like a Shaker these days. No wonder Theodore's been so cranky lately. Anyway, I wouldn't be surprised if Sewell had something going with Julia, and I'm not the only one who thinks so."

"Did you observe anyone else being very friendly with Julia?" Rose asked.

"Too friendly, you mean?" Otis grinned. "I'd have a hard time naming a man who *wasn't*. Eyed her myself, a bit—but she wasn't interested in the likes of me." There was no obvious bitterness in his voice. "Well, let me think. Julia had set her sights on Johnny, that's for sure. She'd get all slinky and bat her eyelashes when he was around."

"How did Johnny respond?"

"Never saw him do anything he shouldn't, if you know what I mean. Which doesn't mean nothing happened. Johnny, he's not above using a person to get what he wants." This time there was an edge to his voice.

"What do you mean?"

Otis shrugged. "Just that he's got himself most in mind."

"How did Theodore get along with Julia?"

"She flirted with him, too, of course. She always liked a man better if he already had a girl. Theodore, he didn't really mind. He'd say how bad she was, but I'd see him eyeing her when he figured no one was watching."

"What about Aldon?"

Otis's genial expression hardened. "Don't like that man. Thinks he's got a telephone line to God's house. I never saw him so much as glance at Julia," he said, with obvious regret, "but he sure is a strange sort."

"In what way?"

"Well, I was wandering around one night—just looking at the snow, you know—and when I got near the old Stone Barn, I heard these sounds coming through the cracks in the wall. Sounded like an animal in mortal pain, but I knew there hadn't been animals in that barn for ages. I got real curious, so I peeked in a window. It was Aldon, and damned if he wasn't kneeling on the ground, with his shirt off, whipping himself with a bit of rope. He was putting some muscle into it, too. His back was all red, and he kept mumbling to himself. Gave me the creeps, I can tell you. I hightailed it on back to my room, and you can bet I stay away from him, if I can. He's not right in the head."

"Did you mention this incident to Fannie—or to anyone else?"

Otis shook his head. "Not till now. I figured it must be one of those weird things Shakers do in private, you know?"

Rose neither confirmed nor denied his belief. Certainly, during Mother Ann's Work, a century earlier, some Believers had tried to purify their souls by denying themselves food and sleep. Sometimes they danced or prayed for days on end. Aldon, who sounded overzealous, probably thought that by punishing his flesh, he was emulating early Shakers. In time, he would surely learn that confession served to purify without destroying the body.

"You did the right thing," Rose told Otis. It was the best way she could think of to keep him from spreading the story to the police. Maybe he would be superstitious enough to think evil would befall him if he opened his mouth. She had enough to handle without worrying about the world whispering rumors about odd, secret Shaker practices.

She'd certainly gotten Otis to loosen his tongue, but she had run out of questions. Best to stop and move on. He seemed to enjoy talking to her now; she could always seek him out again.

"I won't take you away from your work any longer," she said, favoring him with a smile. "Thank you for your insights." She slid off the hay bale and headed for the barn door, aware that Otis hadn't moved. No doubt he intended to take his belated nap right where he was.

Rose hiked toward the Brethren's Workshop, trying to remain grateful for her galoshes, even though her feet were soaked from the snow that had sneaked over the rims and inside. The time spent questioning Otis had felt longer than it actually was, and she was eager to find out as much as possible before the evening meal. Questioning one of the novitiates seemed like the logical next step, and she had settled on Aldon Stearn. She knew he'd been a Congregationalist minister, and she hoped that meant he was honest and forthright. She was also curious to judge for herself whether he was "right in the head."

The Brethren's Workshop was a plain building two and a half stories high. Rose noted at once that it was badly in need of new paint, especially along the windows. When Rose first entered the building, she thought it was empty. Then she heard the gentle swish of straw and realized that someone in the far corner of the building was making flat brooms. She followed the sound and came upon Brother Ricardo, bent over a winder, his back to her. She cleared her throat, and he turned instantly.

"I'm sorry to disturb your work, but I was told I could find Aldon here."

Ricardo smiled and pointed upward, which Rose interpreted to mean that Aldon was upstairs, not that he had achieved Heaven. She thanked the brother, who was back at his work before she'd turned around.

She'd first seen Aldon Stearn when he had filed into the dining room with the other men. He was tall and distinguished, with well-groomed gray hair and a prominent chin. He held his head high, perhaps just a shade higher than humility demanded, but there was time for him to shake off pride before signing the Covenant.

Rose climbed the stairs to the second floor. The afternoon had grown cloudy, and the lights were off, leaving the large room dim and gray. She walked a few steps into the cluttered work area and located Aldon, seated close to a window, which gave him barely enough light to work. He was struggling with a thin strip of wood with swallowtail shapes cut on one end. Rose recognized the beginnings of an oval box.

Aldon wasn't aware of her presence. With mild guilt, she watched him work, hoping for clues to his character. He seemed to be learning how to make Shaker boxes, a task requiring considerable skill. The wood had been soaked in a bucket of water to make it pliable, but it was also slippery. Aldon forced it into an oval shape over a form, only to have it slide through his fingers and pop out again. He grabbed the ends and tried again, his face contorted in frustration.

Rose's guilt overcame her curiosity. She cleared her

throat. Aldon started, dropping the strip of wood, which bounced off his lap and onto the floor. He did not bend down to retrieve it. His dark blue eyes stared at her with fierce intensity. Rose began to wonder if she had made the wisest choice for her first interview of a novitiate.

"Forgive me for ruining your concentration," Rose said. "We haven't met. I'm Rose, and I'm—"

"I know who you are," Aldon said. His rich baritone voice must have held his congregation spellbound. "You are that eldress from North Homage, and you are here to help us with our current dilemma. I must tell you that I find it ridiculous for Fannie to have called you all the way up here for something our police are far better equipped to handle."

Rose dusted some shavings off a ladder-back chair and sat down. "I have had some success with such problems before," she said. "Fannie felt that, as a Believer myself, I might possess knowledge and understanding that the police lack."

"I can't imagine what that might be," Aldon said.

Rose forced her mouth into a faint smile. "Can't you? How interesting."

The two stared at each other for several moments. Rose used the time to pray for a calmness of spirit that she often had trouble attaining. Aldon's face gave little away. Finally, he shifted his eyes away from Rose.

"If Fannie wants you to investigate this tragedy, then of course I will cooperate in any way I can. For the sake of our village, I want this cleared up as soon as possible."

"Thank you. I am told that the police suspect one of your fellow novitiates, Sewell Yates. Does this seem a reasonable suspicion to you?"

Aldon leaned over and retrieved the piece of maple at his feet. He laid it on the workbench, dusted it slowly with a rag, and replaced it in the bucket of water. As he straightened again, he smoothed his thick gray hair back in place with a quick movement.

"Sewell has far to go before he knows the joys of salvation," he said, "but I can't believe he would stoop to killing."

"What would you say are his spiritual weaknesses?"

"He does not fear the wrath of our Father enough."

Rose hadn't planned to argue theology with Aldon, but the harshness of his words disturbed her. "Perhaps Sewell is feeling the light and love of Holy Mother Wisdom," she said.

"That is the argument of a woman."

Though the Shaker way of life placed men and women on an equal plane, Rose was undisturbed by Aldon's patronizing attitude. She had dealt with Wilhelm long enough to know that, while Believers strove for perfection, they did not always achieve it.

"In your estimation, then, why should Sewell become more fearful of God's wrath?" she asked.

"He is weak and undisciplined. He has goodness in him, but his behavior is an abomination, always has been."

"You knew him before you both became novitiates?"

"He was one of my parishioners," Aldon said, avoiding her gaze. "He came to Hancock shortly after I'd settled in, and I was surprised to see him. He had often failed as a Congregationalist, and I'm afraid he will fail as a Shaker. I doubt he'll stay past spring. The life is too demanding for him."

"What did Sewell do to make himself so unworthy in your eyes?"

Aldon fixed her with a bright stare that sent an involuntary shiver down her spine. "He lived loose and fast," he said, in an intense whisper. "He drank and smoked and fornicated, and what little remorse he showed was no more than playacting. I wasted untold energy trying to win him to the ways of the Father, to show him how his behavior pained and angered his God, but Sewell's soul is without strength. He cannot change, and he lures others to follow him. It would be better if he were to leave here and drink himself to death in the world, where he belongs. Then, perhaps, he will understand the depth of God's fury."

Rose digested his words for a few silent moments. Wilhelm at his most inspired could almost shake the Meetinghouse roof, and the evil of carnality was one of his favorite homily topics. Aldon, she guessed, was destined to be an elder, though she hoped he would absorb something more of the Shaker theology beyond the blessedness of celibacy.

"Do you know, has Sewell continued his bad habits after coming to Hancock and proclaiming his intention to become a Believer?"

Rose thought she saw a faint wince cross his face as he nodded.

"Was he involved with Julia Masters?"

"Do you mean, did I catch them fornicating together? Never. However, I observed them many times in deep conversation, apparently thinking they were hidden from view. Knowing Sewell's character, I drew my own conclusions. The girl was a temptress, no better than a whore, and Sewell is weak enough to fall into the flesh."

"Did you know Julia?"

Aldon's jaw tightened. "She, too, was a parishioner, as was her family. Her parents were God-fearing, for all the good it did them; their children were cut from coarser cloth."

"Dulcie, as well?"

"Both of them."

"Did you have occasion to see anyone else paying attention to Julia?"

"More than I can remember, since she was fifteen. She led astray many of the more promising young men in my congregation."

"And since she began working here in Hancock?"

"All the hired men, certainly, including Theodore."

"Theodore Geist, the man Dulcie's is engaged to?"

Aldon raised his face to the ceiling and smiled, as if sharing a private joke with the Heavens. "Their engagement is nothing but a sham."

"Are you suggesting that Theodore is unfaithful to Dulcie? Have you seen this for yourself?"

Aldon did not answer. Rose decided not to press him until she could hear what others had to say. "I'd like to speak with you again later, if you are willing."

Aldon inclined his head in a gesture of noblesse oblige.

Though it would cost her a thorough confession, Rose gave a silent prayer of thanks for those who were obsessed with their own holiness—they watched their "inferiors" so carefully, and they made such willing gossips.

TEN

Gennie had already spent much of her precious free hour wandering around Hancock Village, learning the layout. The number of empty, deteriorating buildings stunned and saddened her. To be truthful, she had no idea how to proceed. In North Homage, it had been easy. She knew everyone, and she knew where each person was assigned to be.

She was at the northwest end of the village, just beyond the Brick Dwelling House. She knew that the buildings just across the road were mostly unused. The old Schoolhouse hadn't heard Shaker children's voices for years, and it had been sold just a few years earlier. The Ministry Shop, where once the elders and eldresses had worked, was far too big and lonely for Fannie, the last remaining eldress, who chose to stay with the others in the Brick Dwelling House.

Just in front of her, Gennie saw the saddest sight of all—the abandoned Meetinghouse. It had held no dancing worship for decades, Abigail had told her, and it was due to be razed soon. The distinctive gambrel roof had been transformed at some point into gables, so the building was two stories high. Lots of room, and no one using it. Soon it would be gone. Investigations notwithstanding, Gennie would never forgive herself if she left Hancock without seeing the inside of their Meetinghouse.

As she approached the building, the effects of its abandonment became clear. The white paint was flaked and discolored in places, and several broken windows had been replaced with boards nailed to the outside. A shutter hung askew, its nails corroded through. Was this the future for Rose and the village that had raised Gennie?

Out of habit, Gennie walked through the unshoveled path to the sisters' entrance. She tried the door, fully expecting it to be locked or nailed shut. It swung open, making a scraping sound, as if it no longer fit the frame. Tentatively, almost expecting to encounter a bevy of dancing Shaker ghosts, Gennie entered the building and stood just inside.

The ghosts were there, in the middle of the dingy pine floor, clustered in a loose circle, jumping and twirling in Shaker dancing worship. Except they were doing it all wrong. The men and the women were mixed together, weren't they? That wasn't right. Gennie blinked several times to clear her vision—and her feverish imagination.

"Mummy," squealed one of the figures, "they've found us. Now they'll make us stay apart, and we'll never, ever be together again."

"Hush, now," said a deeper, calmer voice, which Gennie realized belonged to the only adult in the group. The other figures—five or six of them, as far as she could tell—were children of varying ages, but none older than perhaps ten years. As her eyes adapted to the poor light from the few unboarded windows, she saw two boys and four girls. All of them, including the woman, wore jackets over simple clothing reminiscent of Shaker dress.

"I don't know who you are," said the woman, "but you might as well come on in."

"My name is Gennie Malone. I'm new here, just started helping out in the store."

"You're not a new novitiate then?" There was relief in the woman's voice.

"No, not at all."

A small towheaded creature attached itself to the woman's arm. "Mummy, Mummy, she'll tell on us. Don't talk to her."

"Hush, now, honey. Sarah, take everyone over to the corner and tell them a story," the woman said to the oldest child, a serious-looking girl with blond curls and spectacles. "Run along now, go with Sarah." With some difficulty, she detached the towhead and handed him over to a larger boy, who took his hand and dragged him off.

"I'm sorry about all the fuss. My name is Esther, Esther Jenkins. I'm a Shaker novitiate."

"Are you a teacher?"

Esther glanced over at the children and shook her head. "These are my children," she said. "Have you had much experience with Shakers before now?"

"I've heard about them," Gennie said.

"I see." Esther's shoulders slumped. "Then you know that I am not supposed to be here with my children?"

"Yes, I do, but I assure you, I have no intention of giving you away. I'm not a Shaker myself, nor ever likely to become one, but someday I hope to be a mother." She held out her left hand with shy pride. "I'm engaged to be married."

"Then you understand," Esther said. "I just wanted to be with my children. Giving up the care of my little ones has been the hardest thing I've ever done. They are so precious to me, more precious than my own life."

"I don't understand. Why would you give them up to become a Shaker?"

Esther raised sad gray eyes to Gennie's face. "I truly hope your marriage is a long and happy one, blessed with love and children. Mine was not. Johnny—my husband—he always had such grand plans, and six children slowed him down."

"He left you to take care of six children by yourself?" Gennie was horrified and, to tell the truth, a little frightened.

"Worse. He decided to join the Shakers. He's a novitiate, like me. He pressured me to join, too."

"How could he pressure you?"

"You'd have to know my parents. I came from . . . Well, my parents were dead-set against me marrying Johnny, but I was eighteen and headstrong, and Johnny was so different from the silly boys I'd grown up with. Or so I thought. Anyway, I ran off with him. I wanted children so much. As you can see, we had quite a few." Esther laughed, and her eyes brightened.

"And money became a problem?" Gennie guessed. "The Depression must have been very hard on such a large family."

"I loved being a mother. But Johnny, he got more and more irritated with how much time and money children take. He was lucky enough to have a job, but he didn't earn much. He wanted more, much more. Children got in the way, and after a while, a wife got in the way, too." Esther stared at the floor. "Johnny said the only way he'd contribute any more to raising the children is if I'd join the Shakers, and if I refused, he'd tell my parents I'd left him. They'd come and get me, and they'd take my children away from me. I know them. They'd hire nannies and tutors, and pretty soon, I wouldn't be their mother anymore."

"Your parents are well-to-do?"

"Oh yea. Father never believed in banks or the stock market, so he came through the crash without a scratch. Father would say it's because most people are gullible and stupid. You can be sure he thinks the same of me for marrying Johnny, and he would never let me forget it."

A squeal arose from the corner of the room, as Sarah's story apparently reached an exciting moment. Esther watched the group with tender wistfulness. "I don't want Father and Mother raising my children," she said. "I don't want them to learn the ways of the rich, and I don't want them to learn to value money above all else."

"Then I should think the Shakers would be a good choice to raise them."

"*I* want to raise my children." Fury contorted Esther's delicate features. "Can't you understand that? They are *my children*."

"Yes, of course I understand," Gennie said quickly. "I'm sure no one, not even the Shakers, could do a better job. Anyway, Hancock seems not to have enough spare hands to raise and educate many children."

"No, they don't, but they still don't want me spending time with my own children. They hired a tutor from Pittsfield to teach them in a room in the Brick Dwelling House. The only reason they are with me now is because the teacher and I arranged it. She could get fired if the Shakers find out."

Esther nodded to a dark corner of the Meetinghouse. Gennie made out a figure curled up on the floor, covered with a coat. "She is their tutor," Esther said. "I knew her back in Pittsfield. She's a seamstress at night and teaches during the day, just to make ends meet. She pretends to take the children on an outing, but she really brings them to me, and she naps while I watch them. They are the only children here right now, so no one has reason to suspect. You're sure you won't tell?"

"I promise," Gennie glanced at her watch, a gift from Grady. She had two minutes to get back to the store. For the first day, she supposed she could claim to have gotten lost, but it wasn't the best approach to asking for room and board. "I completely understand your need to be with your children," she said. "In fact, I feel we have a lot in common, and maybe we could be friends."

Esther didn't look appalled by the idea, so Gennie forged ahead. "Maybe we could talk again? I feel rather lonely out here, so far from my home."

"I know what you mean," Esther said. "Of course, we can talk again. I try to see the children every day about this time, though not always in the same place. Just check the abandoned buildings, you're likely to run into us."

"I'll do that," Gennie promised. "Until then . . ."

Gennie entered the store at the stroke of one o'clock, only slightly out of breath. She smiled at Abigail, who glanced up briefly from her knitting.

"You haven't missed a thing, my dear," Abigail said. "Not a single customer. We have so many lovely items for Mother Ann's Birthday, and the world doesn't seem to care in the least."

No sooner had she spoken than a man entered the shop. From Gennie's point of view, he was a bit old, maybe late thirties or so, but he was undeniably handsome. He was tall and broad-shouldered, and his curly blond hair held only a hint of gray. He wore simple work clothes that could be Shaker or could be of the world, but they fit him well. His wool overcoat clearly came from the world; it nipped in at the waist and was far too fancy for a Shaker coat.

Unfortunately he seemed aware of his appeal. He struck a pose as he entered the door, gazing around with a critical eye as if he owned the store. His gaze paused only briefly when he saw Gennie. She had grown used to attention from men, so she wondered if pretty young girls were of little interest to him. He seemed more concerned with the contents of the room.

"Johnny, how nice of you to stop by," Abigail said. There was a distinct chill in her voice, and she returned immediately to her knitting.

Johnny. Gennie's ears perked up. Perhaps this was Johnny Jenkins, Esther's erstwhile husband and father of her six blond children.

"Abigail," he said, acknowledging her with a curt nod.

"You must be the new girl." He glanced again at Gennie, then seemed to find a display of oval boxes more enthralling. Gennie didn't bother to answer.

"I'll need an inventory as soon as possible," he said to Abigail, who peered up at him over the top of her spectacles.

"Whatever for?"

"Well, naturally so we'll know how to direct our efforts in the next few days. Mother Ann's Birthday is nearly upon us, you know."

A pink spot appeared on each of Abigail's cheeks, but she held her tongue. Gennie was both amused and appalled. A novitiate daring to lecture a sister about Mother Ann's Birthday—he was lucky Abigail was such a gentle soul. Rose would have set him straight.

"Aldon is hopeless with wood," he said, with a sneer, "so I doubt there will be more boxes. I suppose the pulpit is the only place for him. And Sewell has his head in the clouds, as usual, planning how to restore all those old buildings."

"Which is precisely what we asked him to do," Abigail said.

"I know," Johnny said. "It's too bad no one has put more thought into what we could do with them once they are restored."

Abigail's knitting needles flew, and Gennie busied herself with straightening the items on the counter.

"I'll need that inventory by tomorrow at the latest, and I also want a list of the prices you are charging. I suspect they are low." Gennie realized he was talking to her. She looked over at Abigail, who seemed to have vanished behind the red scarf emerging from her needles. Gennie gave Johnny a faint, noncommittal smile and began to dust the counter.

"I'll be back first thing tomorrow morning," Johnny said, as if everyone had jumped at his command. With a last proprietary look around, he was gone.

"That man needs a lesson or three in humility," Abigail muttered to her knitting.

"Must we put together an inventory of the entire store by tomorrow morning?" Gennie asked, with a hint of panic.

"Of course not. Such nonsense. Our journal is completely up-to-date; I record every item that comes in and everything we sell. If Johnny Jenkins wants an inventory, he can just copy it from the journal. Fannie assigned Johnny to work under Sewell, and it's more than likely Sewell had nothing to do with this visit. Johnny likes to think he's in charge. He stops by at least once a week with one of these 'orders,' and I give them exactly the time they are worth."

"Will he come by tomorrow, as he said he would?"

"Possibly, if he doesn't get distracted by some other scheme. I'll take care of it, don't you worry. If I'm not here, just hand him the journal and tell him to start copying. An inventory. Of all the silly wastes of time . . ."

Relieved, Gennie finished her dusting and began rearranging the boxes on an oval candle stand. When she felt she'd given Abigail enough time to recover her good temper, she broached the subject of boarding in the Brick Dwelling House.

"It would be so convenient for everyone," she said, "not just me. I mean, if you needed anything carried over after the store closes, or if you wanted to keep the store open a little longer before Mother Ann's Birthday, I'd be right here. You could just call me, and I'd come in a flash. Wouldn't that be helpful?" Gennie hoped her enthusiasm wasn't too overdone. In fact, the last thing she wanted was to spend all her time in the Fancy Goods Store.

"I think that's a lovely idea, my dear," Abigail said. "Perhaps you could help out elsewhere sometimes, too. The day before the celebration, they will surely need help in the kitchen."

Oops. The kitchen was definitely not where Gennie

wanted to be. But it was too late now, so she put on her happiest, most grateful smile.

"I'll speak to Fannie directly after the evening meal," Abigail promised. "Do stay and eat with us, and we'll make the final arrangements before you go back to town. Sewell can drive you; he's quite good at negotiating our slippery roads. I'll send him to pick you up in the morning, as well, so he can carry your luggage to and from the car."

Gennie thanked her profusely and kept her immediate thought to herself—that, as Sewell was suspected of murder, he might not be the best choice for chauffeur.

ELEVEN

A WORRIED FANNIE HAD BEGGED ROSE TO STAY WITH Sewell when the police arrived around 2 P.M. to question him further about Julia's death. Dulcie's doctor's appointment wasn't until late afternoon, so Rose agreed. She intended to listen only. Despite Fannie's hopes, Rose saw it as her duty to seek the truth, not to protect Sewell because he was a Shaker novitiate.

To her surprise, the two young officers, who introduced themselves as Billy and Stan, did not object to her presence. In fact, they seemed almost apologetic to be there, as if they, too, had trouble believing that a Shaker—even a novitiate— could possibly be involved in such a heinous crime. In North Homage, at least in the past, the Sheriff's Office would have been more than ready to accuse any number of Believers of such violence, but Rose was learning that Hancock and Pittsfield enjoyed a friendlier relationship.

They met in the parlor of the Trustees' Office, just across from the Fancy Goods Store. Rose barely recognized the parlor as a Shaker room. Thick curtains covered the windows, blocking out most of the sunlight. Heavy Victorian furniture contributed to the gloom. It hadn't surprised Rose to learn that funerals were often held in the room.

The officers waved Sewell and Rose to two delicately carved chairs with needlepoint seats, placed side by side.

113

Rose pulled hers farther away from Sewell's and sat down. The officers leaned against a nearby wall, their arms crossed. Rose began to suspect they were not as sympathetic as she'd first thought.

"Look here, Sewell," said Stan, the taller and more commanding of the two officers, "you and me, we go way back. Like I told Chief O'Malley, it's tough to believe you'd do something like this without a lot of provocation. And Julia, well, we both know how provoking that girl could be. She always was a tease. That can make a fella real mad. Why don't you just tell us what happened, and I'm sure we can explain it to the chief, so he'll go easy on you."

"Stan, I promise you on a stack of Bibles, there's nothing to tell. I'd tell you, if there was." Sewell looked even thinner than he had the day before, when Rose had first seen him. Layers of bluish circles under his eyes made them seem huge in his narrow face.

"As I remember," Officer Billy said, "you and Julia were a hot item at one time. What happened? She throw you over?"

"We just lost interest in each other. It happens. We were young. But I've left all that behind. I'm a Believer now."

A spot of blood had appeared on Sewell's lip, where he'd been gnawing at it. Something was making this man very nervous.

"Sure, we understand, Sewell," Stan said. "But how much can a man really change? You used to be hell on wheels, and a lot of fun. Are you telling me you just walked away from all that? You never drink or smoke anymore? You never think about girls or sneak in a little sweet talk now and again? After all, aren't Shakers like Catholics—a little confession and you get rid of all those sins?"

"I never took up again with Julia, I swear it," Sewell said. He turned haunted eyes to Rose. She would have loved to give those young men a piece of her mind, but she kept silent. She'd learn more by listening.

"Suppose we told you someone saw you and Julia together just before she was murdered?"

"They'd be lying." Something in Sewell's voice sounded tentative.

Stan dragged a ladder-back across the rug and sat backward on the delicate seat so that he watched Sewell over the top slat. Rose had never seen a Shaker chair used in quite that way. The effect was both intimidating and humorous. A shorter man would have been peering through the slats.

"Everybody in town knows you, Sewell. Do you think you can have a public fight with a young lady—and you a Shaker—without somebody noticing?" Stan asked.

Sewell slumped in his chair. "It was that nosy Mrs. Alexander, wasn't it?"

Stan and Billy said nothing.

"Never mind, I know it was her. She came out of the greengrocer's when we were talking—not arguing, just talking—and she stared at us like we were breaking the law."

"You were breaking your own law, weren't you? You aren't supposed to talk to a woman alone, are you?" Billy asked. He had the softer voice of the two officers, which Rose suspected was intentional.

"It wasn't like that," Sewell said. "It was . . . just two old friends passing the time of day."

"Mrs. Alexander is sure you two were arguing, at least at the end," Billy said, softer still. "You've got to see it from our point of view. You were observed in what looked like an argument with a girl who was murdered just two days later. We got no other suspects. So why don't you just tell us what happened?"

In the silence that followed, Rose heard the tick-tick-tick of an ornate grandfather's clock in the parlor corner. Muffled voices floated from the store across the hallway. The sound of sniffling next to her told her that Sewell was fighting back tears.

"Tell us," Billy said. "We'll try to make it go easy on you."

Sewell pulled a handkerchief from his jacket pocket and blew his nose noisily. "It wasn't what you think," he said. "Julia was my friend. She was angry, but not at me. We were all finished years ago. Matter of fact, we were never really all that . . . Anyway, it was her current beau who was making her angry. She wouldn't tell me his name, so I figured he must be married."

"Or a Shaker, perhaps," Stan said.

"I suppose so." Sewell gave his nose another blow and wadded up his handkerchief in his pocket. "Anyway, she was sure he was cheating on her, and she was furious."

"Why'd she tell you?" Stan asked.

"She trusted me, and she needed to talk to somebody."

"Right across from the greengrocer's? Pretty public, wouldn't you say?" Stan's tone implied he wasn't buying Sewell's story.

"Was it because she was more afraid of being overheard in Hancock Village?" Billy asked. "Maybe because her lover was a Shaker?"

Sewell shrugged. "I told you, she wouldn't say who he was, just that he was cheating on her." His face looked gray in the dim light. "It's no use pushing me anymore. That's all I can tell you. If you're going to arrest me, you might as well get it over with."

The officers looked at each other. "I guess we won't just yet," Billy said. "We'll check out your story first. You aren't planning to go on any of those sales trips, are you?"

Sewell shook his head. "I'll stay put," he said. "I was never any good at riding the rails, anyway," he said, with a halfhearted attempt at levity. "I'd probably break all my bones."

"We'll be back," said Stan.

After the officers had left, Rose sat quietly with Sewell for several minutes. Finally, Sewell stood and moved his chair over to a desk, avoiding Rose's eyes.

"Guess I'd better get back to work," he said to the rug, an Oriental pattern with dark reds and blues.

"Sewell," Rose said, as gently as she could, "I heard you insist that Julia did not tell you the name of her beau."

"That's right."

"But you guessed who it was, didn't you?"

Sewell did not move, nor did he raise his eyes. The rug seemed to fascinate him. "I've been away from my work far too long," he said. Without a glance at her or a further good-bye, he was out the door.

Brother Ricardo turned over Hancock's roomy, well-maintained Cadillac to Rose, giving it a fond pat on the left headlight. Ricardo insisted on the very best for the sisters. Rose promised to take good care of the car. She wrapped Dulcie in a travel rug and drove toward Pittsfield. She was grateful that Dulcie had consented to see the doctor in Pittsfield, since it meant she didn't have to find her way over ice-rutted roads to a farther-flung city. Both women were silent as the countryside rolled past them. Rose concentrated on driving, and Dulcie seemed to be drifting in her own world. The way back would surely be easier, and Rose promised herself she would then have a talk with Dulcie.

Dr. Kendell was elderly, kindly, and a little forgetful, which was just as well. He kept calling Dulcie "Lucy," which seemed to reassure her that her secret was safe. He expressed delight at her impending motherhood. It never occurred to him to ask if she was married.

"Everything looks normal," said Dr. Kendell, "though you're a bit on the thin side. I like to see my expectant mothers gain some weight—it's best for the baby and safer for the mother. Have you stopped feeling sick in the mornings?"

"Mostly, but sometimes I feel sick all of a sudden during the day," Dulcie said.

"Nervousness, that's all. First mothers are always nervous, afraid something will go wrong. You're at least a couple months along, so the morning sickness should disappear soon. Just relax and look forward to your baby. It'll be here before you know it."

This reminder was not what Dulcie needed. She slumped forward and looked as if she might be sick again.

"How can she gain a little weight, Doctor," Rose asked, "when she continues to feel sick?" She'd been surprised and alarmed when Dulcie had taken off her old Shaker dress and revealed matchstick arms and a protruding collarbone.

"Just eat little bits at a time, as often as you can," Dr. Kendell said to Dulcie, giving her a fatherly pat on the shoulder. "Keep some food with you, and eat right before you go to bed. You really must keep your strength up, you know. The baby will drain your energy. We don't want to lose you in childbirth and leave your poor husband to raise the child on his own, do we?"

Dulcie's misery completely escaped the kindly doctor, but it worried Rose. For the first time, she wished she could stay longer in Hancock than it would take to solve the mystery of Julia's death. She wished, too, that Josie, North Homage's Infirmary nurse, was there with her. Josie would know how to breathe strength back into the fragile Dulcie. Rose made herself a promise that she would not leave before turning Dulcie and her coming baby over to the tender care of Fannie and the other sisters.

Rose bundled Dulcie back into the front seat of the Cadillac, wondering if they'd really accomplished any good. Dulcie was under orders to "eat like a horse," something she clearly wasn't capable of doing. At least Dr. Kendell seemed convinced the baby was fine, and nothing was seriously wrong with Dulcie—physically, at any rate.

As Rose pulled away from the doctor's office, Dulcie slid down in her seat and pulled the wool travel rug up to her neck. She looked ready for a nap, but Rose wasn't about to lose her chance to ask some of the questions that had been crowding her mind. She cleared her throat. "Are you warm enough?" she asked.

"Yes, thank you. And thank you for taking me to a doctor. I feel much better now." It was a lie, but surely well-meant.

"No need to thank me. Any sister would have done the same." Rose took a deep breath and plunged ahead. "Dulcie, as you know, Fannie has asked me to help find your sister's killer. I'm sure you'll understand how important it is that I know as much as possible about Julia."

"I suppose." Dulcie sounded tired and cranky, but Rose hardened her heart. The girl could rest later.

The car rattled and slid sideways as they hit a chunk of ice in the road. Rose's heartbeat nearly doubled.

When her breathing was closer to normal, Rose said, "I spoke with Otis this morning, and he mentioned you'd seen your sister's body before the police arrived." She knew she was being brutal, but she hoped Dulcie now trusted her.

"Yes," Dulcie answered, after a moment's pause.

"Can you think of any reason she would have been dressed the way she was?"

Dulcie stared out the windshield, giving no sign of emotion. "It didn't surprise me," she said. "Isn't that strange and sad? It didn't surprise me that Julia would be dressed in a summer dancing gown in February. She'd do anything for fun, anything to be outrageous. It was like she had to grab everything with both hands and squeeze out every drop of fun. She could have dressed that way on a dare; that would have been like her. I once heard that people in Norway or Sweden or somewhere jump into ice-cold lakes in the winter, I can't remember why. Julia was like that—she loved to do anything that was wild and dangerous."

"What other wild things did she do?" Rose asked.

"We were very poor growing up, you know, even before the crash. But Julia loved beautiful things, she loved to be beautiful, so one day, she and . . . She stole a lipstick from the five-and-dime in Pittsfield. She didn't feel guilty at all, and I don't think she would have even if she'd been caught. It was like she was floating on air for days afterwards."

"Who else was with her when she stole the lipstick?"

"Does it matter?"

"It might. If it doesn't, I promise that I will never reveal the person's identity."

"Carlotta was with her. Carlotta was one of our best chums in those days. She was poor, too, and real mad about it. Her family wasn't so bad off before the crash as we were, so she was bitter when they lost everything. She was greedier than Julia. She stole a whole bagful of stuff—lipsticks and a compact and rouge, some combs, anything she could grab. So she was the one who got caught. She was just thirteen, but the store owner pressed charges. She'd never done anything like that before, so she didn't have to go to reform school, but everyone knew about it."

"Julia never confessed her own involvement?"

"No. I think Carlotta getting caught made it more exciting for Julia. Afterwards, things were never the same between them. Carlotta was madder than ever, and I can't say as I blame her. And Julia . . . well, she just didn't seem to care." Dulcie's voice grew softer. "It was almost like Julia knew she wouldn't live very long, so it didn't matter what she did."

"Otis mentioned something else," Rose said. "He saw you lift up Julia's skirt. Why did you do that?"

Dulcie hesitated, just for a moment. "Oh, it was just because I saw something bright-colored sticking out from under her hem, that's all. It was only a piece of old calico, a rag."

"The police didn't find it. Did you take it?"

Dulcie shrugged. "I didn't think it was important. I mean, it was just an old rag. It was kind of pretty, though—red and blue checks. I thought it would make a good handkerchief. I thought the sisters must have left it in the Summerhouse. It wasn't the sort of thing Julia would like."

It struck Rose as strangely cold-hearted that Dulcie would lift her dead sister's skirt to take a bit of fabric. Her excuse—that it might make a good handkerchief—=was farfetched. "Do you still have the rag?" Rose asked.

"When I got back to my room, I started feeling bad about taking it, so I threw it away." Dulcie squirmed under her travel rug. "She wasn't really bad deep down, you know. Julia, I mean. She couldn't help being what she was. We were so poor. We didn't have anything, and she just wanted something."

"You aren't like her, though," Rose said.

"I was younger. What Julia was doing, it scared me. I don't want to be scared all the time."

"Are you scared about your baby?"

"Yes."

"Have you told Theodore yet?

Dulcie picked at the wool rug. "Telling him would be scarier than *not* telling him," she said.

"He's going to find out eventually. From what I've heard about Theodore, he would want to do the right thing. And if he doesn't, perhaps it would be best to know that soon, so you can make some plans for your life. Nothing is hopeless, you know. If you feel you can't raise the baby on your own, there's no shame in asking the sisters for help. They would gladly raise the child themselves or find a family for it, and they would help you in any way they can. I can promise you that."

"I want my baby," Dulcie said. Her tone was emphatic, and so was the silence that followed. She turned her face and shoulders away from Rose and leaned her head against the seat.

After delivering Dulcie to her room and insisting she take a nap, Rose decided to replace her in the kitchen, where preparations for the evening meal were under way. She wanted to try again to loosen Carlotta's tongue.

Two sisters were working with Carlotta in the kitchen when Rose arrived. She assured them she would take over for them, and they gratefully returned to their other duties.

Carlotta moved no faster than usual. "Where's Dulcie? Sick again?"

"She's in need of a rest, so I'm taking her place," Rose said. She stirred a pot of potato stew, which was to provide the substance of the evening meal. She'd grown tired of potatoes, a winter staple, but the rich scent of onions and salt pork sparked her interest in eating again.

Rose peeked sideways and watched Carlotta linger over the slicing of a jam cake, a special treat for dessert. The young woman's face was pinched and tense, as if years of hunger made her uneasy near such a luscious dish. But she didn't even lick the spatula she'd used as a knife. Perhaps her hunger was not for food.

When they had served the stew and brown bread to the silent group in the dining room upstairs, Rose and Carlotta each took a serving and settled at the kitchen worktable. But Carlotta seemed uninterested in any conversation with the intruder to her world, so Rose broke the silence.

"Have you worked in Hancock for long?" she asked, though she knew the answer.

Carlotta took a bite of bread and chewed it before answering. "Nope," she said, "and I won't stick around for long. I'm just helping them get ready for this big party they're supposed to have."

"Mother Ann's Birthday," Rose said.

"Yeah."

"Do you enjoy this work?"

"It's okay. Better than nothing."

"Have you worked at other jobs in Pittsfield? It's your hometown, isn't it?"

Carlotta had thick, dark eyebrows, which lowered to give her eyes a hooded look. "Yeah, I grew up there. Why do you want to know?"

"Just curious."

"No, you're not," Carlotta said. "You're here to pin Julia's murder on somebody, and you sure won't pick a Shaker, if you can get away with it. You'd just love to find somebody like me to blame, wouldn't you? Somebody unimportant, an outsider."

"Carlotta! Is that what you think of us?" Rose pushed aside her empty plate and leaned on the table toward the girl. "All I want to find is the truth. I would never, ever just *pick* someone to accuse of murder."

Carlotta said nothing, but her cynical scowl was eloquent. Rose decided to get tough.

"However," she said, leaning back in her chair, "if you refuse to speak to me, I admit it will strike me as very suspicious. I'll begin to wonder what you're trying to hide."

Carlotta sulked in silence.

"*Do* you have something to hide?"

"Of course not." Carlotta tipped her soup bowl and scraped up a last spoonful of stew, all the while keeping a wary eye on Rose.

"Then there is no reason to be afraid. The sooner you tell me everything you know, the sooner we can resolve this tragedy, and I'll be gone, back to Kentucky."

"How do I know you won't take everything I say and use it against me?"

"Do you believe that any of the sisters here would do such a thing?"

Carlotta shrugged. "Most everybody in town says the Shakers are honest."

"It's the same where I come from," Rose said. "Honesty is part of who we are. You said that I'd rather blame an outsider than a Shaker for Julia's murder. It would hurt me deeply if it turned out a Shaker committed this crime, but I would know that he—or she—is not truly a Believer. I would not protect such a person."

Carlotta's thin, rigid body loosened slightly. "We'd better serve up that jam cake," she said. "Then I'll answer your questions."

"Thank you." Rose realized she'd been tense, as well. Serving the jam cake gave her a chance to relax her shoulders and formulate her questions.

"Leave the dishes awhile," she told Carlotta, when they'd finished serving. "I'll wash them up later." They settled back at the kitchen table, now littered with piles of soiled dishes and cutlery. "Do you have any suspicions about who Julia might have been meeting the night she was killed?"

Carlotta's laugh was short and mirthless. "Could have been anyone," she said, "but it was probably a man. No, I take that back. There's plenty of women mad at Julia, mostly for spending time with their husbands." Now that she'd overcome her initial distrust, Carlotta seemed more than ready to talk. "Honora, for one," she said. "Honora Stearn, who's married to that new Shaker, Aldon."

"Aldon? The minister? Was he involved with Julia?"

"Some minister. Julia wasn't the only girl he had his eye on, though he always claimed they chased after him. I heard that's why he came here, to escape."

"To escape what? Temptation?"

"Maybe. Or maybe he just wanted to escape that wife of his. She's a nasty piece of work. You'd think she'd be glad to be rid of him, but she sure liked being the minister's wife. It made her feel like she was better than the rest of us." Carlotta's bitterness honed her voice to a razor-sharp edge. "She doesn't feel so superior now, and she can't stand it. I wouldn't put it past her to kill Julia."

"Are you certain that Aldon was carrying on an affair with Julia?"

Carlotta hesitated. "Well, I'm not *certain*. I mean, I never actually saw them together since I got here. But I know he was always trying to 'save' her, back when we went to that church of his."

"You and Julia were part of Aldon's congregation? Was Dulcie, too?"

"Oh, yeah, and Sewell and Johnny and Theodore—all of us. That's how we all come to know each other so well, we grew up together in that church. Except Esther, she came later. I mean, we were different ages, but we still knew each other. I remember Johnny and Esther were Sunday school teachers. Julia and Dulcie and me, we all had them as teachers some of the time."

"Did you observe Julia being friendly with anyone else besides Aldon—since you've been here, I mean?"

"Yeah, Sewell, of course. He's friendly with all the girls, but he don't mean nothin' by it. I did see him and Julia go off for a walk together one night after supper. They wasn't hand in hand or anything, but they looked chummy enough to me. I asked Julia about it later, and she just giggled and said that he wasn't a real Shaker yet, so he had some time left for a few sins."

"What about the other men here? Did you ever see any of them with Julia?"

"Well, all of them, I guess. Julia was friendly, if you know what I mean. I never told Dulcie, but that fiancé of hers, Theodore, I saw him have a couple of talks with Julia. I don't know what that was about, and anyway, he ain't a Shaker, so it ain't against the law or anything. I mean, him and Julia was practically family."

Carlotta curled a short piece of dark hair around her finger. "Then there's Johnny—you know, Johnny Jenkins, another new Shaker. I saw him talk to Julia, maybe three times. Julia said he was just bossing her around, but I didn't believe her. He's just the sort of man she'd fall for in a big way. He's tall and *so* handsome. Have you seen those shoulders? Oh, I used to just stare at those shoulders when he was my Sunday school teacher."

Rose knew Carlotta was watching her reaction. She waited, in silence, for Carlotta to go on. It didn't take long; Carlotta was enjoying herself now.

"Julia liked her men rich and important and good-looking. If she couldn't have all three, she'd settle for one while she kept on looking. Johnny, he's good-looking, and he was always figurin' how to get rich. Besides, he's married *and* he's practically a Shaker, and that would've made him real exciting to Julia."

Rose was aware that time was passing, and Carlotta was speculating wildly. Her information might have some use, but it couldn't be counted on. At least Rose was getting a picture of Julia. Unfortunately, she seemed to have been the kind of girl any number of folks might have wanted, at some time or other, to murder.

"Is there anyone else who might have been involved with—or angry with—Julia?"

"Well, Dulcie and her didn't always get along, but I don't think Dulcie hated her or anything. I mean, not unless Theodore was carrying on with Julia, and Dulcie found out about it. Theodore means more to Dulcie than her own life, practically."

"And what about you, Carlotta? Did you and Julia get along?"

The hooded look returned to Carlotta's face. "Yeah, we got along fine. We grew up together."

Rose hesitated. If she confronted Carlotta with the shoplifting story, she'd probably never get any more information out of her. It was best, she decided, to go elsewhere for information about Carlotta's relationship with Julia.

"That's good," Rose said. "I'm very grateful for all the information you've shared with me. If you think of anything more, I hope you'll be willing to tell me; anything can be helpful, anything at all. You can call or visit me in my retiring room—even at night, if you think of something that might be useful."

Carlotta almost smiled. Rose had made her feel important, clearly a rare experience in the young woman's life.

TWELVE

ROSE SPLASHED SOME WATER ON HER FACE AND LAY ON HER bed for a few minutes, grateful the long day was coming to an end. After her talk with Carlotta, she had hurriedly washed the dishes and straightened the kitchen, in hopes of a short rest before the evening worship service. However, no sooner had she closed her eyes than she heard a knock on her retiring room door, followed by a creak as her visitor slipped inside.

"Rose? You aren't asleep, are you?" Gennie closed the door behind her and peered into the gloomy room.

"Nay, come in, Gennie." Rose pulled herself upright. "Have a seat, and tell me why you are still here. I thought we weren't going to meet until early tomorrow morning. I saw you at evening meal, but I assumed Abigail had invited you. Don't you need to get back to the boardinghouse soon?" She hoped Gennie wasn't depending on her for a ride to Pittsfield.

Gennie switched on the light and settled into a short chair next to the small pine desk. "Oh, don't worry about me," she said airily. "I've got everything all arranged with Abigail, who's already spoken with Fannie. Sewell will drive me back after evening worship, which Abigail invited me to stay for. Then he'll pick me up again tomorrow morning." Gennie brushed a speck of lint off her wool skirt and cleared her throat.

128

"What else have you arranged?" Rose asked, resigned to another Gennie-hatched plot.

"It's perfect. Wait till you hear. Abigail said I could bring my things back here tomorrow and room right in this building, with the other hired women. Isn't that wonderful? We can talk anytime we want to. No one will wonder why I'm up here, if I live in the building."

"Gennie, you know I'm not comfortable having you in the thick of things."

"Yes, I'm well aware of that," Gennie said, with dignity. "However, I'll say the same thing to you that I said to Grady before we left—I expect you to treat me like an adult. I'm moving here tomorrow, and that's that."

Rose's heart was caught somewhere between the sadness of letting Gennie grow up and pride in the young woman she had become. "All right," she said, "let it be as you wish. Now, go ahead and tell me what you've learned so far."

When they had shared their information, it was time to leave for the worship service. "After your description, I would like a look at Aldon's wife, Honora," Rose said, as she stuffed some errant curls back under her cap. "She certainly sounds angry enough to do violence."

"If she returns to the village, I'll try to get a message to you," Gennie promised.

By the time they arrived downstairs, at the large meeting room Fannie had designated for the service, everyone else had gathered. Gennie and Rose separated before entering and sat at opposite ends of a semicircle of women, facing a much smaller cluster of men. Rose was surprised and pleased to see both Dulcie and Theodore attending the service, each sitting, as was proper, with the appropriate gender.

In the absence of someone like Elder Wilhelm to lead, the worship seemed tame and gentle. Fannie led them in prayer and several songs, but no one stood for dancing worship. Rose missed the movement, but she was not unappreciative

of the quiet. For once, she could send her prayers to Holy
Mother Wisdom without half of her mind worrying about
what surprises Wilhelm might have in store. She closed her
eyes and gave herself up to worship.

The door hinges in Hancock all seemed to need the attention of an oil can. In the second before the worshipers began
another song, the squeak of the door from the hallway broke
Rose's concentration. She opened her eyes. A tall, middle-
aged woman in worldly clothes stood just inside the large
double doors, looking around as if seeking a place to sit.
Rose supposed she must be a friend of Fannie's; the Hancock sisters had many dealings with the women from Pittsfield, so it wouldn't be surprising if some were invited to
share worship with the Believers.

The woman moved forward, her eyes fixed on the men's
side of the room. An inkling of doubt entered Rose's mind.
Something wasn't right. Gennie glanced up as the woman
passed her chair. Gennie's expression changed from polite
and somewhat sleepy to excited. Her wide eyes sought out
Rose, and her hands twitched as if she wanted desperately
to convey a message without standing up and shouting.
Rose knew instantly what the message was—this was Honora Stearn, come to claim her husband back from the Shakers. She sent a slight nod of understanding to Gennie, who
relaxed.

Honora walked to the center of the room and stood with
her back to the women, facing the men. All attempts to carry
on the song had faltered, and the worshipers watched as
Honora turned to her husband, Aldon. She raised her arm
and pointed a long, bony finger at him. The spectacle mesmerized everyone, including Fannie, and no one protested.
Even Aldon stared in openmouthed silence.

"You," Honora said. "You have offended God. You have
broken His commandments, and His fury is unleashed." Her
voice was deep and powerful, as if she had studied preach-

ing by listening to her husband's performances in the pulpit. "His wrath will smite you down where you sit." She spun around until she faced the women. Her face was contorted with rage. "You are jezebels, every one of you. You have conspired to put asunder a man and his wife, who were joined by God, and *you will be punished.*" She poked her finger toward them as she spit out the curse.

The Hancock sisters were used to quiet dealings with the world, and this exhibition was beyond their comprehension. Clearly, no one knew what to do. Their shock had rendered them helpless. Rose, for better or for worse, had more experience with such behavior. Also, she would be gone soon; it would be easier for her to handle the situation. Any resentments would attach to her, not to the Hancock sisters.

As she stood, however, Honora spun again toward the men and pointed at her husband. "There is only one way you can save your wretched soul," she said to Aldon. Her voice was growing hoarse, and her hand had begun to shake. "You must come with me right now. Return to your marriage bed tonight."

She walked toward Aldon as if to grab him and force him to come with her. This proved too much for Aldon. He leaped from his chair and lifted it up in front of him. Rose had to stifle a chuckle at this picture—the lion tamer fending off a wild animal gone berserk. The men around Aldon jumped up, as well. The novitiates backed away from her to avoid touching a woman, but Theodore pushed through them toward Honora. Afraid he might handle the distraught woman too forcefully, Rose hurried across the room to stand just behind her.

"Mrs. Stearn, I am Theodore Geist. Do you remember me from church?" Theodore's voice and demeanor were firm. Rose stayed where she was.

"Theodore?" Honora lowered her arm.

"Remember you taught me in Sunday school?"

"Of course I remember you—you were such a good student, always knew your Bible verses perfectly. You aren't—you haven't become one of *them,* have you?" Her voice had dipped again into outrage.

"No, of course not. I just work for them. You know how hard it is to find a job these days."

Honora nodded sadly.

"I'm getting married soon, you know," he said. "So I can understand how angry you are. If anyone put me asunder from my wife, I'd . . . well, there's no telling what I'd do. I'd try to leave it up to God, but maybe I wouldn't be strong enough. You know what I mean?"

"Yes," Honora said. "Yes, indeed. Sometimes you have to remind God. He has so much to watch."

"Exactly." Theodore glanced at Rose as if he wanted to tell her something. "But let's just leave it to God this time," he said to Honora. "I'm sure you got His attention." He took her firmly by the crook of the elbow and guided her toward the door before she could protest. Within seconds, he had led her into the hallway and closed the door behind them.

After a moment of awkward silence, a sister began a song quickly, and the others joined in, as if the incident hadn't occurred. Much as she wanted to do so, Rose couldn't stay to finish the worship service. She followed Theodore and Honora. By the time she'd shut the door on the singing worshipers, the hallway was empty. Rose threw her cloak around her shoulders and hurried through the women's door to the dwelling house. A brisk snow had been falling for some time, coating the village with thick, wet globs, and making it difficult to see beyond a few dozen yards. Rose swiped at the snow as if to push it aside. The nearby churn of a motor reached her. It seemed to be coming from the small garage just across the path from the Brick Dwelling House. Ignoring the snow that caked her shoes, she ran toward the sound. As she came in view of the entrance, an ancient Model T emerged and skidded toward the main road. Rose recognized the car Brother Ricardo kept for the use of the hired hands. Theodore was behind the wheel, and Honora sat beside him.

Rose watched as the car reached the main road and headed toward Pittsfield. It occurred to Rose to wonder, as the car bounced over ruts in the icy road, how Honora had made the trip to Hancock Village in the first place. According to Gennie, Honora had been mired in poverty since Aldon left, and her clothing showed it, so it was unlikely that she had a car. If she had walked, wouldn't she have been soaked to the bone? Her clothes had been dry, and her cheeks only pale pink, as if she had ridden in a cold car. Had Theodore driven her to Hancock, knowing what was likely to happen? What reason would he—or anyone—have to encourage such a scene? For that matter, how did she get to the Fancy Goods Store on such a regular schedule, as Abigail had told Gennie she did?

Rose stripped off her wet clothing and hung it from hangers on pegs to dry overnight. She knew her shoes would still be damp in the morning unless she helped them along, so she had found some rags in the kitchen and now stuffed them into the toes to absorb moisture. She slipped into her warm, blessedly dry winter nightgown and knelt for prayer.

Still shivering, she snuggled under her wool coverlet, closed her eyes, and waited for sleep. And waited. By the time the evening worship service had replayed itself three times in her mind, she accepted defeat. Sleep would elude her until she had organized her thoughts on paper. Giving in to frustration, she yanked the coverlet from her bed, wrapped it around her shoulders, and settled at the small desk in her room. She'd had the forethought to request paper and a pen for her retiring room, so she didn't have to go roaming through the huge, cold dwelling house searching for writing materials.

First, she wrote a list of the folks she or Gennie had met during their first day in Hancock. All of them had known Julia, so she first noted the ones who had an obvious motive. Honora Stearn led the list. Rose suspected that Theodore had been trying to convey that message to her while he was calming Honora. Honora wanted Aldon back, and she thought Julia had tempted him to stray. Had Julia purposely sought the job in the Fancy Goods Shop simply to be near Aldon?

What about Aldon himself? He was a minister of God, but that did not protect him from temptation—or excuse him, if he caved in to it. Had he fallen into the flesh with Julia, either before his conversion to the Shaker faith, or both before and after? His devotion to the Shaker faith seemed genuine, if somewhat harsh, and he might easily become an elder, once he'd signed the Covenant. Would he kill to protect his future in the Society? It seemed farfetched, but not impossible.

Rose had grown fond of Dulcie, and hopeful for her future. Yet, according to Carlotta and to Dulcie herself, she and Julia were not on the best of terms. Otis and Carlotta both suspected Theodore had been too attentive to Julia. Suppose Julia, with her competitive carnal instincts, had set out to seduce her sister's fiancé, just for the sport of it? Would Dulcie have been angry enough to kill her sister—especially to protect her own unborn child? Why had Dulcie rushed to see her sister's body? Did she remove the calico rag because it somehow incriminated her or someone she loved?

Dulcie loved Theodore Geist—or at least she needed him desperately. Theodore clearly considered himself to be upright, a man of high moral character. If he had allowed himself to yield to Julia's charms, might he have killed her in a fit of rage, misdirected at her, rather than at himself? Theodore also needed and valued his job as manager of Hancock's farmhands. If Julia had threatened to reveal his sinfulness, perhaps even threatened blackmail, might he have killed her to keep her silent?

Then there was Carlotta, the source of so much gossipy information about others. She was unwilling to admit to her past troubles with the law, which, according to Dulcie, Julia had led her into. Carlotta was a bitter young woman. How far might her resentment drive her? A woman could certainly have strangled Julia from behind with the fabric of her own dress. But could a woman, especially Carlotta, have persuaded Julia to meet at night in the Summerhouse in a flimsy summer dancing dress?

Sewell Yates. Rose stared at the name. This was the man the police suspected of Julia's murder, and Rose had yet to uncover any evidence to clear him. Of all the men she had met so far, he was most likely, she believed, to have had a carnal relationship with Julia. Something haunted the man, that much was clear. By all accounts, he flirted with the women, seemingly driven to charm even the older sisters. His protestations of chastity were intense, yet somehow unconvincing. Rose felt certain that Sewell had a secret, perhaps of profound depth, which she must discover before she could eliminate him as a suspect—or confirm his guilt.

Finally, Rose listed Johnny and Esther Jenkins. Esther did not really want to be a Shaker sister. She wanted to raise her own children. She might be hoping Johnny would eventually return to her. Julia had set her cap for Johnny, and what Julia wanted, it seemed, Julia got. Suppose Esther considered another woman more of a threat, in the long run, than the Society? From Esther's point of view, six children and her own survival were at stake. Would she have killed Julia, rather than take the chance of losing her ambitious husband to another woman?

As for Johnny, Gennie had described him with cold clarity. Johnny seemed uninterested in women, even disdainful of them, but Rose knew better than to believe she knew his heart. He could be playing a part, or he might be trying to keep his distance from the temptation of women. Others had agreed that Johnny wanted to be important. This horrible Depression severely limited the opportunities available to men who wanted power and wealth. The Shakers might seem like the answer to a prayer for a man like Johnny—so few men to fill leadership positions, and still comparatively large land holdings. If he had fallen into the flesh, particularly if he had done so after becoming a novitiate, he might want to eliminate the evidence.

Rose rubbed her tired eyes. Morning would come all too soon. It would still be dark and cold when the wake-up bell rang, and she would have had far too little sleep. She thought longingly of North Homage, and of dear Sisters Josie and Agatha. Josie always seemed to appear with a revivifying tea when Rose had spent half the night puzzling out a problem. Agatha, Rose's dear friend and mentor, would listen with wisdom until the problem seemed to solve itself. She wanted to go home. She shoved the paper and pen back in the desk drawer and slid into her bed. This time she fell into instant and dreamless sleep, her mind blissfully emptied of all the information that had kept her awake.

THIRTEEN

WHEN THE MORNING WAKE-UP BELL RANG, ROSE LAY FOR several minutes in groggy confusion. She had slept as if drugged by a pot of valerian tea. In the early morning darkness, her room looked familiar, yet wrong somehow. Slowly, she dredged up the memory of her train ride, her arrival in Hancock Village, and, finally, Honora Stearn's startling disruption of the previous evening's worship service.

She switched on her bedside lamp, tossed off her covers, and swung her legs over the side of her bed. As soon as her bare feet touched the cold floor, she whimpered and yanked them back up and under her nightdress. Kentucky could be damp and cold in the wintertime, but Massachusetts was unlike anything she had experienced—or ever wanted to again.

Time was passing. Holding her breath, Rose slid her feet to the floor and ran across the room to where her clothes hung from wall pegs. Her dress and shoes from the previous evening were still damp. Though normally she would wear her work clothes until they were ready to be sent to the laundry, she couldn't bear the thought of clammy fabric touching her skin. Ignoring her guilt, she selected her second work dress, a dark blue wool, of the same loose design as the other. She pulled it over her shivering body, then quickly swung a large white kerchief across her back and shoulders, like a shawl, and crossed it over her chest. She tied an apron

137

loosely around her waist and tucked the ends of the kerchief inside the apron's waistband. With each additional layer, her shivering eased. She pictured the dead girl, Julia Masters, wearing a sleeveless summer gown on a freezing evening. How could the girl have stood it? Were Easterners made of sterner stuff, or was the girl driven by something powerful enough to make the cold endurable?

Rose rushed through the rest of her morning preparations, purposely slowing down when it came to her prayers. With no chores to perform, she arrived outside the dining room well before the rest of the village. She sat in a rocking chair and pulled from her apron pocket the sheet of notes she had written the night before, intending to use her free minutes to formulate a plan for her day.

Someone shouted in the distance. The sound was unexpected at such an early hour—or at any hour in a quiet Shaker village. Rose stuffed her notes back into her apron pocket and ventured into the hallway to investigate. No one was about.

A second shout sounded as if it had come from outside. Rose opened the women's front door. A blast of wind and snow hit her in the face and dampened the wood floor. It was snowing thickly, and Rose could see only partway down the path. A man appeared through the white curtain, running toward the Brick Dwelling House. He slipped on the snow and fell on one knee. Without any sign of pain, he struggled back up and continued toward the building. As he drew closer, Rose recognized Theodore Geist, Dulcie's fiancé. He was carrying a bucket, which he held out in front of him as if it contained something important.

"Where's the eldress?" he panted, as he reached the door. "Gotta talk to her right away."

"I'm the only one who has arrived for breakfast so far," Rose said, "but I'll find her. What's wrong?"

"No time. Get Fannie."

"You can afford a few seconds to tell me what's wrong," Rose said.

Theodore scowled, but she stood her ground. "Look at this bucket," he said, finally. "Look at it." He held it close to her face. A few inches of liquid splashed around as the bucket swung under her nose. She saw nothing alarming.

"What am I supposed to see?" she asked.

"Well, *look* at it. Look at the inside and around the rim. Can't you see?"

Rose peered inside the bucket. In a wavy line, which followed the edge of the sloshing water, was a coating of some powdery substance. It also covered the rim of the bucket, though the falling snow had washed it off in spots. She leaned closer to sniff the powder, but Theodore yanked the bucket away from her.

"Don't do that," he said. "It's poison."

"How do you know?"

"It's all over the water buckets in the barn, the feed buckets, too. I didn't notice it at first, so I used one of them to get some feed for the cows. I fed the first one, and she sniffed it and backed away. Cows are smarter than humans sometimes. She knew."

"What is it?"

Theodore shrugged. "Rat poison would be my guess. We've had problems in the barn, and the cats weren't doing the job, so we got something from town to take care of it."

Rose stifled her first impulse, which was to ask whether they'd thought about how many innocent cats they might have poisoned, along with the rats.

"Where are the other tainted buckets?"

"I put them all in an empty stall, with a note warning the other men not to use them to feed the animals."

They turned at the sound of footsteps in the hall.

"Goodness, you two are early for breakfast." Fannie's smile turned to puzzlement as she saw the bucket in Theodore's hand.

"Oh dear, it's just like the old days," she said, when he had explained the situation to her. "We've gotten along so well with the world for so many years. Why should this be happening again?"

"This has happened before?" Rose asked, horrified. North Homage's neighbors had been unfriendly almost to the point of violence on occasion, but they had never resorted to mass poisoning.

"Well, it has been quite a long time," Fannie said. "At least a century, as I recall. I remember reading about it in Elder Amaziah's journal—someone had put arsenic in the buckets and on the water pump. He couldn't say who'd done such a thing, just that he assumed it was a few of the village's neighbors, angry over something or other." Fannie's small frame began to shiver, and Rose led her to a chair. "I thought those days were far behind us," Fannie said. "And now this, so close to Mother Ann's Birthday."

"We'll get to the bottom of this," Rose promised. "Are you all right? I feel I must act quickly, but I don't want to leave you alone, if you are unwell."

"Run along, Rose. This is far more important than my shakes." She shooed Rose with her hand.

A group of sisters was descending the stairs, and Rose wanted to avoid hysteria. She turned to Theodore.

"We'll delay breakfast," she said, "until we are certain it is safe. I want you to make sure everyone understands that the pails mustn't be used. Then check all water sources and the food stores for any sign of this powder, although I fear the snow would have washed off anything outdoors. We must warn the children not to eat any snow," she murmured to herself. "Also, try to locate the rat poison. Leave it where it is until I get there, and don't let anyone touch it. I'll call the police, and then I will join you in the Barn Complex."

Leaving Fannie, who had regained her composure, to explain why breakfast would be late, Rose made her call to the police. The officer named Stan said he'd be along as soon as possible, but the roads were getting difficult because of the snow. Rose didn't argue; she still couldn't imagine how the East managed to carry on with anything approaching normal life in such a climate. She grabbed her cloak and heavy palm bonnet, and headed for the Barn Complex. By the time she reached it, her bonnet and the bottom edges of her cloak and work dress were caked with fresh, wet snow.

Inside the barn, Theodore had gathered the hired men, including Otis, and the male novitiates. Aldon, Johnny, and Sewell stood apart from the others, separating themselves from the world as much as possible.

"Did you find the box of rat poison?" Rose asked Theodore. He shook his head.

"Where was it kept?"

"Over there." He jerked his head toward an untidy stash of farm implements piled against one of the long concrete walls of the rectangular building.

"Do you mean to tell me that an opened container of rat poison was simply tossed on the floor, along with all that equipment?" She clamped her teeth shut to quell a tirade about the importance of tidiness. Now was not the time, though she couldn't believe the novitiates hadn't ordered the area straightened up long ago. "Was it at least kept out of sight?"

Theodore shrugged. "We were using it a lot lately—the rats come inside for the winter, and they were getting to be a real problem."

"Who was in charge of spreading the poison?" Rose was struggling to keep the disapproval out of her voice, and she was losing the battle.

"No one, really," Theodore said. "We all knew where it was. Anyone could have taken it." He glanced over at the novitiates, who scowled back at him.

"Young man, if you think that any one of us could have engaged in such destructive behavior, you know nothing about our faith," Aldon said, his booming voice filling the two-story structure. "It was most certainly someone from the world."

"You've got no right to go accusing my men," Theodore shouted. He grabbed a nearby pitchfork and started toward the novitiates.

"Stop it, instantly," Rose commanded. "There will be no more violence, not if I can help it. The police could arrive at any moment, and if you don't control yourselves, you will *all* look guilty. Theodore, put that pitchfork away, *now*."

Theodore hesitated just long enough to convey defiance for Rose's authority, then he stabbed the pitchfork into a nearby hay bale. He crossed his thick arms over his chest and glowered at Aldon.

It was Sewell who broke the tension. "The eldress is right, you know," he said. "If we lose our tempers and go around accusing each other, we'll all end up looking like we have something to hide. I think we should answer her questions. After all, maybe it wasn't one of us. Maybe someone from a neighboring farm sneaked in and did this, to teach us a lesson. I know I've chatted with folks in the area about the rat problem this year, so probably lots of people would know we had poison about—and we didn't exactly hide it, did we? Maybe it was just a prank."

"It's a prank that might have cost lives," Rose said.

"I know," Sewell said, "but it could have been just a couple of kids, who didn't really know how dangerous the stuff is."

"Farm kids know about rat poison," Theodore said.

"I think we can assume," Rose said, "that whoever did this

meant to cause harm. Who was the last person to leave the barn yesterday evening—besides the person who did this, I mean?"

"I guess I was," Sewell said. "I'm in charge of repairing buildings, and I'd been so busy with the unused buildings, figuring out how to save them, that I hadn't gotten around to looking at what the Barn Complex needs."

Johnny snickered with contempt.

"Was the poison in its place when you left?"

Sewell spread his hands in a gesture of confusion.

"Think. Did you put away any implements once you were through with them?"

"Well, no. I suppose I should have tidied up a bit, but—"

"Never mind that."

"Wait, though," Sewell said, brightening. "I was examining a crack in the cement along the wall just next to where we usually kept the poison." The frown lines already imbedded along the corners of his mouth deepened as he tried to remember. "It wasn't there," he said. "I'm sure of it; the poison wasn't in its usual place."

"Why should we believe you?" Theodore stepped toward him, and Sewell backed away.

"It's true. I love architecture, and I'm very good at remembering what buildings look like, inside and out. Sometimes I dream about them." Sewell looked startled and a little embarrassed by his own admission. "Anyway, I remember how that wall looked last night, and there was no box of rat poison on the floor."

"Good, we'll accept that for now," Rose said quickly, to cut off further argument. "When did the rest of you last visit the barn?"

The men looked at her, at each other, then back at her. "We all left together," Theodore said. "It was after supper and before the service. We finished up with the animals and put everything away, and then we left Sewell here alone. I

sent the men to their rooms to get some sleep, and I decided
to go to the service." He turned back to Sewell. "I noticed
you were slow getting to the service," he said. "Just what
were you doing all that time?"

"I wasn't poisoning buckets, I just—well, I told you, I
started taking some measurements, and the time got away
from me."

"All right," Rose said quickly, to forestall another attack
from Theodore. "Does anyone remember seeing the rat poison while you were putting your tools away before the worship service?"

Some of the men shook their heads, and others shrugged
their shoulders.

"We were in a hurry," Theodore said. "We didn't think
about it."

"When was the poison last used?"

"I guess it must have been night before last," Theodore
said. "We always used it at night, last thing, because that's
when the rats were more likely to come out."

"I remember seeing it when I got here yesterday morning,
just before breakfast," Sewell said. "I just stopped by to pick
up a couple of tools to take around with me while I looked at
the other buildings, and the can was sitting right where it
was supposed to be."

"All right, then we'll assume the poison could have been
taken anytime from breakfast yesterday until sometime before the worship service."

"If we believe Sewell, that is," Theodore said. "He's the
one the police think killed Julia, so it stands to reason he
could be the one trying to poison everybody. He could have
taken the poison before breakfast, and no one would have
noticed."

"That's enough," Rose said. "We'll make no assumptions
about guilt—or innocence, for that matter. We will keep to

the facts, as best we can. Now, Theodore, have you found evidence of the poison anywhere except in these buckets?"

"Nope. The food stores look fine, and so do the water faucets. Whoever did this probably didn't have much time, so they settled for some buckets."

"Perhaps," Rose said. "Where any of these buckets used just before the worship service last evening?"

"Well, yeah," Otis said. "I grabbed some to feed and water the animals. Didn't see anything wrong with any of the buckets I used, and the cows didn't get sick or anything. That was maybe half an hour before everyone left for the service." His weather-worn face crinkled into a pugnacious ball. "I didn't go to the service myself, but I was done with my chores well before it started. Anybody else could have gotten to those pails after I was done with them."

"So the actual poisoning could have been done just before or during the service—or sometime overnight." Anyone could have done it. Rose felt a wave of weakness and realized how hungry she was. "All right, that's enough for now. The police should be here soon, and you need to get your breakfast. I know you've missed several hours of work already. Theodore, do you have a padlock you can use to lock away the tainted buckets? Good, then we'll eat, since it seems clear the food supply was not touched. If any of you thinks of something else I should know, please tell me immediately."

She led the way outdoors, where the snowfall had thickened and gave a ghostlike appearance to the Brick Dwelling House. She wondered how long it would be before the police managed to plow their way through the rapidly deepening snow.

FOURTEEN

IT WOULD BE A VERY LONG TIME, ROSE THOUGHT, BEFORE she again found a snowfall enchanting. The storm had finally tapered off by early afternoon, leaving nearly a foot of sloppy snow, already shrinking into a sodden mess as the sun appeared and pushed the temperature above freezing. Worry had frayed her temper, and stomping along Hancock's cold, wet paths wasn't helping. She prayed for patience, but even more than that, for a speedy resolution to the village's troubles.

Rose had found no reason to suspect the Shakers themselves, but she could not yet eliminate any of the hired workers or the novitiates from her list. No one had an alibi for either Julia's murder or the poisoning of the village's buckets. Even Honora Stearn could have accomplished either or both. At first glance, she seemed a likely suspect for the poisoning, given her threats during the worship service. Rose had watched Theodore drive her toward Pittsfield, so she could only have done the poisoning before the service started.

Rose had no clear ideas about why any of the novitiates or hired workers would have dusted the buckets with poison. To distract or to divert suspicion to outsiders, perhaps? It didn't make sense.

The police had yet to arrive, but there was little that they could do, anyway. She had spoken by phone with Chief O'Malley, who had listened respectfully to the information she had gathered from the men. He'd promised they would send someone, when the road was passable, to pick up a bucket and see if a pharmacist could verify that it was rat poison. That's all she could hope for at this point.

For now, all she could do was carry on with her questioning. She'd had no luck finding Johnny Jenkins, so she was trudging back to the Brick Dwelling House, where she knew there was a sewing room. Esther Jenkins was supposed to be in it. With Mother Ann's Birthday close upon them, the sewing and cooking were in full swing. Esther had been assigned to make Shaker dolls, which were proving popular with worldly customers looking for Shaker mementos for their children. The Shakers were hoping to sell many more on March 1, when they expected crowds of visitors to come for the celebration.

Rose hung her heavy cloak on a wall peg just inside the dwelling house door, to allow it to dry after being dragged through the snow. She noticed that a collection of rags had been spread on the floor to catch the drips from soaked outdoor clothing; it was untidy, but efficient. She could already hear the chattering of female voices from farther down the hall. She followed the sound to a meeting room, converted to a sewing room.

Rose had begun to feel like an executioner. As soon as she entered the open door, conversation stopped and needles halted. Two elderly sisters smiled and nodded to her, then went back to their stitchery. Dulcie and Esther remained frozen in mid-stitch. Dulcie hunched over a Singer sewing machine, apparently putting a seam in a long length of red wool. Her right foot hovered an inch above the foot pedal. Rose gave her a reassuring smile and walked instead to Esther, who sat at a sewing desk, hand-stitching a small piece of butternut wool.

"We haven't had a chance to talk yet," she said, keeping her voice low and soothing. "Why don't you leave your work for a moment, and we'll walk in the hallway. It won't take long. I know how busy you are."

With obvious reluctance, Esther secured her needle in the wool and laid the doll dress on the desk, next to a cloth body with a dried-apple head. Rose studied Esther's profile—fine pale skin, an upturned nose, and golden-blond hair pulled in a neat bun. Though an avowed novitiate, she wore neither an indoor cap nor a Shaker work dress. Her dress was worldly, yet shapeless, as if it were too large for her or had once been worn with a belt. She moved with smooth grace, and Rose wondered if at one time in her life she had been trained in dance. When she turned, Rose noted her perfect oval face and serious gray eyes.

Rose led her into the hallway, where they settled on a wooden bench backed against a wall. "You know why I am here," Rose began.

"There is nothing I can tell you," Esther said. There was a hint of command in her voice. "I barely knew Julia. I know her sister, Dulcie, only slightly better, since I did one kitchen rotation with her."

"I understood that you grew up in Pittsfield. Is that correct?"

Esther shook her head. "I grew up in Boston and moved to Pittsfield as a young woman, after my marriage."

"I see. I was led to believe that the novitiates and the hired workers all knew each other, at least to some extent, before coming to Hancock."

Esther blinked rapidly, but otherwise did not respond.

"Was that information inaccurate, as well?"

"I knew the others, but not well at all. We . . . ran in different circles."

"Do you mean because you were somewhat older, were married and had children?"

"In part."

Something about the young woman's demeanor led Rose to an unexpected line of questioning. "Are your people still living in Boston?"

"My family? Yes, they are."

"Do you see them often?"

Esther's lips parted to reveal teeth in need of care. "I don't see how my family can be of any concern to you, or to this . . . this incident."

Rose could sense she was poking at a tender spot. In her experience, tender spots often proved quite useful. She poked from another angle. "Your people were wealthy, weren't they? Did they lose their wealth in the crash, or are you estranged from them?"

Esther's eyes flashed. "I have little contact with my family. That's the way I prefer it. All this has nothing to do with Julia's death. They never met her, and they would never have occasion to do so. *I* would never have had anything to do with such a person, if it hadn't been for . . ."

"If it hadn't been for the Shakers?"

One of the older sisters left the sewing room and walked past them, toward the sisters' stairway. Rose nodded a greeting. Esther hardly glanced at the sister. Her straight back and elevated chin conveyed barely controlled anger.

When the sister was out of sight, Rose asked, "Your association with the Shakers has led you into contact with people you consider inferior, hasn't it?"

"Is that a reason to suspect me of murder?"

"Nay, not yet."

Esther's eyes turned to granite. "But I suppose you will keep looking until you find a reason?"

"I only want to find the truth," Rose said. "It troubles me that a novitiate so clearly despises those with whom she lives and works. That is all I meant. You might want to consider again whether you are called to this life." She'd poked enough, and she'd only raised yet more questions. Class arrogance was not an obvious motive for Julia's murder, yet Rose knew there was more to Esther's story than she was willing to discuss. She had offered nothing about attending Aldon's church in Pittsfield.

"I have just one more question," Rose said, "and then I'll let you get back to your work. Where were you last night between the evening meal and the worship service?"

"I had no reason whatsoever to poison anyone."

"Then you won't mind telling me where you were."

To Rose's surprise, Esther flushed. Could it be that the woman had a lover? Or perhaps she still had contact with her husband? Then Rose remembered Gennie's quick report about discovering Esther in the abandoned Meetinghouse, playing with her six children. Quite likely, she'd been with them again. Since she wasn't assigned to the kitchen, it would have been a perfect time to sneak off, with no one the wiser. The children lived in the Brick Dwelling House, along with everyone else, and would probably have been put to bed right after the meal. She could have gone to their rooms to spend bedtime with them. But if Rose mentioned her suspicions, she'd be giving away her connection with Gennie.

"It will help me to prove your innocence if you tell me where you were. If you decide to do so, or if there is anything else you wish me to know, you may call upon me anytime."

Esther nodded and headed back to the sewing room, not bothering to wait for a formal dismissal.

"Ma'am? Sister Rose?"

Rose was reaching for her still damp cloak and formulating questions in her mind for her coming interview with Johnny Jenkins. She recognized Dulcie's voice.

"I was just working in the kitchen, and Sister Elizabeth

said you were up here, and I asked her if I could have a word with you."

Dulcie looked just as pale as she had before her visit to the doctor, but there was a brightness in her eyes that Rose hadn't seen before.

"Of course, Dulcie. Let's go to my retiring room, shall we? We can be private there." Rose's cloak could do with more time to dry out, and to be honest, she was glad to delay yet another foray into the snow.

"What's on your mind," she asked, as she offered Dulcie her rocking chair and settled on top of her bed.

"Well, you said I could talk to you anytime . . ."

Rose nodded encouragement.

"It's about my baby." Dulcie laid her palm on the small mound forming under her waist. "I want my baby to be okay. I want it to have a good life, better than Julia and me had. We didn't really have a father, not to speak of, anyway. Even before we lost everything because of the crash, he wasn't around much. He'd just show up now and again to get money. Mother took in laundry and mending, and we made do, even with Father showing up like he did. But then we lost our little house, and we all had to live in this one room in a boardinghouse, and it was so cold, and Mother could only do mending, because there was no way to take in laundry anymore." Dulcie rocked gently, as if comforting her child while reliving her own deprivation.

"You had a terribly hard life," Rose said, inviting her to continue.

"Yes, it was very, very hard. Then it got even worse. Father would come and take the little bit of money we had, so sometimes we couldn't eat if we wanted to pay our rent. Julia got really wild, which hurt our mother so much she cried every day, sometimes right over her mending. All that sadness, I know it's what killed her." Dulcie lifted her small chin. "I stayed in school. It made Mother happier, and I wanted a better life." She stopped rocking and leaned toward Rose. "That's what I want so much—a better life. I don't want my baby to know what it feels like to be poor and cold and hungry."

"How can I help?"

Dulcie sat back and rocked again. "Theodore is a good man," she said. "He doesn't drink. He works hard. Sometimes he's a little hard on people, but it's only because he expects everyone to do their best. I know he wants to protect me."

"You are thinking of telling him about the baby?"

"Yes. But I'm scared."

"Your fear is understandable," Rose said, "but I am so glad you are gathering your courage to take this step. I agree completely—your baby deserves the best life you can give it. If Theodore will accept responsibility and be a father, your baby would have a good start in life." She slid off her bed, pulled a chair close to Dulcie, and took her hand. "Remember, too, that if Theodore is unwilling, the Shakers will help you. Your baby can have a safe life, either way."

But Dulcie did not seem to hear her. She rocked gently, caressing her abdomen. "Theodore will take good care of me and the baby. He will, I know he will," she said. "I'm going to tell him as soon as possible. Maybe we can be married right away, so the baby won't ever have to feel fatherless. Nobody will ever know, except you. You promised you wouldn't tell," she reminded Rose.

"Yea, I promised."

"I'd better get back to the kitchen," Dulcie said, sounding lighthearted for the first time since Rose had met her. She turned at the retiring room door and looked back at Rose. "I'll let you know when the wedding is," she said. "We'll want to keep it quiet, but I'd like you to be there."

"I would be honored."

Rose frowned at the door for several minutes after Dulcie

had closed it behind her. She felt ill at ease, but she couldn't say why. Surely it was best for everyone if Dulcie would confront Theodore with their dilemma. He seemed an upright man, one who would accept responsibility for his mistakes. He was perhaps a bit strict, but wasn't that far better than drunken and shiftless? He would provide a safe haven for Dulcie and their child. If any man could find a way to care for a family during these dreadful times, it was Theodore. So why this niggling, nameless fear?

The bell rang for the evening meal, and Rose took it as a reminder that she didn't have time to sit in her retiring room, fussing about everyone else's life. She had work to do, and the days were passing too quickly. Best to let Dulcie and Theodore sort out their own lives, with no more help from her than prayer could provide.

FIFTEEN

GENNIE YAWNED BEHIND HER HAND. THIS WAS HER THIRD morning in the Hancock Fancy Goods Store, and each minute seemed longer than the last. The day before, she'd eagerly settled into a retiring room in the Brick Dwelling House, having arrived in the wee hours, just before the snow, with Helen Butterfield. Helen had wangled a room in the village as well, but at least it wasn't right next to Gennie's.

Then the excitement about the poisoned buckets started, and there was Gennie, trapped in the store, nibbling candied sweetflag for breakfast. For most of the day, the snow had kept them indoors and the customers away. Gennie tried to walk outdoors during her hour off, but everyone else stayed inside. She couldn't find a soul to talk to or spy on or anything. For hours and hours, it was just her and Abigail and Helen. At least Helen went across the hall to the parlor for half an hour or so. To look over the furniture, she'd said, though Gennie had heard her voice once or twice, as if she might be using the telephone.

Today was busier, now that the roads were passable and the sun was slicing through the clouds in pale slivers. Several folks had come to buy eggs and inquire about the upcoming celebration. Mainly, they seemed interested in the free foods, which no one begrudged them. Abigail had brought several cakes to the store, and she handed out sam-

154

ples to each customer, often slipping the children an extra bite.

Gennie was tired and, to be honest, thoroughly thwarted. None of her scheming had worked so far. Rose had filled her in on everything she'd found out, which only served to demonstrate how boring and useless Gennie's life was in contrast. She'd barely slept all night, waiting for something to happen, but of course nothing did, except that Helen had knocked on her retiring room door and stayed chatting for nearly an hour. Gennie had been raised to be polite to her elders, but Helen Butterfield would be a test to anyone's good breeding. Gennie had pleaded exhaustion to get rid of her.

Gennie's hour out of the store was still far off. She couldn't help wishing that Honora Stearn would make another visit, or that one of the other suspects would arrive and do something, well—suspicious. When she heard the front door of the Trustees' House open and shut, she hoped that perhaps God had taken pity on her frustration.

Dulcie Masters stood shivering in the doorway. She took a tentative step into the room, while her gaze took in the glorious colors and textures. Gennie wondered if she'd been in the store since her sister had worked there.

Seeing Gennie behind the glass counter, Dulcie gave her a tremulous smile. As she handed a basket to Gennie, she leaned over the counter and whispered, "Could I speak with you for a minute? Right away?"

Gennie glanced at Abigail, who, as always, sat across the room, rocking and knitting. "I suppose, but—"

"Please."

Gennie had to admit her curiosity was intense. "Go across the hall to the parlor," she whispered. "I'll meet you there in a few moments."

"These are all the dolls we were able to make yesterday," Dulcie said, in a normal tone. "What with the excitement, and all." Without a word to Abigail, she left the store. There was no sound of the front door opening; Gennie hoped Abigail hadn't noticed.

Gennie grabbed a rag and dusted the counter, rubbing hard at a palm print left by a child reaching for some candy. She stood back as if to examine her handiwork, then folded the rag and stowed it in a basket on the floor behind the counter.

"Abigail," she said, as she walked toward the door, "I'll only be a minute. I'm just going to . . ." She pointed vaguely in the direction of the washroom down the hall.

"Of course, dear," Abigail said, peering over her spectacles. "Take your time. We seem to be in a lull."

Gennie crossed the hallway and eased the parlor door shut behind her. Dulcie was pacing in circles on the rug.

"Thank you so much, Gennie. I was worried you wouldn't take me seriously."

"I knew you were serious, but, frankly, I can't imagine why you'd want to talk to me," Gennie said. She gestured to a settee, but Dulcie kept pacing. Gennie figured the conversation might take a while, and she might as well be comfortable, so she claimed the settee for herself.

"I can't find Rose anywhere," Dulcie said.

"Yes?"

"You've got to help me find her. I must talk to her right away."

"I would help you if I could," Gennie said, trying for just the right touch of innocent confusion, "but I can't imagine what you think I can do."

Dulcie turned on her with impatience. "I know you two are friends. I *need* to find her. My . . . Everything has gone wrong. She's the only one who can help me. Can't you tell me where she might be?"

It took several moments for Gennie to recover from her surprise. Dulcie resumed her pacing.

"How did you know?" Gennie asked.

"That you two are friends? It wasn't that hard, really. I saw her go into your room yesterday after supper. She didn't come out for a long time."

"Weren't you supposed to be working in the kitchen?" Gennie's question came out more accusatory than she'd meant, but she and Rose had been so sure it was a safe time to meet in the hired women's wing of the dwelling house.

"I had something important to do," Dulcie said. "I asked the kitchen sisters to let me go for the evening. I sat in the hallway for a while, thinking. I was in the shadow, I guess. Anyway, Rose didn't see me."

"Couldn't you just tell me what you need to see Rose about? Maybe I could help you."

"No! I mean, it's just between Rose and me."

Gennie felt a twinge of jealousy. Rose had confided nothing about Dulcie that might lead to such agitation—except, of course, that Julia had been Dulcie's sister. But her anguish was immediate; perhaps it had nothing to do with her sister's murder. Unless Dulcie had a suspicion about who killed Julia. But why would Rose keep such information secret from Gennie? Was she still being the protective mother hen, afraid her little chick would rush out into danger?

Gennie's irritation dissolved when she noticed that Dulcie had slumped into a chair and begun to cry. Her tears were silent, the tears of despair. Gennie knelt at her side. "Dulcie, I know something is terribly wrong, and Rose has been helping you, but I promise she would urge you to let me help, too. Whatever it is, I won't tell anyone else. You've got to trust someone right now. Rose is so busy tracking down this . . . the person who hurt your sister. She could be anywhere, even off in Pittsfield talking to the police or something. Why not just confide in me, and we'll work out a solution together?"

Dulcie's tears stopped. She turned dull eyes toward Gennie. "There's no solution," she said. "You can't help me.

Rose can't either, but I always feel better when I talk to her. But this—she probably can't help with this." Dulcie stood— with some difficulty, Gennie noticed.

"You'd best get back to work. Abigail will be wondering. I'm sorry I bothered you. Please don't worry about me. There's nothing you can do."

With her frustration near the bursting point, Gennie was relieved when her hour off arrived. Dulcie would be in the kitchen, helping to wash up after the noon meal, so there was no point in making another attempt to pry her secret out of her. Maybe later.

Rose's description of her interview with Esther Jenkins had intrigued and puzzled Gennie, since Esther had seemed friendly when they'd met two days earlier. *Maybe,* Gennie thought, not without some worldly pride, *I'll be able to get more information from Esther than Rose can.* She decided to visit the deserted Meetinghouse again, in hopes of finding Esther with her children.

A sharp wind sliced through her wool coat as she crossed the slushy road to reach the north end of the village, which was now mostly abandoned buildings. The one drawback of pleading poverty so she could live in the Brick Dwelling House was that she couldn't just whip out twenty-six dollars to buy a Shaker cloak. Maybe Abigail would let her use one if she offered a small down payment and another reduction in her dwindling pay. It was worth a try. She could already feel the sniffles coming on, and she wouldn't be much of a sleuth if she ended up sick in bed.

Gennie turned back and gazed over the whole village, or as much as she could see. No one seemed to be wandering about. Good. She didn't want to be seen making a habit of entering unused buildings. On the other hand, it probably wouldn't be long before the whole village knew of her connection with Rose. Dulcie had certainly tumbled to it easily, and she might mention it to someone else. All the more reason to work fast.

As Gennie trudged toward the Meetinghouse, she came upon footprints in the snow. They looked fresh. She tried matching her steps to them. They were much larger than her small feet, and her legs couldn't span the spaces between the footsteps. Her suspicions were confirmed when she traced the imprints to the men's entrance. The feet had not belonged to Esther and her children. Two men had recently visited the Meetinghouse. She examined the snow nearby and saw no evidence of footsteps leading back toward the road. The men might still be inside.

Gennie's heart picked up speed in a most pleasant way. Probably the visit was innocent, but Gennie was desperate for excitement, and this was the closest she'd gotten to anything out of the ordinary. She decided not to announce her presence just yet, in case she might hear or see something helpful to the investigation.

The large windows to either side of the men's entrance were boarded up, so Gennie rounded the corner of the building and headed for the back, where no one could see her from the village. She was aware she was creating a new path in the snow, but she tried to walk on her tiptoes, to make it look more like animal tracks. Thank goodness Abigail had insisted on lending her some galoshes.

Two windows along the north end of the Meetinghouse still contained glass. She hugged the wall and edged close to the first window until she could see inside. The building looked dark and empty. The old glass was thick, so she couldn't hear even a mumble of voices. She leaned back against the wall and thought a moment. Her hands lay flat against the wood, and through one glove she could feel a rough edge that came off as she nervously picked at it. In her hand was a good-sized sliver of white paint. The back of her coat must be covered with bits of peeling paint. She'd have to remember to clean it off before going back to work.

This was getting her nowhere except frozen. On impulse, Gennie crouched below the bottom of the window and scooted underneath, gasping as the snow scraped her thighs. Once past, she stood again and edged toward the next window. This time, luck was with her. A corner of the glass had cracked and worked loose from the window frame, and no one had yet thought to cover the hole with a board—or perhaps no one had even noticed it.

Gennie peeked through the glass and still saw nothing. She pushed her ear as close as possible to the open corner of the window and listened. Now she heard voices—men's voices. No wonder she hadn't heard them before; they sounded calm and easy, like two friends discussing crops. There was nothing the least bit mysterious about them. She was disappointed. However, she wasn't about to give up so easily on her first chance at excitement.

She wanted to see who the men were, but it meant looking straight into the window and taking the risk of being seen. She thought a minute. Okay, if they did look over and see her face, she would wave eagerly and go right inside, as if she were just out on a jaunt, exploring the village, and was delighted to find someone to talk to.

Her courage bolstered, she peered directly into the building and looked around. There they were, in the southeast corner, standing close together with their heads bent over a large piece of paper that looked like it might be a map. She recognized them at once—Aldon Stearn and Sewell Yates. Her excitement dimmed as she remembered that Sewell was an architect assigned to see about renovating some of Hancock's deteriorating buildings. Aldon, as she recalled, worked with him. So all she'd discovered was two brothers doing their work.

Disappointed, she pulled away from the window and leaned back against the peeling wall. She hadn't used much of her hour yet, she thought. She still had time to search some of the other abandoned buildings for Esther and her brood. Still, she was here. She might as well watch for a spell, see if they got into a discussion of Julia's murder or something. Her feet weren't frozen to numbness yet; when they were, she decided, she'd give up and leave.

Again, she placed her ear against the hole in the window. The men's voices had become more animated. They were discussing future plans for the Meetinghouse, and the prospects pleased them.

"We could do a great service for the Society," Aldon said, in his rich baritone.

"The space may seem too big for us now, but just think if we could dance again in here." Sewell's higher, gentler voice quavered with excitement. "Others would join us, I'm sure of it. It would take some work, though. The roof leaks, some of the wood is rotten, and all the windows will need to be replaced."

Gennie pulled back as she imagined the men looking around the building and gazing at each window. After a few moments, she felt safe enough to listen again.

"We'll talk the others into this," Aldon was saying. "Mother Ann's Birthday is bringing in some extra funds; I'll approach Fannie about using some of them for building supplies. It's for our future. You have done well, Sewell."

Sewell's response was muffled and husky, as if the compliment had choked him up. Gennie couldn't resist a quick peek through the glass. Both men were gazing at the drawing in Sewell's hands, and Aldon had stretched a fatherly arm around Sewell's shoulders. Surprise was not a strong enough word for Gennie's reaction; she was stunned. Was no one in this village what he or she seemed? From Rose's description and from her own observation, Aldon seemed so harsh and distant, more intent on fire and brimstone than on human compassion. Yet here he was, offering warm encouragement to another.

Gennie peered through the window once more. The men had moved apart and appeared to be examining the Meetinghouse floor and walls. They neither spoke nor looked toward each other for several minutes, and Gennie grew bored. And very aware of her cold, wet feet. They weren't numb yet, but maybe it was time to move on. With luck, she could still find Esther and have a quick talk with her before the Fancy Goods Store beckoned again.

She slogged back to the front of the Meetinghouse and out to the path leading east to the unused Ministry Shop. Esther might be there. Gennie's thoughts were occupied with what she'd just heard and seen, and with what she hoped to learn from Esther, so it wasn't until she'd reached the path that she thought to look around her. Just across the main road, on the path next to the Brick Dwelling House, stood Carlotta. She was carrying a large basket, as if she might be transporting items to the Fancy Goods Store. If so, however, she was heading in the wrong direction. It crossed Gennie's mind to wonder if Carlotta had been spying on her from a north window in the dwelling house and had hurried outdoors hoping for gossip fodder.

So much for her chat with Esther. Carlotta would probably follow her and pretty soon all the hired workers, if not the whole village, would know that Esther was sneaking time with her children. Gennie sighed a puff of warm air and crossed the road toward Carlotta.

"Is this how you spend free time?" Carlotta asked, as Gennie came into earshot. "I could think of lots better things to do. Come on, I'm freezing. Let's go to the kitchen and fix some tea. There's nobody there now the washing up is done." The word "washing" sounded more like "warshing," and Gennie wondered if her own accent was so obvious that everyone, including Carlotta, already knew she'd come from Kentucky with Rose to work on the murder investigation. She wondered if they were all snickering behind her back about her feeble attempts at subterfuge. Gennie was not in the best of moods.

The basement kitchen seemed damp and cold to Gennie, but she removed her galoshes and soaked shoes, while Carlotta lit a small, and probably forbidden, fire in one of the ovens.

"Pull up a chair," Carlotta said, "and toast those frozen toes. What was you doin' out tramping around in the snow like that? A soft Southern girl like you, I thought you'd stay bundled up indoors."

A small kitchen clock told Gennie she had only about ten minutes before she had to return to the store. Ten minutes was about all the time she could stand with the sharp-tongued Carlotta. Best to ignore Carlotta's jabs and change the subject, Gennie thought.

"How do you like it here, Carlotta?"

"Okay, I guess. The work is pretty boring, but at least some exciting things are happening."

"Julia's murder, you mean?"

"Yeah, and this poisoning. I mean, I'm glad no one got sick, but you gotta admit, it spiced up the day. It's got those high-and-mighty new Shakers and the hired men at each other's throats, which is fun."

"Who do *you* think killed Julia?"

Carlotta stiffened, like a wild animal ready to flee an attacker. "Why ask me?"

Gennie shrugged. "Just curious. You seem to be really observant, so I wondered if you'd picked up any clues that the police missed."

Carlotta relaxed but didn't answer.

"I know the police suspect Sewell, but he seems like such a nice man," Gennie said. "Do you think he could have done such a terrible thing?"

"The police can't see what's in front of them," Carlotta said, with a toss of her stringy hair.

"Who else should they be suspecting?"

Carlotta poked at the small oven fire, smiling to herself. "Just about anyone *but* Sewell."

Gennie asked casually, "What about Dulcie? They weren't really close, were they?"

"Dulcie? Not likely. She's too puny, for one thing, and too timid, for another. They wasn't close, though, that's for sure. Julia brought shame to poor Miss Dulcie. Not enough to kill her for, though. That fiancé of hers, though, that's a different matter."

"Theodore?"

"Yep. Theodore acts all upright and good, but he's a mean one. I saw him slap Dulcie once, over nothing. He expects her to follow orders, and if she doesn't, well . . ."

"But why would he kill Julia? What reason could he possibly have?"

Carlotta looked at Gennie as if she were a pathetically innocent child. "He's a man, ain't he? Julia was beautiful, I'll give her that, and fun, too. I never met the man that didn't want her, since way back when she was a kid. Wouldn't surprise me if Theodore settled for Dulcie because Julia wouldn't have him."

"You think he carried a torch for Julia all these years?"

"You don't know much about men, do you? They always carry a torch for the ones they can't get."

Gennie glanced at the clock. Just a few minutes.

"I can call over to the store and tell Abigail I found you soaked and you need to dry out," Carlotta said. Obviously, she wanted to talk more, and Gennie was loath to stop the flow.

"Thanks."

Carlotta called from the kitchen telephone, while Gennie stoked the fire and pondered her next questions.

"What about the novitiates?" Gennie asked, when Carlotta returned.

"The novitiates," Carlotta said, with an unpleasant sneer in her voice. "It's hard to see any of them as Shakers. Except Sewell, maybe." Her voice softened. "He's sweet. He's real nice to me, but he's never so much as touched me."

Gennie thought that he might more easily touch one of the other women. Carlotta obviously was sweet on him, but she wasn't especially alluring.

"The police are just stupid. Sewell couldn't hurt anyone. He's as gentle as they come." Carlotta threw more kindling into the tiny fire. A spot of red brightened each of her cheeks. It could just be an effect of the heat, but Gennie suspected her feelings for Sewell were more than a crush.

"What about Johnny Jenkins? I don't know much about him, but he seems rather arrogant, for a Shaker novitiate."

"Johnny Jenkins. His family wasn't no better than mine or Julia's and Dulcie's, but that man puts on airs. Always wanted to be important, no matter what it took. He's a good looker, though, no denying that."

"Shaker novitiates usually learn to be humble," Gennie said.

"That'll be a long time coming for Johnny Jenkins," Carlotta said, with a laugh. "He wants to be the richest man in the world, does Johnny Jenkins. I've seen him looking over the furniture like he's pricing it for sale. One night I was going to the washroom, and I saw him heading for the attics— probably to see what treasures he could find up there that'd make him rich. I figure that's why he's here."

"Here in Hancock, you mean? To get rich? How could he get rich as a Shaker?"

Again, Carlotta turned her pitying gaze on poor, innocent Gennie. "The Shakers *are* rich. Haven't you figured that out yet? Look around you. Everybody else is poor, digging stones out of the ground to grow a potato or two. But the

Shakers, they've got crops and businesses, and buildings they don't even use. There's lots of money to be had here. Johnny probably figures he can get at it if he becomes one of them. That's the way Johnny always thought. That's why he married Esther, you know."

"What do you mean?"

"I forgot, you're not from here. Esther's from a rich Boston family. Johnny went to Boston when he was eighteen, and, the way I hear it, he wanted to find a wife with money. He thought he'd really made a catch when he latched onto Esther. Her family thought different, though. I heard her father tried to buy him off with a fat chunk of dough, but he figured he could get more if he got her to elope with him and then have a bunch of kids. He figured her parents would soften up and open their pockets when the grandkids arrived."

"It didn't work?"

Carlotta laughed. "Nope. Esther's folks are hard as nails, just like she is. They cut her off, right out of their will. They're still alive, far as I know, and they haven't changed their minds. She's their only child, too."

"Doesn't she have children?" Gennie asked.

"Yep. Six of 'em. They're around here somewhere. Johnny doesn't want 'em, that's for sure. If they don't soften up the grandparents, what good are they?"

"What about Esther? Doesn't she want them?"

"Esther's hard to figure. She thinks she's better than the rest of us, but I guess she loves her kids."

"I don't understand why she's here, then. Why not take her children and go back to Boston? Wouldn't her folks welcome her?"

"Too proud to admit she messed up. That's my guess, anyway. Julia knew her better." Carlotta grinned. "Probably because Julia knew Johnny so well. He wasn't exactly loyal to Esther, never mind the six kids. He pretends not to notice girls now because it suits his purpose."

"Did he have a fling with Julia?"

"Didn't everybody?"

"And Esther knew about it?"

Carlotta shrugged. "She'd be stupid if she didn't."

Both women were silent for several moments as they stared at the fading fire. Gennie knew she'd have to get back to the store soon, but she wanted to cover as many suspects as she could.

"What about Aldon Stearn?" she asked. "Did he have any reason to kill Julia?"

"Aldon," Carlotta said, poking at the sticks. "He was the preacher in my church, you know. We were all in the same church—Sewell, Julia, Dulcie, Theodore, Johnny and Esther, and me. Honora was there, too, of course—strange, as ever."

Gennie glanced at the clock. "I'd best get back. Abigail will be wondering." She reached for her damp shoes. "Aldon seems very strict," she added. "Do you suppose he has a soft side?"

"Oh, he can be kind enough," Carlotta said, "when he thinks you're ripe for salvation. But he sure can put the fear of Hell into a person. To this day, I look over my shoulder to see if the devil's watching me."

SIXTEEN

ROSE COULDN'T STILL HER FEARS THAT THE ATTEMPTED poisoning was a prelude to something worse. Since no one was hurt, the police seemed uninterested in identifying the perpetrator. "Probably just a kid's prank," Chief O'Malley had concluded, when Rose spoke with him on the telephone. To Rose, however, Honora Stearn seemed a possible culprit, after her threats at the worship service. A visit was in order.

Rather than stop for the noon meal, Rose waited until the kitchen workers had finished their breakfast clean-up, then gathered some bread and cheese in a cloth. She took an extra hunk of bread and another of cheese, three eggs, and a bit of butter, all of which she wrapped in cloth and packed in a basket. As an afterthought, she added some candied sweet-flag she found in the pantry, probably meant for the Fancy Goods Store. She worked quickly, hoping no one would come in and catch her raiding the food supplies. She had a good reason, but she preferred not to reveal it just yet.

Ricardo didn't need the Cadillac for the afternoon, so she drove off at noon, while everyone else was in the dining room. She waited until she'd reached Pittsfield to eat her lunch, sitting in the car. It gave her time to gather her thoughts—and to utter several prayers for guidance. The novitiates and the hired workers were all linked to one another, it seemed, through their membership in Aldon Stearn's former church.

Surely Honora would be able to tell her more about them—their secrets, old hurts they had inflicted upon one another, thwarted loves and violent hates. Honora might just be bitter enough to dredge up such information about those she believed had wronged her, including her own husband. In the process, she might reveal useful information about herself, as well.

Rose followed Fannie's directions and found the Pittsfield First Congregational Church, tucked into a side road still clogged with snow. She parked as close as she could, lifted the basket of food from the passenger seat, and walked the rest of the way, staying near the center of the road, where cars had packed the snow into dirty mush. The church itself was small and stark, built of gray stone that looked as if it had never been cleaned. Nor had the windows, which looked black from the outside.

Fannie had told her that the congregation, out of respect, allowed Honora to live in a room at the back of the church. A new minister had replaced Aldon, and he and his large family had taken over the cottage the church provided for its clergy. Without her little room, Honora would be on the streets. A hard fall for a prideful woman.

Rose entered the church and shivered. It felt even colder than the outdoors, but perhaps it was only the effect of the darkness and the damp air. Rose had not spent much time in the world's churches; they hadn't been welcoming places for her. St. Christopher's Episcopal Church, back in Languor, was beautiful, with stained glass windows and statuary, and she'd heard that the Catholic church was similar. She preferred the simplicity of the Shaker Meetinghouse, but she didn't mind most of the churches she'd seen. This church, though, disturbed her. There was something harsh about it.

She walked quickly through the sanctuary to the other end, where she found a door leading to a hallway and three more doors. From one of the rooms came the sounds of typing, of the hunt-and-peck variety. The door was open, so Rose looked in. An earnest young man hunched over an old Remington typewriter, frowning at what he'd written as if it had come out in some language other than English.

"Excuse me," Rose said.

The young man jumped. "Heavens, I'm sorry, I didn't see you there. This sermon is giving me fits. Our secretary is out for lunch. Can I help you?" He took in her Shaker outfit without comment.

"I'm looking for Honora Stearn. I was told she lives here."

"Ah. Yes. Honora lives in the room at the end of the hall, but I'm afraid she's not too keen on visitors."

"I'm not surprised," Rose said.

"You know her, then," the young man said, looking relieved that he wouldn't have to handle a scene. "Well, go on ahead and knock on her door. Truth be told, she needs more company. I've urged her to get out, see people, but, well, you know Honora." He squinted at the paper in his typewriter, and Rose withdrew. An odd group, these Eastern Congregationalists, she thought—though she supposed an outsider meeting Wilhelm for the first time might think the same thing about the Shakers.

Rose knocked on Honora's door and waited. Nothing happened. She knocked again, more loudly. She could hear shuffling inside, but after a couple of minutes it became clear that Honora had no intention of answering her door. Rose took a deep breath, prayed for forgiveness, and turned the knob herself. As she'd suspected, the door was unlocked. She opened the door slowly and peered inside, hoping to find Honora without having to enter where she hadn't yet been invited. She could see no one, though, so she took a tentative step over the threshold.

She found herself in a small room that served as both parlor and bedroom. A rumpled day bed was pushed up against a wall. It was covered with wrinkled clothes, so it must also serve as Honora's closet. The living area held one easy chair, with some of the stuffing showing through a rip in the fabric; one small table; and a crooked lamp. A large black Bible, the kind passed down through generations, lay on the table, along with a pair of reading spectacles. The small window was covered with grime. On the sill, Honora had placed an empty vase made of green glass.

"What are *you* doing here? How dare you invade my privacy?" Honora stood in a small doorway leading to a tiny kitchen.

"I'm sorry," Rose said. "You must have been cooking, so you didn't hear my knocks. I was concerned you might not be well, so I thought I'd better check."

Honora crossed her arms and stood her ground, looking like an Old Testament prophet in a patched dress.

"You haven't answered my question," Honora said. "And I don't care anymore. Just leave."

"Well, I will in just a moment, but first I've brought you a gift." She held the basket out in front of her.

"What makes you think I need food?"

"Oh, it's not because I think you *need* it. I just thought you might like to have some treats around for visitors." Honora made no move toward the basket, so Rose placed it on the easy chair, the only clear surface in the room. Then she moved back toward the door, so Honora would feel safe.

Honora's suspicious eyes darted back and forth between the basket and Rose. The basket won. She picked it up and held it tightly, as if she were afraid Rose would snatch it back.

"May I stay and chat for a minute?"

"Why?"

"Well, as you may know, I'm just a visitor to Hancock Village, and frankly I feel a bit at sea." She counted on Honora's isolation to have kept her from learning of Rose's real mission in Hancock. "Such terrible goings-on—murder, poisonings, and who knows what else. I wondered if you had some idea why all this is happening?"

"What poisoning? Who was poisoned?" Honora's normally distrustful demeanor made it impossible to tell if she was surprised to hear of the poisonings or hopeful it had killed someone.

"Rat poison—that hired man, Theodore, found it spread all over the animals' food and water buckets. No one was injured, thank goodness, not even an animal." Rose watched closely, but Honora's face gave nothing away.

Honora turned abruptly and deposited the basket in the kitchen. When she returned, she crossed her arms and said, "It was no man put that poison about."

"What do you mean?"

"It was God's own instrument. God has sent someone to smite you Shakers. I told you this would come to pass, and now it is beginning."

"Do you mean that there will be more?" Rose closed the door to the hallway, in case their strange conversation should attract eavesdroppers. "Do you think there is someone who is in particular danger?"

Honora's dark eyes lost their fire, and she leaned against the doorjamb as if weary. "I'm afraid for my husband," she said, "for Aldon."

"You fear your husband might be the next victim?"

"If you could get them to send him back to me, I could take care of him, keep him out of danger," Honora said. Her wild bitterness had disappeared. Suddenly she was a wife, pleading for her husband's life.

"You know that is his choice," Rose said gently. "But I can promise you, if I learn Aldon wants to come back, I will urge him to do so."

Honora's face changed expressions several times, as if she were carrying on an inner dialogue.

"Honora? Can you name the danger that threatens Aldon? Is it one of the other novitiates, or one of the hired hands?"

Honora's short laugh sounded more like a yelp. "They are all dangerous, every one of them. He can't protect himself. He seems so strong; *they* all think he is strong, but the devil is stronger."

Rose wondered if the time had come to give up. Honora drifted in and out of reality. She seemed unable to distinguish individuals, except for Aldon. To her, everyone else was *them*, and they were all evil.

"Perhaps I should go now and let you rest," Rose said.

Honora looked straight at her. "I'll never rest until Aldon is safe from the evil he has chosen," she said. She disappeared into the kitchen and left Rose to show herself out.

Rose sat at the small desk in her retiring room with all her notes spread out in front of her. It was close to the dinner hour, and she and Gennie had just managed a quick exchange of information. Rose felt overwhelmed with tidbits and impressions, and she needed to update the list of suspects she'd made shortly after arriving in Hancock. She wrapped the thick wool blanket from her bed more tightly around her shoulders. If she weren't wearing her indoor cap, she was quite certain she'd be tearing out her hair. Starting on a fresh sheet, she divided her paper into eight sections. In each section, she wrote the name of a novitiate or a hired worker who had been connected in any way with Julia Masters. They were still little more than strangers to her, yet somehow she must sort through their stories and find a killer. As quickly as possible, she jotted down her observations and questions next to each name, writing very small so that she could fit everything on one page and see it all at once.

She began with Dulcie Masters, Julia's sister. Dulcie was the "good girl," compared to Julia, yet she was pregnant out of wedlock. Dulcie had been alone with her sister's body and had removed a piece of calico—was this to protect someone else or herself? Dulcie defended her sister, but clearly the two girls hadn't gotten along well. Julia had enjoyed pursuing men who belonged to other women. Might Dulcie have been frightened that her sister would steal her fiancé, leaving her pregnant and alone?

Carlotta DiAngelo had been caught shoplifting, and Julia had escaped punishment. Carlotta was a bitter young woman, but would an old grudge be enough to set her on the path to murder? Carlotta was sweet on Sewell. Did she believe that he would have been hers, if only Julia had not pursued him?

Sewell Yates seemed to like and be liked by everyone, even Aldon, who pronounced him weak, yet with good in him. He'd been observed in animated conversation with Julia shortly before her murder, and there had been rumors of a carnal relationship with her. He seemed incapable of violence, but Rose knew better than to trust appearances. There was something about Sewell—his haunted eyes, his sunken thinness, everything about him hinted at some hidden anguish. Might he have continued his affair with Julia, then killed her in a jealous rage upon discovering her dalliances with other men? It seemed unlikely. The murder seemed carefully—indeed, cold-heartedly—planned. Yet sometimes the gentle ones are slow to burn.

Theodore Geist, Dulcie's fiancé—Rose admitted her dislike of the man. He could be disrespectful, even cruel, to Dulcie, and—again, according to Aldon—he had been unfaithful to her with Julia. His character was harsh, demanding. He had a quick and violent temper. He was the sort of man who believes a woman must be obedient and faithful, while a man may do as he pleases. But he also considered himself to be good and upright. Carlotta had mentioned that he might be relieved not to have Julia as a sister-in-law.

Might he have regretted an affair with Julia and killed her to protect his reputation and his job? No one had provided any real evidence of such a relationship.

Aldon Stearn reminded her of Elder Wilhelm. His faith was deep, strong, and tended toward fire and brimstone. Though celibacy was a central tenet of Shakerism, he seemed unduly concerned with it, and with suspicions that everyone else was violating it. He was condescending to women. He cherished and celebrated his own holiness. What secrets might he hold inside? Honora said she was afraid for him and that he could not protect himself. What did she mean by that? Were her words the ravings of a woman driven over the edge? Or did she know something about her husband that no one else suspected?

Then there was Honora herself, a proud woman who had lost her respected place in the community. By all accounts, she had always been odd, but since her husband left, her behavior hinted at insanity. She had lost her husband and her position. She'd been left in poverty, living in one room in a church that used to be her husband's. Several informants had claimed that Aldon had been unfaithful on numerous occasions. Honora had turned the other cheek, but her Christian forbearance had not kept her husband at her side. An insanely jealous wife might have planned such a bizarre murder to avenge her husband's unfaithfulness—if Aldon had indeed dallied with Julia.

It had become clear that Johnny Jenkins was driven by the desire for wealth. He used people, including his wife and children, to achieve his goals. Though he showed no interest in women, there were hints from his past that he was not above illicit carnal liaisons. On the other hand, Rose suspected his obsession with riches superseded all other desires. If Julia had been a threat to him, it was more likely because she had found evidence that he meant to drain the Shakers' resources.

Esther Jenkins's behavior seemed contradictory. With Gennie, she had been friendly and open, expressing disapproval of her rich parents' values; but when Rose questioned her, she had adopted an upper-crust arrogance and revealed as little as possible. Was she afraid that Rose might have the power to take her children away from her? She had denied knowing much about Julia and showed low regard for her "sort." To Rose, it seemed that Esther had trapped herself with her own pride. She could not bear to admit her parents were right about Johnny, nor could she allow anyone else to raise her children. She needed Johnny back. Julia had set her cap for Johnny—indeed, she might already have captured him. Rose could envision Esther, with cold-hearted calculation, eliminating Julia to save her own economic security and allow her to keep her children.

Rose read back through her notes, then added one more name to the bottom: Otis Friddle. He didn't have an obvious motive for killing Julia, and he didn't seem to have the energy to plan such a meticulous murder, yet he had found her body, and he hadn't given a good reason for being near the Summerhouse. Had he been more attracted to Julia than he'd admitted? How might he have reacted to a cruel rebuff of his passion? It seemed farfetched, but she would keep him on the list for now.

On the edge of the page, she wrote two questions: (1) What does the attempted poisoning have to do with Julia's murder? (2) Who was Julia's lover at the time of her death—the one Julia believed was cheating on her? Rose wasn't ready to write down any speculations yet. Unless someone was trying to muddy the waters—perhaps to make it seem like an angry outsider was the guilty party—she couldn't see any logical connection between the two incidents.

When the bell rang for the evening meal, Rose was more than ready to put her work aside. She stowed it in the drawer of her desk, under some blank sheets of paper, just to be safe. She wished she could make better sense of what she had learned, and she prayed most fervently that nothing more would happen before she could do so.

SEVENTEEN

AS SOON AS ROSE ENTERED THE DINING ROOM, SHE KNEW that something must be wrong in the kitchen. Normally, the kitchen help had already arranged dishes, cutlery, bread, and pitchers of water on the tables by the time the diners arrived. Rose and Fannie sat down with the sisters, and they all waited in silence. And waited. With a gesture to Rose to stay put, Fannie went downstairs to find out what had happened. Within moments, she reappeared and signaled to Rose to follow her back down.

Carlotta was alone in the kitchen, hacking at a loaf of bread. "Don't expect supper anytime soon," she said. "Not if you expect me to do everything around here."

"Why on earth didn't you call for help?" Fannie asked. "Where's Dulcie?"

"Dulcie couldn't be bothered to show up. Don't ask me where she is, because she sure didn't tell me. I got a good mind to quit right now and let you cook your own meals."

"Dulcie is usually so reliable," Fannie said. "I hope she isn't ill again. The sisters told me she's been having dizzy spells."

"Oh, she's snuck off before, without you knowing, you can be sure of that. She just figures somebody else'll do the work for her."

Fannie shook her head. "That doesn't sound like her. I'm worried."

178

"So am I," Rose said. Gennie had told her of Dulcie's frantic visit to the Fancy Goods Shop. She should have paid more attention. "When did you see her last, Carlotta?"

"She was here at noon, not that she was much help. She was a real nervous Nellie, kept dropping things and forgetting what she was doing."

"Did she leave before you did?" Rose asked.

"No, at least she stayed through the washing up. We left together and walked upstairs to our rooms. I told her she'd better have a nap or she wouldn't be no good to anybody. Not that she listened to me." Carlotta scooped up a pile of bread slices and dumped them on a platter.

"What do you mean?" Rose asked.

"I mean she went right out again. My room is just two doors down from her, and not more'n five minutes later, I heard her door open and close again. She was trying to be quiet, but I got good ears. I opened my own door a little, and I saw her going down toward the staircase. I knew she was going outdoors because she was wearing that ratty old jacket of hers."

"I'd better go search for her," Rose said.

"I agree," Fannie said. "You go on ahead, and I'll help Carlotta get the evening meal put together. On your way out, tell everyone to be patient, we won't be long. Here, take some bread with you." She grabbed a slice from the cutting board, narrowly missing Carlotta's next swipe at the loaf.

Rose hurried back upstairs to reassure the hungry diners. On her way through the dining room, she caught Gennie's eye and tried to tell her to stay put. She knew Gennie's curiosity, but if they left together, everyone in the room would know of their connection. Gennie was much more valuable if she remained independent.

Despite Carlotta's observation that Dulcie had been dressed for the outdoors, Rose knew it would be foolish not to search the Brick Dwelling House first. Dulcie might have returned. She might be unwell and resting in her room, or even hiding for unknown reasons in another room. Dulcie might just have wanted privacy—perhaps Carlotta had made one of her typical insensitive remarks. But what if something had gone wrong with her pregnancy, and she was desperately ill, yet afraid of discovery? The thought sent Rose's feet into a run.

She began with Dulcie's room. It was empty, and there was no sign of her jacket. Either she had never returned, or she had returned but kept her jacket with her, perhaps for warmth.

The Brick Dwelling House was huge, with three floors, plus two attic lofts used for storage. Most of the retiring rooms were unused but held furniture and could be inhabited comfortably at a moment's notice. If Dulcie wanted to be alone, she could be anywhere. Now Rose wished she'd brought Gennie along. But it still wasn't the time to raise an alarm—not until she knew that Dulcie wasn't just trying to avoid curious, prying eyes by hiding in an unused part of the building.

For the sake of thoroughness, Rose quickly searched the two first-floor communal rooms; the large meeting room, where worship was held; the waiting rooms; and all the Ministry rooms, even Fannie's. Taking the sisters' staircase, she moved to the second floor, to the retiring rooms inhabited by Believers. She included her own retiring room, in case Dulcie might be waiting for her. She skipped the brethren's side, since she couldn't imagine Dulcie seeking refuge in the retiring room of a Shaker brother.

Rose's arms were feeling the strain of opening and closing doors, one after another after another. She had found no sign of Dulcie on the second floor or on the third floor, where the hired workers lived. She was not waiting for Theodore, that much was clear. Time was passing. Even with the delay in serving the evening meal, the diners would be finished soon, in a hurry to return to their duties.

She'd best search the attic lofts. It would be cold and dark and dusty up there, but she had to be certain. She climbed the staircase to the first attic level. She'd never examined the Hancock attics before, and she saw at once that they would be brighter during the daytime than she'd expected, due to a clever system of double skylights, which would allow natural light to penetrate both levels. However, the sun had long ago set, and grime had collected on the skylights, blocking the weak moonlight. Rose could see the dark shapes of furniture piled everywhere. She stood a few steps from the landing and listened intently. She heard no movement or sound of breathing but her own—and blessedly, no little rodent sounds, either.

She moved on to the top attic level. The air was stale and musty, but moonlight from the roof skylights made it slightly brighter than the attic below. She could make out shapes more clearly. None of them moved. She looked around for anything out of the ordinary helter-skelter of hastily stored items. One recessed corner, off to the left of the stairwell, struck her as odd. It was filled with furniture, as was the rest of the attic, but there was something almost roomlike about their arrangement. She went closer. A small pine desk, with a scratched surface, stood just inside the alcove. Behind it, facing outward, was a ladder-back chair with a woven seat. Despite one broken tape, the chair would surely hold an adult without collapsing.

The setting gave the impression that someone had recently been working at the desk, perhaps arising to go down five flights to evening meal. A small jar of ink rested in one corner, the ancient label stained with drips of black. Rose saw no pen. The alcove was cut off from the skylight, so it was far too dark for someone to work in. Rose looked around and found an old oil lamp set on the floor to the right of the chair. She picked it up. It still held oil.

Rose was torn. Dulcie could be in trouble, and she shouldn't waste any time in finding her. Yet something drew her to investigate this strange little attic corner. She took a step and her toe kicked a small object. She reached down and picked up a box of matches. She struck a match and lit the lamp.

She turned around slowly in the small area, using the lamp to light the back corners. Nothing unusual caught her eye, just dust and spiderwebs. She examined the desktop. For a moment, her breath caught in her throat. A spot of blood had run along one of the deeper scratches. It looked as if some attempt had been made to wipe it off, but the red tinge remained. Rose leaned closer. *Nay,* she thought, *surely dried blood would not still be so red.* It had to be ink.

On impulse, she picked up the ink jar. There was liquid inside. She placed the lamp on the desk and unscrewed the lid. The jar was half full of a bright red substance. She sniffed it. Paint. Scarlet paint, still quite fresh. She replaced the lid and put the jar back precisely where she'd found it.

The desk had one drawer, which she pulled entirely out of its enclosure and laid on the desk. It held paper; a dried-up, old fountain pen with a black-stained nib; and, pushed to the back, a rolled-up rag. Her hands shaking, Rose unwrapped the cloth. Inside were three small paintbrushes, of the sort that might be used for spirit drawings—drawings once given as heavenly gifts to Believers who were dreaming or in a dancing trance. One of the brushes had been used and crudely cleaned. It still held traces of red paint.

Rose's instincts told her she'd found something significant, but she had no idea what it meant. This was no time to dawdle and figure it out. She'd return later. She placed the lamp and matches back on the floor, put the spent match in her apron pocket, and headed back downstairs.

The evening meal was ending as Rose reached the first-floor landing. Lines of silent men and women filed into the hallway and began to scatter. Fannie's worried, questioning eyes sought out Rose, who shook her head slightly.

"No sign at all?" Fannie asked.

"None. As far as I could tell, nothing but her jacket is missing from her room, so she probably did not intend to leave the village. I believe it is time to raise the alarm. With everyone helping, we can do a village-wide search in quick order."

"I agree."

Fannie called to everyone to regather in the hallway, and she explained the situation. She sent the Believers and novitiates to search the buildings they knew best, while Theodore, looking more angry than worried, ordered the hired workers to search the farm buildings and all the abandoned buildings. With regret, Rose stayed behind so that anyone with news could report to her immediately. Gennie followed a group of sisters, and Helen Butterfield tagged along.

When the last of the searchers had left, Rose paced the empty hallway. Waiting idly was not in her nature. Whenever she passed a window, she peered out into the darkness. Light appeared and disappeared inside buildings and the swinging brightness of lanterns punctuated the outside air. The minutes passed with aching slowness. Rose almost expected dawn to appear in the east, but the hall clock told her it had been only half an hour.

She couldn't stand the waiting much longer. She pulled on her galoshes, half inclined to step outside, but instead she resumed her pacing. As she looked out a corner window facing southeast, she saw a light emerge from the Round Stone Barn and begin to bounce toward the dwelling house. Someone was running. She grabbed her cloak and threw it around her shoulders without bothering to tie it around her neck.

Ignoring the paths, she ran toward the light. Sewell came into view. As soon as he recognized her, he stopped and bent over to catch his breath before she reached him.

"You've found her? Is she all right?"

Sewell straightened and held up his lantern, which gave his gaunt face an unearthly pallor.

"Sewell, tell me quickly." Rose wanted so to grab his shoulders and shake him.

"She's . . . she's alive. Not by much, though, far as I can tell. She fell from the upper level of the Round Stone Barn— you know, from where we used to push hay down to the animals. She must have been ill and gotten dizzy or something."

Fell or was pushed? "Did you move her?"

Sewell shook his head. "I put an old blanket over her, and I came right out to get you."

"Good. Run now to the dwelling house and phone the doctor in Pittsfield. Tell him it's an emergency, a girl's life depends on him. Then tell the others to meet me in the barn. Go now!" Rose took the lamp from Sewell's hand and sprinted awkwardly toward the Stone Barn, giving no heed to the snow that caked inside her galoshes.

Under a filthy blanket, Dulcie lay in a crumpled heap, her face drained of color. But she was still breathing. Rose lifted the blanket and looked her over, trying not to move her and risk worsening her injuries. She had landed on a pile of old hay, which might explain why she was still alive after such a fall. She had probably broken some ribs. Moving her out of the barn would be dangerous, but they couldn't leave her here to freeze to death. She might also have a concussion and who knows how many other internal injuries. One could only pray that her back was not broken.

Rose noticed a wet spot on Dulcie's dark blue dress. She ran her finger across it and smelled it. Blood. Gingerly, she lifted the girl's skirt to her waist. Her undergarments were soaked with blood. Rose covered her quickly and sat back on her heels, fighting back tears. The baby. The baby was dead.

She heard shouts outside and knew the others had arrived. For the sake of Dulcie's privacy, it would not do to let them all know about the baby. Not yet.

The barn door flew open, and, to Rose's astonishment, the first person to enter was Helen Butterfield, who ran with surprising agility toward the injured girl. She knelt and took Dulcie's pulse, then lifted the blanket before Rose could stop her. As the others approached, Helen quickly dropped the blanket.

"I'm a nurse by training," she said. "This girl is alive but seriously injured. We need to move her with the utmost care. You two men," she said, pointing to Johnny and Otis, "find another blanket and bring it back. We'll make a sling and lift her onto it. Then we'll have at least four men carry her back to the dwelling house with as little movement as possible. Go! Now!" she ordered, as Johnny and Otis hesitated. They took off, cooperating for once.

Helen pointed to Aldon and Theodore. "I'll need you two to help carry her, when the others get back, so you stay put. The rest of you, I'll need a room prepared for her, first floor. It must be warm, or at least bring extra blankets. In addition to her injuries, she'll be in shock. Go on now, scoot!" Everyone obeyed, except Rose, who had other plans.

As Helen knelt again by her patient, Rose backed away. She left the barn after the others, but she did not follow them. Instead, she walked around the outside until she found the entrance to the next level, the one from which Dulcie had fallen. The door was slightly ajar, so she slipped inside without making any noise. She walked delicately to the edge of the fall-off and looked over. Directly underneath, Helen still bent over Dulcie, apparently taking her pulse again. Across the radius of the barn, Johnny and Otis were shaking out an old blanket they'd just found.

Rose pulled back from the edge and began her search. She had a strong hunch that everyone, including the police, would treat this as an accident—especially once they discovered Dulcie had been pregnant and hadn't been well lately. They would assume she wanted some air, had a dizzy spell, and fell over the side. It was the most convenient story for everyone.

There was little light, so Rose dropped to her knees and examined the area from which Dulcie must have fallen. She was counting on the fact that no one had been available to sweep the barn for years. Bits of hay, dust, and dirt were scattered across the wood floor. She examined the floor inch by inch. By the time she heard Helen giving orders about how to lift Dulcie from the ground, Rose knew that her hopes had been in vain. She found evidence that someone had recently been there—wet spots indicated melted snow from boots or galoshes, and the heavy layer of dust had been pushed about. However, she couldn't find anything that looked like skid marks that would indicate a struggle. She couldn't even tell if more than one person had been up there recently. It was possible that the would-be killer had already subdued Dulcie and simply carried her into the barn to throw her down. That would explain what wasn't there. But then, the police could only work with what *was* there.

Feeling discouraged and very alone, Rose stood and looked over the side. Four men were lifting Dulcie, who was wrapped in a blanket so she would move as little as possible. Helen guided them, her hands waving about as if she didn't quite trust the men to be careful enough. Finally, eight strong arms securely held the Dulcie bundle, and the group moved like a centipede toward the barn door. Helen watched them leave, then glanced back at the hay on which Dulcie had fallen. She crouched down, pushed the hay aside, as if she'd spotted something. She picked up a small object and stowed it in her coat pocket. Kicking the hay back into a pile, she followed the others out of the barn.

EIGHTEEN

"I⊤ WAS JUST AN ACCIDENT. THAT'S WHAT THE DOCTOR AND the police both said." Johnny Jenkins's gaze flicked up at Rose and back again to his journal, where he was listing a series of numbers. Since they were in the Brethren's Workshop, surrounded by thin strips of wood, she assumed he was recording the production of oval boxes for sale to the world.

"Nevertheless," Rose said, "I want to know where you were yesterday afternoon between two and the time we gathered for the evening meal." She did not bother to justify her request. Johnny was a novitiate and should by now have grasped the need for obedience to an eldress, even if she was from a different village.

Johnny paused just long enough to be insolent before putting down his pen. "Yesterday afternoon, I was, as usual, working. I came here immediately following the noon meal, and Aldon and I worked on oval boxes until the bell rang for the evening meal. Does that satisfy your curiosity?"

"Did either of you leave the building at any time?"

Johnny's jaw tightened. "We are not in the habit of interrupting our work for pleasure outings," he said.

"You might have needed something in another building. Perhaps one of you carried some items over to the Fancy Goods Store?"

"We did not leave the building." He picked up his pen, signaling the interview was over.

Though she prayed for patience, Rose felt her own pride tripping her, clouding her mind. As Johnny began writing again, she stood her ground and willed her temper to cool. Too much depended on her ability to find the truth. Dulcie hovered between life and death. If her "accident" was really a murder attempt, she was still in danger. There was no time for injured pride.

"That's good," she said. "The doctor and the police may be quite right, of course, but you can understand why I want to be certain Dulcie was alone when she fell."

Johnny's pen hesitated above the page. "Dulcie did sometimes go to the Round Stone Barn alone, you know," he said.

"I didn't know."

Johnny tapped the top of his pen on the desktop. "I saw her go in alone, now and then. I can't imagine why she would choose such a cold place, but maybe she thought no one would think to look for her there. So I'm not surprised that's where her accident happened."

"Did you ever see her go there with anyone else?"

Johnny shrugged. "Sorry. Now I really must get back to work."

"Of course."

Rose descended to the first floor of the Brethren's Workshop and found that Aldon had arrived to make brooms. Apparently, brooms were just as irritating to him as oval boxes had been, because his aristocratic face puckered in a frown. His frown deepened at Rose's question.

"Johnny and I worked together all afternoon," Aldon confirmed.

"And neither of you left the building for any reason? To deliver finished items to the store, anything at all?"

"I do not lie."

"Of course not. But when one is working intently, the memory can falter."

"Not mine."

"I see. Then I won't keep you longer from your work." When she reached the door, she turned back to Aldon. "Just one last question," she said. "Were you aware that Dulcie sometimes visited the Round Stone Barn alone?"

"Unlike some others, I took no notice of Dulcie's comings and goings, nor those of any other female."

"Which others took more notice of her?"

Aldon picked up some broom straw and stuffed it awkwardly in the winder. "I should think her fiancé would be better able to tell you her habits."

"I see. Thank you for your help."

So Aldon and Johnny alibi each other for the time of Dulcie's "accident," Rose thought as she crunched through the snow toward the Barn Complex. And Aldon seemed to hope she would look with suspicion on Theodore. She might as well follow the lead, vague as it was. She had no other ideas at the moment.

She found Theodore and Otis inside the Barn Complex, cleaning and repairing some farming equipment, so they would be ready when spring arrived. With Theodore nearby, Otis appeared to be hard at work. They both looked up at the same time as she approached them. Theodore gave her a cold stare, while Otis's face crinkled with pleasure as he put aside his work with no sign of regret.

"You think Dulcie had some help falling all that way?" Otis asked, when Rose had begun her questions.

"That's ridiculous," Theodore said. "Nobody'd bother to hurt Dulcie. She got dizzy, and she fell. That's all."

By some miracle, Rose had prevailed upon the doctor, Helen, and Fannie—the only ones who had found out about Dulcie's pregnancy—to keep the information under wraps for the time being. Theodore must think that no one knew.

Wouldn't it occur to him that the baby must have been injured in Dulcie's fall? Perhaps he didn't care, as long as his reputation was safe.

"I'm not sure of anything at this point," Rose said. "I just think it wise to clarify at once where everyone was when Dulcie fell. After all, someone might have seen something that would help pinpoint the exact time of her accident."

"Well, I guess we're both suspects, then," Otis said cheerfully. "Theodore and me, we worked all over the place yesterday afternoon, both together and alone."

"I worked here most of the afternoon," Theodore said. "All this stuff has to get fixed soon. Spring is coming."

Rose had trouble believing that spring would ever come again to this frozen land, let alone soon, but she could appreciate the urge to work efficiently.

"As for me," Otis said, "I was in and out. Had to deliver some frilly stuff to the store—for the sisters, you know. Got rags and so forth for cleaning and oiling. I was all over the place."

Rose believed him. He probably walked well out of his way whenever possible, if his previous habits were any indication.

"Otis, if you were around the village, perhaps you saw something that might be helpful. Did you catch sight of Dulcie at any time?"

Otis pulled down the corners of his mouth until he looked like a frog about to flick his tongue at a fly. "Now you mention it," he said, "I might've seen Dulcie, but I can't be real sure. If it was her, then I saw her a couple of times. She always wears that old Shaker dress, so it's hard to tell her from a sister sometimes, especially from a distance—but I'm pretty sure it was her jacket I saw."

"Where did you see her—and when?"

"Well, let me see. I saw her heading out of the store—no, wait, that was before supper. You don't care about that."

"Tell me anyway." She'd probably just talked with Gennie, Rose thought, with regret. If only she had stayed in the village yesterday afternoon, maybe Dulcie would have found her, and none of this would have happened.

"She took off at a run, and I remember thinking that was strange," Otis said. "She's been feeling poorly lately, so I was surprised she could run like that through the snow. She was heading west, probably back to the dwelling house."

"Did you watch where she actually went?"

"No, but I did see her stop and talk to one of the baby Shakers—Sewell, I think. He wasn't so much taller than Dulcie, so I figured it was Sewell. Those other two, they're real tall. I had to get back here with some rags, so I didn't wait around to see where she went after that."

"And after the noon meal?"

"Well, it must've been around the middle of the afternoon when I had to go out again—the sisters wanted me to deliver some things to the store. I saw Dulcie come out of the dwelling house as I was walking toward it. I think she must have seen me, too, because she went way off the path into the snow so she wouldn't pass close to me. We've always been friendly, Dulcie and me, but maybe she just didn't want to talk to anyone. She gets like that once in a while." He glanced sideways at Theodore, who showed no interest in the conversation.

"Did you see where she was heading?"

"Yeah, I watched her a bit. I mean, she was acting strange, and I guess I was curious. She sort of circled wide around me and went straight for the Round Stone Barn. That's the last I seen of her."

"What time was that?"

"No idea."

"Did either of you see or hear of anything else that afternoon that struck you as unusual?" Rose asked.

Theodore shook his head without looking up from the hay rake he was scraping clean of dirt and rust.

"You know," Otis said, "there was one more thing, now you ask. I didn't think much of it at the time." He frowned. "Of course, I could be wrong, too."

"Tell me."

"Well, it seemed like one of the barn doors was open. The Round Stone Barn, that is. Might not mean anything, though, come to think of it. Sewell's been going around to all the old buildings a lot, so he might've been inside or just left. It's dark in there; maybe he wanted more light." Otis shrugged and picked up a rag, as if he might actually put in a few minutes of work.

"Do you have any idea where Sewell might be now?" Rose asked.

For once, it was Theodore who answered. "He said he was going to the old Meetinghouse to take some measurements. Wanted me to come along and help, as if I didn't have enough of my own work to do, with spring planting getting closer."

Rose noticed he did not mention a need to spend time watching over his fiancée. Perhaps he was one of those men who kept their emotions secret. It seemed she'd met more such men up here than back in Kentucky. Maybe it was her prejudice showing through—or maybe it was an effect of the climate.

"How is Dulcie? She isn't . . . ?" Sewell watched with anxious eyes as Rose crossed the Meetinghouse toward him.

"As far as I know, she is the same," Rose said. She thought she saw his expression relax. Was he truly concerned about Dulcie, or was he relieved she was still unconscious?

"I need to ask you a few questions about yesterday."

Sewell held a large sheet of paper that crackled as his hand twitched. "Yes?"

"Right now it looks like Dulcie fell accidentally, but with Julia's murder and all, I thought it best to find out where everyone was yesterday afternoon—just to be safe, you know." In the lantern light, Rose could see the fear in Sewell's eyes.

"Of course. That's the wisest course, I'm sure." He ran a hand through his dark hair and knocked a pencil from behind his ear. "Sorry," he mumbled, as he knelt to retrieve it.

"When you spoke with Dulcie yesterday, did she mention if she was planning to meet someone later?"

"When I . . . ? I'm sorry, I don't remember speaking with her for several days."

"You were seen, Sewell. Just take your time, I'm sure it will come to you."

Sewell's eyes darted around the room as if looking for a crack to fly through. "I suppose we did pass the time of day, but it was no more than that."

"No one is accusing you of forbidden behavior," Rose said. "I wasn't here yesterday afternoon, so I need others to remember for me. That's all."

"It may be nothing to you," Sewell said, "but the police still think I killed Julia. Why wouldn't they blame me for Dulcie, too?"

"The police are convinced Dulcie fell by accident."

"They won't be for long, if you keep asking these questions."

"And if you refuse to help me," Rose said sternly, "I will have to wonder what you are trying to hide."

"I haven't hurt anyone, not a soul. I swear it before the Holy Father. I don't understand why this has fallen on me. Hasn't my life been hard enough? Why am I being tested like this?" Sewell had spread out his arms and reached his shaking hands toward the heavens. From anyone else, it would have seemed a calculated gesture, but Rose believed

Sewell's anguish. He was a tortured soul, but by what, if not murder, she could not guess.

"Help me prove your innocence," she said. "Tell me everything you remember from your conversation with Dulcie yesterday."

Sewell clenched his hands prayerfully before his chest. "All right," he said, "I will try. I will trust that God has sent you here. Dulcie was upset. We were friends, in my former life, good and trusted friends. She confided in me. When she saw me, she came running right up to me as if I was the only person she could talk to. She said everything had gone wrong, and she had only one chance to set it right."

"Do you know what she meant by that?"

Sewell bowed his head over his hands for a moment, then looked Rose in the eyes. "I knew about the baby," he said. "She had told me before. Yesterday she said that Theodore was furious with her, blamed her for everything and didn't want her or the baby. She kept saying, 'My baby needs a father,' over and over."

"Did she tell you her plan—how she intended to 'set it right'?"

Sewell shook his head slowly. "I told her she must tell the sisters about her condition and let them talk to Theodore. Then she began to cry and said she couldn't talk anymore. I urged her to go to bed and rest; she looked so pale. She said she had to fix everything right away or she'd never be able to sleep again. As she walked away, I heard her say, 'Why has he left me like this?' I thought she might have meant God."

"Did you see where she went after she left you?"

"I was in a hurry, so I only watched for a few moments. She walked very slowly toward the east. She could have been going anyplace—the Round Stone Barn, the Trustees' Office, anywhere. I'm sorry I can't be more helpful. Do you believe me?"

"I think I do," Rose said. "But I would find it easier to believe you if I understood you better."

"There is nothing to understand." His haunted dark eyes refuted his statement.

"You are afraid of something," Rose said. "I've sensed it ever since we first met. My guess is that you have not confessed this terrifying fear to anyone. Tell me. Perhaps I can help. As you well know, confession itself can give you the peace you so clearly lack."

Sewell turned still as stone. Even his breathing stopped. For an instant, Rose wondered if he had slipped into a trance. Then his body sagged as if all hope had burned away and melted his sinews. "I appreciate your concern," he said, "but there is nothing to tell. I'd best get back to work now."

Rose gave up, for the moment. He had seemed close to confessing something—if not murder, then another torturing sin. She would try again.

"I have just one more question," she said, "and then I'll let you work in peace. Where were you yesterday afternoon between the noon and evening meals?"

Sewell seemed relieved by the question. "That's easy," he said. "I spent all afternoon listing materials we would need to repair the Meetinghouse, the Round Stone Barn, and the Ministry Shop. I'd just finished in the Round Stone Barn and was heading for the Meetinghouse when I spoke with Dulcie."

"Was someone helping you?"

"I was alone. We have too few hands for all the work to be done."

"Did you see Dulcie while you were in the Round Stone Barn?"

"Of course not. If I had, I would have said something."

"Might you have left the barn door open?"

"It's entirely possible. When my mind is on my work, sometimes I forget simple acts, like closing doors. It's a problem

I'm working on, but I could improve more, obviously. Is that all?"

"Thank you, Sewell. That is all, for now."

She did not add that the situation looked bad for him. If the police began to suspect that Dulcie's fall was not an accident, Sewell had no alibi whatsoever for the entire afternoon. Everyone else had at least a partial alibi. Theodore and Otis were apart at times, probably long enough to have met with and pushed Dulcie, but they would have had to work fast. Aldon and Johnny claimed to have worked side by side all afternoon. Rose herself was Honora's alibi. She knew from questioning the sisters that Esther had been with them all afternoon, sewing Shaker dolls, and Carlotta had been trapped in the kitchen. While it was possible that any one of them might have managed to get away at some point, Sewell had the shakiest alibi of them all.

NINETEEN

GENNIE HAD GROWN TOO USED TO BEDTIME IN THE WORLD. Here it was only 10 P.M., and the Brick Dwelling House might as well be a mausoleum. She gave up her attempt to sleep and tossed off her bedclothes. She was instantly sorry. She kept forgetting this wasn't Kentucky. Dragging a wool blanket off her bed and wrapping it around her shoulders, she plunked down into the rocking chair by the window of her retiring room and began to rock vigorously. It wasn't enough to use up her energy.

Rose was definitely having all the fun this time around. Even moving into the Brick Dwelling House had not assured Gennie a central part in the investigation, and she meant to change the situation. To be truthful, it was more than lack of excitement that frustrated her; she felt deeply responsible for what had happened to Dulcie. She should have found some way to convince the girl to confide in her. She agreed with Rose that Dulcie's "accident" had probably been a murder attempt. It was the only thing that made sense. Maybe Theodore had pushed her to get rid of the baby, which would make him horribly evil. Or maybe Dulcie knew something about Julia's death and had intended to use the information to secure a future for herself and her child. Gennie bounded out of her chair. She could sit and think of possibilities all night. She needed to *do* something.

She was feeling especially irritable because she'd had a phone conversation with Grady earlier in the evening, followed by a chat with Rose, and they'd both said the same thing—stay out of it. It was beginning to look as if they would never, ever let her grow up. She freed her left hand from the blanket and watched her diamond engagement ring dance in the moonlight. She loved the ring, and she loved Grady, but marriage was another matter altogether.

Her retiring room was on the third floor of the Brick Dwelling House. From her window, she could see much of the village. New snow had begun to fall. Since most of life took place within the dwelling house, the other buildings looked cold and empty, as if they'd been covered in white sheets until the inhabitants returned. Despite her longing for adventure, Gennie was grateful not to see any mysterious lights that required investigating.

As she considered another attempt at sleep, Gennie heard a creaking sound above her head. It was probably nothing—the old dwelling house surely creaked incessantly, and she just hadn't noticed it. On the other hand, she knew that no one lived above her. The fourth and fifth floors were attics, used for storage. Then she remembered—Rose had mentioned finding evidence that someone was using the top attic. She hadn't had time to give details, just that she'd found some fresh ink or something, and a lamp. What if it was the killer's hideaway, where he—or she—hid anything that might be a clue?

Gennie stood in the middle of her room, clutching her blanket around her shoulders, and listened intently to the night sounds of the building. They were many, as she'd suspected, and they seemed to come from all directions. A cracking sound reminded her of cold snaps at home, when the roof sounded as if intruders were running across it. In the distance, a door opened and closed—probably a nocturnal trip to the washroom. Steps—were those steps on a staircase? Surely not, she was too far away from the stairs.

vacy? Was it a killer, planning his next attack? Could it be
that more than one person met up here—lovers perhaps? No,
surely there wasn't room for lovers.

Rose had revealed little about her search of the desk, so
Gennie repeated her movements, noting the red paint in the
inkpot and the brushes wrapped in a rag. Two of them had
been used and cleaned without benefit of liquid, leaving
them stiff. Why would someone put red paint in an inkpot,
and what on earth would it be used for?

Gennie picked up the lamp and moved around the small
nook, examining the dark corners. Aside from dust and spi-
ders, she found nothing. She stepped out of the nook and
held the lamp high as she gazed around the rest of the attic.
It was full of old chairs, boxes, and a few chests of drawers.

Drawers—what if something important was hidden in
those drawers? Too excited now to worry about making
noise, Gennie started pulling open drawers and riffling
through their contents. Most were neatly filled with old and
out-of-season clothing, as well as odds and ends that she
couldn't identify and didn't care about. Then she reached the
bottom drawer, closest to the desk. She pulled it open and
gasped—two grotesquely wrinkled faces stared up at her
with evil black eyes.

She forced herself to bend over and examine them more
closely. They had small, soft bodies. One was covered in
light brown wool, and the other in dark blue. Shaker dolls—
a sister and a brother, dressed for Sabbathday worship. She
picked up the sister and held it close to the lantern. Her heart
had regained its normal rhythm, now that she saw what it
was—a doll with a dried apple for a face. She'd seen a few
in the store, she remembered. Abigail thought the china-
faced dolls would be more appealing to customers, but these
were less expensive. The dolls in the store hadn't looked this
frightening, though. This poor sister's face had been decorated with more than rosy cheeks and button eyes. There

were spots of scarlet on her forehead, showing just under her white cap. Gennie untied the cap and lifted it off. Someone had painted two red horns on the sister's head.

Gennie's entire body began to shake, and it was not from the cold. She felt herself in the presence of evil. She retied the cap over the profaned sister's head and placed her back in the drawer. With deep foreboding, she picked up the brother. Like the nineteenth-century brethren, he wore a wide-brimmed, flat-topped hat that shadowed most of his face. With a shaking hand, Gennie lifted off the hat. Two red horns had been painted across his forehead and up to the top of his head. The work was careful, horrifying in its precision.

Gennie felt a sudden, intense need to talk to Rose. Adventure was all well and good, but this was more than she could handle alone. She smashed the brother's hat back on his defiled head and closed him back in the drawer. Blowing out the lamp, she replaced everything as she had found it. She turned to the stairs. Then she heard what she should have been listening for all along—the slow, steady sound of feet ascending the staircase.

The tap-tap sounded like hard shoes on wood steps, still a floor or two away. Maybe the nocturnal wanderer was going downstairs, rather than up, and Gennie could hear the feet only because their owner saw no need to be quiet.

No, the steps were growing slowly louder. Someone was coming up the staircase to the attics.

Thank goodness she had extinguished the lamp and put everything back in place already. There was a slight odor of smoke in the air, but perhaps the visitor wouldn't notice or would assume it had lingered for a long time, trapped in the attic. However, without the lamp, Gennie wasn't sure which of the shapes around her might prove to be a good hiding place. She'd just have to take a chance.

Better to move to the other side of the stairwell, she decided. She desperately wanted to be able to see who was coming up those stairs, but it was more important not to get caught. It was a good bet this was a murderer coming inexorably toward her. Hoping her small body would fit into a hidden crevice, Gennie tiptoed past the railing that encircled the stairs on three sides. She selected a dark corner as far away as possible from the secret nook, which she assumed was the visitor's destination.

The corner was so dark, she discovered, because it was full of one piece of furniture pushed up against another. She'd have to slide into the midst of the mess somehow. Thank goodness she no longer wore the long, loose work dress of the Shaker sister. Her slim-fitting wool dress was less likely to catch on something and pull the whole pile down on her.

She edged in back of a stack of ladder-back chairs, piled up next to a small chest. The sloped roof stopped the chairs and the chest from quite reaching the wall. If she could slip behind the chairs and get to the chest, surely no one would see her. The steps now sounded less than a floor away. Small as she was, the stack of chairs left her only a slit to move behind. She had to move faster, if she hoped to reach the chest and hide behind it.

Two more tiny steps, and she'd be there. She leaned sideways to reach the edge of the dresser. She instinctively tested the dark corner for cobwebs by reaching her left hand in back of the dresser. Her right arm began to follow on its own. She felt the fingers of her right hand catch on the back of a ladder-back chair, and the whole stack began to fall toward her. Her breath stopped in her throat. She held off the stack of chairs with one very shaky hand and slowly brought her other hand from behind the dresser.

The stack was balanced on the two back legs of the bottom chair. If she tried to right it, she would inevitably make a thumping sound. If she held on, the chairs might still slide outward from the bottom and come crashing down on top of her. Worst of all, if she stayed where she was, she might be visible to someone with a lamp.

She had no choice. Praying as she hadn't since childhood, Gennie held on to the teetering stack of chairs and kept as still as she could on wobbly legs. She comforted herself that if she was about to be discovered by a heartless killer, at least she could make an unholy racket and wake the whole dwelling house. Maybe she'd be able to run for it, leap over the banister and drop onto the stairs below before she was captured and turned into a hostage. A broken leg would be a fair exchange for escape.

She heard a faint scratching sound in the wall behind her. Mice. As she steeled herself not to cry out if something furry brushed against her ankles, the back of a head appeared through the railing in front of her. Then shoulders and a large body followed. The intruder seemed shapeless, as if wearing a loose-fitting overcoat. He—or she—seemed to be laboring after climbing all those stairs. Gennie felt a prick of doubt. What Shaker would be winded by climbing a few flights of stairs? A very old one, perhaps. Might this be merely a Believer who couldn't sleep and thought to make a nostalgic visit to the attic?

The figure reached the top step and paused, breathing heavily. Gennie peered through the maze of slats in front of her, looking for clues to the person's identity. If it was a sister, Gennie thought she should be able to see at least the shape of a white indoor cap. Something covered the intruder's head, but it didn't look as smooth as a cap.

Gennie's arms ached, and her muscles were starting to twitch from the effort to keep still. If only the creature would move. Gennie was almost ready to push the chairs over and make a run for it. She doubted she'd be able to hang on much longer.

The figure moved, lumbering toward the dresser next to

the secret niche. To Gennie's enormous relief, he or she did not light the lamp, but instead opened the bottom drawer of the dresser and reached inside. Holding something in both hands, the figure moved to the left to catch what little light the skylight offered. As the figure turned in profile toward Gennie, the light was just strong enough for her to recognize who she was—Helen Butterfield. The soft shape around her head looked like pincurls, and she was wearing a heavy robe.

Gennie stifled a gasp. Helen Butterfield. Of course. She always seemed to be around, claiming to be collecting furniture, yet somehow never spending much time doing it. But why? Was she seeking revenge for some unknown crime against herself or her family? How did she know about the dolls in the drawer? What did they really know about Helen? She had shown up so conveniently right after Julia's murder, and she'd insinuated herself into the lives of the Hancock community. *And on top of that, she used me to get here,* Gennie thought, with a surge of resentment that almost toppled her precarious stack of chairs.

Gennie renewed her grip, now determined to escape and expose Helen Butterfield as an impostor—and probably a murderer. She willed her arms and legs to stop shaking and her breathing to be silent. Without the lamp, she had a chance to escape detection.

Helen took her bundle and quickly replaced it in the dresser drawer. She stood a moment, staring at the dresser, as if lost in thought. Then she turned full toward Gennie and headed for the staircase. Gennie wanted to close her eyes, like a child, and become invisible, but she had to see what was coming. Helen looked directly at her, or she seemed to. Gennie stiffened as something small and quick scurried between her feet and right toward Helen. Helen squealed, grabbed the railing, and bounced down the stairs.

Gennie dared to breathe again. She forced herself to wait until the footsteps had faded before she pushed the stack of chairs away from her and tried to steady it on the floor. Her weakened arms couldn't hold on tightly enough, and the stack swayed too far in the opposite direction, threatening to fall toward the staircase railing.

The image of ladder-back chairs tumbling down the stairs after Helen Butterfield gave Gennie renewed strength. She clutched the pile and held it until it stabilized, then she slowly released her shaky grip. The chairs stayed put. Gennie wilted against the wall and closed her eyes. She had no desire to move, ever again. Finally, her breathing slowed to normal, and the eerie attic room became a less desirable place to spend the night. Besides, she was freezing, and she could feel a sneeze coming on—and she wanted more than anything to tell her story to Rose. Imagine—Helen Butterfield. It had never occurred to either one of them to suspect Helen of anything more than thoughtless nosiness. Now it seemed she might be something far worse than a busybody.

TWENTY

WHEN THE BREAKFAST BELL RANG, GENNIE AT FIRST thought it must be a middle-of-the-night emergency. Surely breakfast couldn't have arrived so soon. It seemed only a few hours since she had snuggled under her covers. In fact, she remembered, it had been about four hours. After her adventure in the fifth-floor attic, she had rousted Rose from a sound sleep, and the two women had sat up sharing information and speculations for quite some time.

A burst of renewed excitement gave Gennie the strength to toss off her warm blankets and dress. She was eager to find out how Rose would deal with Helen Butterfield after learning of her midnight visit to the attic. Not that Gennie would have much opportunity to observe anything first-hand. With Mother Ann's Birthday so close now, Fannie had asked if Gennie could be spared to help out in the kitchen. The very thought almost sent her back to bed. The kitchen wasn't even cozy and warm, like the one at North Homage. And working with Carlotta was nearly as unpleasant as working with Sister Elsa. On the other hand, with Carlotta's gossiping skills, Gennie would surely hear about anything exciting soon after it happened—though perhaps not accurately.

Gennie splashed some water on her face and ran a comb through her tousled curls. She missed having a warm bath in the mornings, like she could in her boardinghouse back home. She strongly suspected she was growing soft, and it was okay with her. When she and Grady married, she'd have a bath whenever she wanted, and she'd enjoy it. And she'd have a cook and a housekeeper, and she'd only go to the kitchen to check on dinner. Although working in the Hancock kitchen might not be all that bad, she told herself— Fannie had said they'd be baking lots of Mother Ann's Birthday Cakes, with rosewater frosting on top.

Footsteps outside her room told her the hired women were heading for the washroom or downstairs to gather for breakfast. Gennie was eager to get there early, so she wouldn't miss anything. It would probably be her last time outside the kitchen until after the evening meal. Thank goodness she hadn't been asked to help with breakfast, or she would have had no sleep at all.

A knock on her door was followed by Carlotta's uninvited entrance. "Come on, sleepyhead," she said. "You can't stay in bed all day, not around here. We'll be on our feet for the next twelve hours in that kitchen—not that it will matter. No one is going to show up for this big birthday party, not with all this snow coming in."

"I've been ready for ages," Gennie said. She couldn't decide whom she found more irritating—Carlotta or Helen. She wished she'd caught them both wandering about in the middle of the night.

Carlotta slipped into the room and closed the door behind her. "Did you hear the news?"

Gennie managed to shake her head innocently, as she wondered if Rose had already called the police, and they had arrested Helen Butterfield for murder.

"Honora is here."

"Honora?"

"Yes, silly, Honora—Aldon's wife. The crazy lady— remember?"

"Of course I remember. You mean she's come for a free breakfast?"

Carlotta sighed. "No, that wouldn't be news. She'll take a free meal whenever she can get away with it. What I meant was, Honora came last night and just told the sisters she was gonna nurse Dulcie back to health. Can you imagine? She claims she was some sort of nurse during the war, so she thinks she can work miracles. I think it's real funny—all of a sudden, Crazy Honora is helping the Shakers."

"But why would Honora care about Dulcie?"

"Gennie, you're so innocent. She don't give a hoot about little Dulcie. My guess is she thinks Dulcie was one of Aldon's many lovers—or at least she thinks Aldon and Julia was lovers, so she figures she can get the story out of Dulcie while she's weak. Maybe she plans to murder Dulcie before she can talk," Carlotta added, with a ghoulish grin.

Gennie grabbed her sweater from a wall peg. "Come on," she said, "time for breakfast." She'd had quite enough of Carlotta DiAngelo, and she found the thought of spending the entire day working with her thoroughly unpleasant. Maybe a full stomach would help.

Rose had been dressed and ready for the day long before the breakfast bell. Her sleep had been far from peaceful, and a howling wind hadn't helped. She opened her curtains to black-gray clouds moving quickly toward the village. The snow never seemed to stop for long.

Rose didn't yet know what to make of Gennie's revelations about Helen Butterfield. She needed to find out more about the woman, which would take time. Meanwhile, she would relieve Helen of any nursing duty with Dulcie. Rose couldn't shake the fear that someone might try again to harm Dulcie. As soon as Fannie stopped by her retiring room to mention that Honora had come to help out with the nursing, Rose's fear redoubled. The offer seemed out of character. In fact, Honora's character could best be described as demented—and wasn't it most likely that a demented person had made those devil dolls Gennie had found in the attic? What if Honora had a wild plan to kill everyone she perceived to be stealing her husband from her? Whoever had poisoned those buckets might indeed have seriously injured many people, if the buckets had been used for drinking water. A minister's wife might not know that they were intended for use with animals. She was in Hancock the night of the worship service. She might have gone to the barn looking for Aldon, seen the poison and the buckets, and simply acted on impulse.

On the other hand, Honora had an alibi for the time of Dulcie's fall. What if someone wanted to give the impression that the killer was insane? Honora was the perfect dupe.

A few rooms in the Brick Dwelling House had been set aside for the care of ill Believers, and Rose headed directly for the one in which Dulcie lay comatose. According to Fannie, Honora had shown up near bedtime the night before and offered to watch Dulcie all night, so the sisters could get some rest. Luckily, one of the sisters had insisted on staying, so Honora had not been alone with Dulcie, as far as Rose knew.

Rose reached Dulcie's room as Sister Abigail was closing the door behind her.

"She's the same," Abigail said. "I'm going to get some breakfast. I'll be as quick as I can."

Rose entered the room without knocking. Honora sat in a rocker next to an adult-sized cradle bed, crooning a hymn and gently rocking the unconscious Dulcie. It wasn't the scene Rose expected to see.

"She has lost a child, you know," Honora said, as Rose approached the cradle bed. "I lost a child, too. It is always a judgment, to lose a child, but not on the mother. No, not on the mother. It's a judgment on the father, the sins of the father. The mother only bears the pain. It's the way of God."

Rose had no inclination to argue the point. "How did you know Dulcie lost a child?" she asked. "Did someone tell you?"

"A woman knows."

"Fannie said that you arrived last night, offering to watch over Dulcie to relieve the sisters. That was kind of you."

Honora nodded in rhythm with her rocking.

"It's quite a storm coming in, isn't it?"

"Nothing we don't deserve," Honora said.

"I was wondering, how did you manage to get here last night? Surely you didn't walk, did you?"

"I could have, you know. We grow up strong around here."

"But last night, you didn't have to?"

"God sent an instrument," Honora said, with a smile. "Someone to help."

"Really? Who did God send?"

Honora squinted at Rose as if she were unbelievably stupid. "Sewell has always been God's instrument, ever since he was a child. That is why he bears so much pain. God bestows great pain on those he treasures most. It is a test."

"Has Sewell picked you up and brought you to Hancock before?"

"Of course. He is a good boy, always thinking of others."

"Indeed," Rose said. "Was it Sewell who brought you here the other night for the worship service?"

"Such a dear boy. He knew without asking."

"Honora, you must be hungry after your vigil. Breakfast is about to begin. Let me watch Dulcie while you eat. You must keep up your strength, you know."

Honora slowed the cradle bed until it came to a gentle halt. "Yes," she said. "I don't know how many more nights I will be called upon to stand watch over this poor bereft mother. I will eat something." She walked toward the door with tall dignity, as if God were calling from the dining room, leaving Rose sad but relieved.

Gennie ate every bite of her biscuits and oatmeal. Lack of sleep had increased her appetite. She noticed both Helen and Honora at breakfast, as well as Rose's absence. Since it was unthinkable that Rose had slept through breakfast, she must be with Dulcie. So, Dulcie must still be alive.

For once, the basement kitchen was warm when Gennie arrived to help clean up and then bake for Mother Ann's Birthday celebration. The sisters had started fires in all the ovens, in preparation for baking dozens of loaves of bread, numerous birthday cakes, and sundry cookies. If she had to cook, Gennie thought, baking was her choice.

To her relief, she was not alone with Carlotta in the kitchen. Esther had also been assigned to help out. She didn't look happy about it, either. Gennie guessed that the demands of so much baking would make it difficult for Esther to sneak off to be with her children.

Gennie gathered the ingredients for Mother Ann's Birthday Cake and began measuring. She reached for the rosewater and, to her astonishment, Helen Butterfield appeared by her side.

Smiling brightly, as if she'd had a full night's sleep, she said, "I've come to lend a hand. Gennie, I see you've got the cakes. I've always wanted to make Mother Ann's Birthday Cake. I'll work with you."

Gennie couldn't suppress a shudder. It was bad enough Helen wasn't under arrest, but now Gennie would have to work side by side with the woman who nearly gave her a heart attack just hours earlier. A woman who might be a killer. On the other hand, at least Gennie could keep on eye on her, maybe wheedle some incriminating information out of her.

"I do so love the feel of flour. So silky," Helen said, as she used her hands to dump flour into a bowl. "Now, I've heard that the Shakers used to stir the batter with the branches of a peach tree, but apparently we aren't going to do that?" Helen smiled, and Gennie's heart chilled.

"Are you all right, dear?" Helen asked. "You look ill."

"I'm fine," Gennie said, with feigned cheerfulness. "Have you been satisfied with your stay here?" she asked. "I mean, have you found what you were looking for?"

"You mean furniture and so forth? Oh yes, more than I imagined. Such precious items, just lying about unused. I'm thinking of opening a store, an antiques store. Shaker furniture is so simple and lovely. Even with times being what they are, I'm sure I'll be able to make quite a bit of money selling what I've been buying from the Shakers."

"This has been quite an exciting time, too, hasn't it?"

"Yes, it has."

"What do you think is going on? I mean, who do you think murdered Julia and hurt Dulcie?"

"I can't imagine, my dear. Furthermore, I thought Dulcie simply fell. Do you think differently?"

Gennie busied herself with measuring butter. "I've no idea," she said, after a while. "After all, I just got here. I never met Julia, and I barely knew Dulcie."

"Of course."

Gennie tried a different approach. "I noticed Honora Stearn showed up for breakfast. Why do you suppose she's here?"

"I heard she offered to help nurse Dulcie," Helen said.

"Do you think that's safe?"

"I can't imagine why not. I also heard that Honora had nurse's training, so she might be quite helpful to the sisters, and I'm certainly glad to share the work with another nurse. Why? Do you have reason to believe Honora isn't capable— that she might hurt Dulcie in some way?"

"Well, it seems odd, that's all. Honora hates the Shakers

and seems to think every woman here has been involved with her husband."

Helen measured and stirred in silence. Finally, she reached over with a floury hand and touched Gennie's arm. "Curiosity killed the cat," she said. She released her hold on Gennie and picked up the rosewater.

Gennie had to restrain herself from throwing her bowl of cake batter at the unbearably irritating Helen Butterfield. Instead, she poured the batter into a pan and started another batch, to give her temper ample time to cool. She had no intention of giving up.

"Where do you intend to open this antiques store?" she asked, forcing her voice to sound casual.

"What? Oh yes, the shop. I hadn't really gotten that far. Pittsfield, perhaps."

"What about back in your hometown? Where did you say that was?"

"Oh no, it's far too small. Perhaps I'll even try Boston—there are still wealthy families in Boston."

Helen was almost as skilled at not answering questions as Grady, when he didn't want Gennie to know something. Why was her life so filled with frustrating people? The more Helen avoided answering her questions, the more suspicious Gennie felt, and the more determined she became.

"I hear the Shakers stored dozens of items up in the attics in this building," Gennie said, "Have you had a chance to explore up there?" She pretended to test her batter for lumps while watching through her lashes to note Helen's reaction.

"Yes, so I've heard," Helen said. She poured her batter into a pan, which she carried over to a table near one of the large ovens. When she returned, she gave Gennie a sunny smile and said, "Well, that was great fun. I have a few little things to do just now, but I'll return in a while to help some more."

Gennie had picked up a few curse words around the Sheriff's Office, and she used them silently on herself. She was

certain she had just caused Helen to fear that Gennie was
planning to explore the attics herself. Helen was probably
going right now to move those grotesque dolls to a safer
place. And Gennie was stuck in the kitchen. Maybe someday she'd learn to keep her mouth shut.

Several hours passed as Rose watched over the silent Dulcie. The sisters had stoked up a fire in the old black cast iron
stove to keep the room especially warm. For once, Rose
wasn't chilled, but the air was getting stale. She poured
some rosewater into a bowl and placed it on a table near the
head of the cradle bed. Maybe it would add a hint of sweetness and summer to Dulcie's troubled dreams.

The room darkened as if evening had arrived, though the
noon meal was still a ways off. Rose rubbed some moisture
off the window to discover snow falling thicker and faster
than she'd ever seen before. She had planned a trip into
Pittsfield, but it would have to wait. She would have to make
use of the Society's telephone to find answers to some of her
questions.

Finally, one of the sisters arrived to take over Dulcie's
care, and Rose left her with strict instructions not to leave
the injured girl alone with anyone other than another sister.
It was the best she could do, and she feared it might not be
good enough. It was already almost noon, and it seemed that
each hour took her further away from a solution to these terrible events.

With everyone so busy, Rose decided to use the phone on
the sisters' floor in the Brick Dwelling House, since they
would be least likely to take time for a rest in their retiring
rooms. She took along her notes and a ladder-back chair and
settled down for a long conversation. The connection crackled ominously, but she managed to reach the Pittsfield police
and the soft-voiced officer named Billy. To gain his assistance, she told him everything she had uncovered so far.

"Sure, I guess I can give you some time," Billy said, "but it sounds like you've found as much reason as we have to think Sewell killed Julia. Even if you figure Dulcie's fall wasn't an accident, Sewell seems the most likely bet. He'd've had the most time of anyone to go to the old barn and push her."

"I realize that, but neither of us has proof yet. I was wondering if you could tell me more about some of the others. You know them all, don't you?"

"Yep, went to church with them up until I left."

"You left Aldon's church? Any particular reason?"

"Nothing that has a bearing on this case. Let's just say Aldon and I came to a parting of the ways. I don't want to say anymore. Not to a lady, especially a Shaker lady."

"I've heard about his reputation with women. You certainly won't shock me."

"Still, I won't say anything more. Honora's got it bad enough already. I don't have a lot of time, so you better get on with your questions." Billy no longer sounded so genial, and Rose knew she would get nothing more about Aldon from him.

"Tell me about Johnny Jenkins. He seems ambitious to me."

Billy laughed. "You can say that again. Ambitious as they come. I always figured that's why he married that snooty girl from Boston, because he thought he could get his hands on her family's money. But they wouldn't give him the time of day, didn't even come to the wedding."

"Why do you think he wants to become a Shaker?"

"What? The snow's weighing down the lines, I can't hear you."

Rose glanced up and down the long, dark corridor. No sign of another living being. Perhaps it would be all right to shout. "I asked, why did Johnny become a Shaker novitiate?"

"Good question. Only one reason I can think of—he suspects there's money to be had in Hancock. Probably spends his nights digging up the graveyard, looking for it. That'd be like Johnny Jenkins."

"Don't you think it's possible that Julia got in his way somehow—maybe she tried blackmailing him, threatening to tell Fannie about his passion for wealth?"

"Nah, that wouldn't bother Johnny. He'd just go on to the next scheme."

Rose was less certain, but there wasn't time to argue. "Do you know Helen Butterfield, by any chance?"

"Helen Butterfield? The name's familiar, but . . . Is she from Pittsfield?"

"I don't think so. She's a rather stout, older woman—arrived the same day I did, though I don't remember seeing her on the train."

"That name . . . You know, if she's a widow lady from Williamstown, she just might be the Helen who was married to old Jake Butterfield. Retired years ago, Jake did. He was a good cop, knew his job."

"Helen is a police officer's widow?"

"If it's the same lady," Billy said. "You know, I gotta hang up. This weather will be causing accidents, and I'm the only one here just now."

"I understand. Could you just tell me if the Helen Butterfield you knew had any connections with anyone here at Hancock?"

"Not that I can think of. All I ever heard was what a good cook she was."

"Thank you, Billy. I'll try calling some other folks in town and let you get back to work."

Aldon's church would be a good start, she thought. Maybe she could learn more about the other suspects, and especially about Billy's disagreement with Aldon and the effect on Honora, from the church secretary. Church secretaries knew everything.

She picked up the receiver and jiggled the cradle. The line was dead. Maybe it was temporary—snow on the line, as Billy had mentioned. She hung up, waited a minute, then tried again. Nothing. Taking along her notes, she climbed the sisters' staircase to the third floor, where the hired women lived, and tried their phone. It was dead, too.

The bell rang for the noon meal. Rose reached the staircase and hesitated. She was so close, she might as well go up and have a look at those dolls Gennie described. She passed by the fourth-floor attic without encountering anyone. The fifth-floor attic seemed deserted as well, and dark as dusk with the noon sun in hiding behind snow-filled clouds. Nevertheless, she easily located the dresser and opened the bottom drawer. She found one doll, not two. She picked it up and held it close. It was a Shaker sister, and, as Gennie had said, the dried-apple head was obscenely decorated with painted red horns. She replaced the doll and felt around the drawer, then checked all the other drawers in the dresser. She found rags and kerchiefs, neatly folded, but no sign of a Shaker brother doll.

"Oh, don't worry about the phones," Fanny said, as Rose pulled her aside before she could enter the dining room. "We have weather like this so often in the winter, and the phones go dead all the time. They will be back."

"But isn't this rather dangerous? Perhaps we should suspend work for the day, keep everyone in the dwelling house and together. We could have a worship service."

Fannie stared at Rose as if she had drifted into lunacy. "A worship service when there is so much work to be done? My goodness, how would we ever be ready for the celebration? Surely we can give our hearts to God and still keep our hands at work. Don't let this storm alarm you, Rose. We are used to it. Everything will be back to normal by tomorrow. You'll see."

Rose gave in. She didn't want to frighten Fannie without good reason. She would just have to trudge around in the snow and gather information as fast as she could, and hope it was fast enough to protect Dulcie.

The meal was blessedly simple and quick. As they left the dining room, Rose slipped out of the sisters' line and reached the hallway before anyone else. She watched everyone head for their afternoon work, so she would have a chance of knowing where they would be, if she wanted to question them again.

Rose sat on a bench and pulled her notes from her apron pocket. She added what she had learned from Billy, the police officer, and had just begun to describe the violated Shaker doll when she heard rapid footsteps on the stairs.

"Rose, I'm so glad I found you. Hurry." It was Abigail, who had closed the Fancy Goods Store, due to the weather, and had volunteered to help with Dulcie. "She's coming around," Abigail said. "Quickly, come with me."

Rose grabbed up her skirts, for once not concerned to hide her legs, and followed Abigail, who was already half a flight ahead of her.

"Abigail," Rose called after her. "You didn't leave Dulcie alone, did you?"

"Don't worry," Abigail said, panting with exertion. "I've left Honora with her."

TWENTY-ONE

"STOP THAT INSTANTLY!" ROSE SHOUTED, AS SHE RAN INTO Dulcie's room and saw Honora aim a hypodermic needle at the girl's arm. "Drop it on the floor. Now!"

Honora stared over her shoulder at Rose, needle suspended in mid-air. "I was just—"

"Don't argue, just drop that needle."

"But it's the only one I have, and Dulcie is in terrible pain. I just wanted to ease her pain." Honora straightened and spread her arms in a gesture of innocence, still holding the needle. "It's a sedative. You see, I brought my little kit with me. I've had it since the war." She pointed to a small cracked-leather satchel, lying open on the seat of a chair.

Rose reached up and slipped the needle out of Honora's hand. Honora didn't fight. "Dulcie is in pain," she repeated.

Dulcie did look as if a sedative might be helpful. Her eyes were closed, but she was thrashing about so much she was throwing herself against the sides of her jerking cradle bed. Rose handed the needle to Abigail and signaled both her and Honora to back away. She placed a cool hand on the girl's forehead. Dulcie's eyes shot open.

"Dulcie, can you hear me?"

The girl stared at her with a puzzled frown, which suddenly relaxed into a rapturous smile. "You are an angel. I'm in Heaven. God has been merciful with me and brought me to Heaven."

"Nay, Dulcie, I am not an angel, and this is not Heaven."

"Hell? I've been sent to Hell?" Dulcie's voice squeaked with panic. She tried to sit up and cried out in pain. Rose gently held her down.

"Lie still, Dulcie. You are badly injured. I'm Rose, don't you remember me? I am your friend. You've told me about your troubles, and I've tried to help you."

Dulcie seemed to crumble inward. "Rose," she said. "You are a Shaker."

"Do you know where you are now?"

"I'm still in Hancock Village, aren't I?" Her voice was thick with grief. "I'm still here, on earth." She grabbed Rose's wrist and pulled her down. "My baby—my baby is dead, isn't it?" she asked in a whisper.

"I'm so sorry," Rose said. "The child did not survive."

Dulcie released Rose's wrist and began to whisper frenetically. Rose leaned close to the girl's face to hear better.

"No, no, no," Dulcie cried. "He took my baby and left me. I shouldn't be here. I shouldn't be here."

"I know you grieve the loss of your child," Rose whispered, "but *you* are alive, and that is a reason to rejoice."

Dulcie shook her head.

"You need to rest," Rose said, "but could you just try to answer one question for me? Can you remember the accident?"

"Accident?"

"Yea, when you fell in the Round Stone Barn. Can you remember what happened? What I mean is, did you slip or did someone push you? It's terribly important that I know if someone pushed you, and who it was. Can you try to think back and remember?"

Dulcie's eyes filled with tears of unbearable sadness. With a surge of strength, she pushed Rose away and tried to sit up.

The cradle bed rocked so sharply it nearly tipped over as Dulcie struggled to free herself from her blankets.

"Abigail, Honora, help me," Rose shouted over her shoulder. The three women gently pushed Dulcie back into the cradle and held her while she squirmed. As suddenly as it had begun, the fit ended, and Dulcie's body went limp. Slowly, the women released their grip. Dulcie turned on her side and curled up like a baby, hiding her face with her arms as if she expected to be disciplined with a rod.

"A sedative might be a good idea," Abigail suggested. "We've got something we use for pain, and it will put her to sleep, as well. Just let me. . . ." She pulled open several drawers built into the wall and rummaged around until she found a bottle. "Ah, this is it."

"Are you sure it's safe?" Rose asked. She wished more than ever that Josie were there.

"Oh, of course," Abigail said. "I take it myself when I have one of my headaches. And it's certainly safer than a hypodermic full of something that might be more than twenty years old," she whispered to Rose.

"Here, dear, swallow one of these and you'll feel better." Abigail helped Dulcie prop herself up on one elbow and handed her a glass of water with the pill. Without resisting, Dulcie swallowed the pill and lay back down. "We'll let you rest now, won't we, Rose?"

Outside in the hallway, Abigail said, "Why don't you two get away for a while. I'll be glad to watch Dulcie."

"My sedative would have worked just as well," Honora said

"Yes, dear, now why don't you go on and take a nap? You've been working so hard, and I can see how tired you are."

"I *have* been working hard."

"You, too, Rose. I know you have tasks to manage."

With Honora out of the way for a while, Rose gratefully left Dulcie in Abigail's care. She did indeed have tasks, and very little time to accomplish them. With Dulcie awake, sooner or later she would reveal what happened to her in the barn, and someone was likely to be very nervous about what she might say. Rose intended to push the issue. It was risky, but she had to act quickly. She needed to be sure that Dulcie was safe. She would relieve Gennie of her dreaded kitchen work and send her to Dulcie's room, with strict instructions to let no one else in. If necessary, they could barricade the door. It was the best she could do. She only hoped it was enough.

"Rose, I promise I would never hurt Dulcie—or Julia. Why won't anyone believe me?" Sewell looked and sounded like a wounded little boy. The effect was enhanced by the setting. They stood almost knee-deep in snow on the north side of the Meetinghouse, where Rose had found Sewell poking at areas of rotted wood with a screwdriver. The snowfall hadn't paused since morning, and Sewell was so caked with it that he looked as if he'd been rolling around making snow angels.

"Still, I believe someone pushed Dulcie and that it was the same person who killed Julia," Rose said, nervously eyeing the screwdriver in Sewell's hand.

"But why? It doesn't make sense. Julia—well, I admit Julia could be a tease, and she always went after the wrong man. I told her so all the time, but she wouldn't listen. I guess someone might be angry enough with her to kill her. But Dulcie? Dulcie is so gentle."

"Maybe Dulcie guessed who killed her sister."

"She would have told me."

"Maybe she thought it was you."

Sewell's bony face turned nearly as white as the snow. His eyes bulged and his mouth hung open so that he looked like an emaciated fish in a frozen sea. Rose pushed ahead.

"Sewell," she asked, "do you believe in the cleansing of confession?"

"Absolutely."

"Then I want you to confess to me now."

"What do you mean?"

"I want you to confess to me the terrible secret that you carry in your heart. I have watched my sisters and listened to their confessions long enough to know when someone's soul is tortured. Tell me."

"I had nothing to do with Julia's death or Dulcie's . . . accident. I promise you by all that is holy to me. I try so hard to be good. I'm a Shaker, or I will be as soon as I am allowed to sign the Covenant."

"You must confess all your sins to become fully a Believer. And if those sins have nothing to do with these recent tragedies, then I promise to keep your confession a secret. You will have cleansed your soul, and unless you repeat those sins, no one here need know about them. I can offer you that."

Sewell sighed with deep weariness and leaned against the Meetinghouse. "To have a cleansed soul . . ." he said, closing his eyes. Rose waited in silence, praying he would make the right choice. He opened his eyes and straightened. "May I have time to think about it?"

"There isn't much time."

"Just a few hours. I will let you know soon. I promise."

"All right," Rose said, with reluctance. "Soon."

The Brethren's Workshop was the next stop on Rose's list. Both Aldon and Johnny were working upstairs, putting the finishing touches on the last batch of boxes being made especially for the celebration. Privacy was impossible, so she would be forced to confront them together. Perhaps that might work in her favor. Rose could hear raised voices as she climbed the stairs to the second floor. Aldon and Johnny were already battling, even without Rose's instigation. They quieted at once when they saw her.

"I have come with news and with several important questions. I need quick and honest answers." She noticed that the men watched her guardedly, but they did not exchange glances. "I must tell both of you that Dulcie has regained consciousness and is able to speak, though she has yet to make much sense. I'm sure she will, in time. If someone pushed her in the Round Stone Barn, the truth will come to light. And although she has survived, there has been another murder. Dulcie was expecting a child, who died as a result of her fall. Was either of you aware of that?"

Throughout her speech, Rose had watched their faces, but neither had shown more than the slightest of reactions—whether shock or fear or regret, she could not tell. These were men whose passions were well hidden.

"I had no idea," Johnny said. "Not that I paid much attention to the women."

"Theodore has much to answer for," Aldon said.

"Perhaps," Johnny said, without looking at Aldon. "I wonder, though. Theodore made much of his uprightness. He bragged to me one day that he wouldn't even kiss Dulcie on the mouth, nothing at all until after they were married. He insisted they wouldn't even be together *after* they were married, not until they could afford to have a child. He was quite proud of himself for his determination."

"A man can say anything he wishes," Aldon said. "He is judged by his deeds, which may be performed in secret."

"Well said, my brother." Johnny's response was edged with sarcasm.

"Which brings me to my questions," Rose said. "If Theodore was not the father of Dulcie's child, who was?" She gazed expectantly at the men.

"I'd say it's obvious," Johnny said. "Sewell. He has never been able to stay away from the women, and becoming a

Shaker novitiate doesn't seem to have helped him control himself."

"Do you have proof of your accusation?"

"If I had actually caught him falling into the flesh, I would naturally have told the eldress. But he certainly seems compelled to flirt with every woman around."

"He is friendly," Aldon said to Johnny. "Almost childlike in his innocence. Something you could learn from. He certainly does not possess your greed."

"How dare you—"

"That's enough," Rose said sternly. "Johnny, I'm afraid I must ask you—why have you spent so much time in the attics and unused retiring rooms? You've been seen, at least once in the dead of night."

"Who is telling these lies about me?" Johnny jumped to his feet and stepped an inch too close to Rose. She felt the menace of his muscular body.

"Take care, Johnny," Aldon said, "or soon everyone will know you for who you are. They aren't lies, and you know it. You've been taking inventory of everything in the village."

"So what? Someone has to do it."

"In secret, in the middle of the night? I think not. I have seen for some time that your purpose in joining the Society comes from the world and the devil. You are worse than a bread-and-butter Shaker, because you want so much more than food and shelter. You want everything. You perceive wealth around you, and you want it for yourself. That is why you spread tales about the others, especially the men. You hope we will all be denied the right to sign the Covenant, and you will be the only young man left in the village. Then it will all be yours, or so you think. It wouldn't surprise me at all if you were the father of Dulcie's child—if you sinned with both her and her sister—and you decided to get rid of them when they wanted a share of the wealth."

Johnny's fair complexion flushed a deep red and his hands

tightened into fists. Rose wondered if she would have to throw herself between the men to prevent violence. Then Johnny stretched out his fingers as if forcing himself to relax. "You have good reason to lie," he said, his expression calculating. "You are the one with secrets. Poor Sewell, I've seen you pretend to be a friend to him, and then you turn around and say how weak he is, how lacking in faith. It suits your purposes, doesn't it, that everyone sees Sewell as the carnal one. But it's really you, isn't it?" Johnny's voice had dipped dangerously low.

The air crackled with rage, and Rose's mind raced. If she calmed them down—as indeed she should—she might learn no more. If she allowed the anger to escalate, she might be responsible for violence. She took a grave chance.

"Aldon," she said, "I had a recent chat with a Pittsfield police officer named Billy about your activities in your former church. Why don't you tell me your side of the story?"

She expected fury, denials, almost anything but what happened next. Johnny looked puzzled but intrigued. Aldon moved not a muscle. His dark eyes burned through her as his lips curved into a smile. "I don't have to do any such thing," he said. "Billy told you nothing. And now, I have work to do. This conversation is over."

Both Rose and Johnny gaped at him as he picked up an oval box and began to sand the rough edge of a swallowtail joint. Doubts flooded Rose's mind. How could Aldon have known she was bluffing? Did he know there was nothing to tell? Did Billy have his own reasons for insinuating what he did? She was certain of only one thing—that Aldon would not say another word to her, perhaps ever.

The snow showed no inclination to stop or even to taper off. Rose had given up keeping herself dry below the knees as she plodded toward the Barn Complex, where she hoped to complete her questioning of the men. Then she could change into dry clothes and talk with the women, who were all in the Brick Dwelling House. The thought of dry, warm feet kept her moving toward what was likely to be another trying interview, this time with Theodore Geist. Perhaps Otis, too, though she had yet to find a compelling reason why he might have killed Julia and injured Dulcie. It would surprise her greatly if he proved to be the father of Dulcie's child. She still favored Theodore. Aldon was right that words are easy to utter, and they prove nothing about the purity of one's actions.

"What brings you out in this weather?" Otis asked, favoring her with an amused grin as she dripped clumps of snow on the floor. Theodore and Otis had returned to their pre-spring task of cleaning, oiling, and repairing the farm implements. "I'd sure stay warm and dry, if I had the choice."

Theodore glowered at Otis and then at Rose before returning to his work. He was chipping hardened dirt from the tines of a hay rake, a job that seemed to absorb his attention far more than was reasonable.

"I don't intend to stay out any longer than I must," Rose said. "I have some questions for both of you."

"More questions?" Theodore rolled his eyes as if to imply that a smarter woman would have solved Julia's murder and gone home by now. Rose ignored him.

"Had you heard yet that Dulcie is awake and able to talk?"

"Why, that's wonderful news," Otis said. "She'll be all right then?"

"It looks hopeful."

"You must be so relieved that your fiancée will recover," she said to Theodore. He nodded. His face was unreadable, but at least she'd gotten his attention. "I am so sorry that the child did not survive."

Otis's eyebrows shot up nearly to his hairline. "Child? Theodore, you old rascal. Why didn't you tell me?"

"Shut up, you fool. It wasn't mine."

"So that's why Dulcie wore those big old Shaker dresses—to hide her condition. Theodore, I'm sorry about the babe, I really am, but you two were getting hitched anyway, so what's the difference? Why didn't you just marry her? She's a sweet girl, she'll make a good wife for you."

Theodore's knuckles whitened as he squeezed the handle of the hay rake. With a furious growl, he flung the rake through the air. Both Rose and Otis hunched over instinctively, though the rake hadn't come near either of them.

"It was *not* my baby!"

"Well, whose then?" Otis was asking just the right questions, so Rose listened.

"She wouldn't tell me, the little—"

"She probably figured you'd kill the guy," Otis said.

"Damn right I would have. And her, too, if I'd caught them together."

"She didn't want you in prison. You can hardly blame her for that." Otis seemed to be enjoying himself.

"Why, because she's so sweet and good?" Theodore laughed without mirth. "I used to think so, too. A lot we knew. She's a whore. I brought her to work here to keep her pure for our marriage—to get her away from her tramp of a sister. But Julia showed up working in the store and brought her whorish ways with her."

Otis laughed. "Well, Julia sure was Julia. She went after anything in pants, and it was more fun for her if he was married or celibate."

"She went after me," Theodore said, "but I stayed true to my future wife, and how did she repay me?"

"Did it occur to you that Dulcie might have been forced?" Rose asked.

"She wasn't. She admitted it, right to my face. Wanted to be honest with me, she said, so we could start our marriage without secrets. Hah! As if I'd marry her after what she'd done. I told her the engagement was off, and she could go crying to her lover. I'm not fool enough to take on a whore with a bastard."

"Theodore, it is vital that I know who was the father of Dulcie's baby. If you have even a suspicion, please tell me."

"If I knew, he'd be dead by now." He stalked past her and left the barn without stopping to pick up his coat.

Fearing he might be angry enough to hurt Dulcie, Rose turned to follow.

"Sister," Otis called after her. "Could you wait a minute?"

Rose turned but stayed where she was, ready to leave quickly.

"It's just that . . . Well, there's something I wanted to tell you. It might not help, but I can't get it out of my mind."

Rose nodded to encourage him.

"I didn't say this in front of Theodore because Lord knows what he'd do. I mean, I don't mind teasing him a bit, but it ain't smart to rile him too much, if you know what I mean."

"Are you trying to say that you think he might be the killer, because of his temper?"

"No, no, not at all. He does have a temper and a half, that's a fact, but I believe him when he says he doesn't know who the father is. Not just 'cause he doesn't lie worth a damn, either. Sorry, Sister."

"I'm in a bit of a hurry," Rose said.

"Yeah, I'm rambling, I know, it's just hard to explain, that's all. I've been thinking it's not so unbelievable that Dulcie cheated on Theodore. She really is sweet, and she tries to be good, but . . . I watched those girls grow up, Julia and Dulcie. They had a rough life."

"I know that." Rose thought of just walking away, but something kept her listening.

"Julia, she grew up real tough, and she went after what she wanted. But Dulcie was different. I was a little sweet on Dulcie, I guess, so I kept an eye on her. Because of Julia's reputation, lots of men thought they could get the same from

Dulcie, and mostly she stayed good, but there was this certain type of man could get to her."

"What type?"

"Well, really all they had to do was treat her gentle, at first, anyway, and maybe seem like they could take care of her real good—you know, someone who seemed real strong. If you're looking for the father of her baby, it'd probably be a man like that."

"Do you mean someone like Theodore?"

"Well, yeah, I guess." Otis's face crinkled in confusion. He shrugged and grabbed an oily rag, as if he'd done his best and that's all he could do. Rose wasn't sure she understood everything he had said, but she was inclined to believe his notion that Dulcie might indeed have strayed. However, it only meant she was right to believe Dulcie was still in danger.

TWENTY-TWO

ROSE PAUSED ONLY TO RIP OFF HER GALOSHES BEFORE RUN-
ning upstairs to Dulcie's room. Fannie sat on a bench in the
hallway, squinting at some knitting she was trying to do in
the poor light.

"All is quiet, Rose," Fannie said. "I knew you were worried, so I posted myself outside the door. Abigail and Gennie
are with Dulcie."

"Has Dulcie awakened again?"

"Not a peep out of her, poor child."

"Has anyone else come up here?"

"No one."

"The phones?"

"Still out, but that's not unusual. The snow should let up
fairly soon, I think, and then the lines will be repaired. Run
along and dry off now. I had one of the sisters put some
clean dry clothes and shoes in your retiring room."

"Bless you."

Rose gratefully slid a dry wool dress over her head. Her
retiring room smelled of wet wool and a hint of mildew, so
she was glad to leave quickly. She went immediately to the
kitchen, where the cakes and pies were getting more attention than preparations for the sparse evening meal. The fragrance of onion and potato was barely perceptible under
waves of apple, cinnamon, rosewater, and yeast. For once,
the kitchen was warm, with every oven fired up.

233

Carlotta was grumpily stirring a cauldron of soup, and Esther was nearby, crimping the edges of a piecrust. Rose decided to question Carlotta first.

"If you've come to tell me Dulcie woke up and that she was pregnant, forget it. I already know," Carlotta said.

"Obviously, but how?"

"Did you really think Honora could keep her mouth shut? She couldn't wait to make an appearance down here and tell us all how she lost a baby, too. Like anybody cares."

"Has there been any discussion about the father?"

"Everybody else thinks it's Theodore, of course. Not me. I'd bet money on Sewell."

"Why?"

Carlotta gave her a pitying look. "No man and woman can be such good friends without it going a lot farther, not to my way of thinking."

"You sound jealous," Rose said. "After all, Dulcie had two men paying attention to her."

Carlotta shrugged. "I didn't care."

"Between them, Julia and Dulcie didn't leave many men for you, did they?"

Carlotta's raised her sharp chin. "I do okay," she said. "Not that it's any of your business, but I got a boyfriend in Lenox. I don't have to run after Shakers and married men. If you want my opinion, it was Dulcie killed her own sister, probably for going after Theodore *and* Sewell."

"Then who pushed Dulcie?"

"Chances are, she did it herself. Probably wanted to kill the baby and herself, both, out of shame."

Rose was shocked into silence—not so much by the suggestion that Dulcie might want to kill herself and her baby, which was the sort of behavior she had encountered too many times in the world. Rather, she was stunned that the idea had not occurred to her before now. She tucked the notion away in a corner of her mind and left Carlotta to her work.

Esther was already rolling out another piecrust when Rose arrived at her side. "Go ahead with your crusts," Rose said, "but I have some questions that can't wait."

Esther did not look pleased, but she nodded.

"I know that you've heard all about Dulcie. What I want to know is—do you suspect that Johnny might have been the father of Dulcie's child?"

"*What?* How dare you suggest such a disgusting thing." She'd shouted, and several curious faces stared in their direction. Esther saw them and rolled her piecrust so hard she pushed the roller through to the table.

"Then why does Johnny wander around in the middle of the night? Is he meeting you?"

Esther's shoulders sagged. "No, he isn't meeting me, or our children. He cares little about any of us. Is that what you wanted to hear?"

"Nay, of course not. I want to know the truth."

"The truth is that Johnny cares only for money. If he is wandering around at night, it has something to do with money."

"Would he kill for money?"

"If you are asking whether he might have killed Julia, only if she threatened his grand plans in some way."

"Such as with blackmail?"

Esther mashed the piecrust back into a ball and began to roll it out again. "I had six children with him," she said, "and I never really knew him."

Bringing with her a small oil lamp, Rose took Fannie's place on the bench outside Dulcie's room. When she was alone in the hallway, she pulled her notes from her apron pocket and began to jot down answers to her questions. She now knew a great deal, but the final answer still eluded her.

Rose closed her eyes to think. Theodore was probably not the father of Dulcie's child, but who was? Otis and Johnny seemed least likely. Esther had confirmed the recurring accusation that Johnny cared deeply for wealth. Dalliance with a kitchen worker promised to another was surely something Johnny would avoid. At the least, such behavior would interrupt his single-minded pursuit of control over Hancock's assets.

The bell rang for evening meal, and doors opened and closed, but Rose sat still, willing the pieces to fall into order. Theodore had rejected Dulcie after discovering her sin. Had the real father turned her away, as well? Might she truly have tried to kill both herself and her child, out of shame and despair? Rose's heart ached at the thought that Dulcie had been so alone in her torment—and that no one, including Rose, had been there to help her.

Rose heard a faint clicking sound and opened her eyes. Except for the light from her small lamp, the corridor was now in complete darkness. The room to Dulcie's door opened, and a small figure peeked out. "Fannie? Are you out there?"

"It's me, Gennie. It's Rose. It looks like all the lights have gone out."

"Abigail said this happens sometimes in a snowstorm. What should we do?"

"You two must be hungry," Rose said. "I'm sure they'll have plenty of candles and oil lamps in the dining room. Why don't you and Abigail have your evening meal, and I'll watch over Dulcie."

Gennie disappeared inside the room for a moment, and then reappeared. "Abigail said that would be okay, but she will eat quickly and return to spell you."

"The poor dear's been quiet," Abigail whispered as she and Gennie turned the sickroom over to Rose. "I'll be back in a jiffy."

Rose could no longer read her notes, so she watched Dulcie's shadowy face and worked from memory. She thought there was one person she could eliminate from her list of suspects, and it was going to make Gennie furious. The recent conversation with Officer Billy had given her the clue. Helen Butterfield was surely not the killer. Rose had a strong suspicion that Grady had a lot to do with Helen's convenient ever-presence. If so, he might find that Gennie was even less inclined than before to marry him right away.

In the dark, quiet room, Rose found her eyes closing. She hadn't realized how tired she was. It wouldn't hurt to rest a few moments, surely. If the night held more surprises, she wanted to be strong enough to face them.

The click and creak of an opening door jolted Rose out of a sound sleep. "Rose? It's Abigail. I'm back. If you hurry, you can still have a bit of company for the evening meal. Has Dulcie said anything?"

"Not a word," Rose said, hoping it was true. She wished she hadn't fallen quite so deeply asleep.

"Well, you run along then. Fannie said we should all eat and go right to bed. The kitchen workers had to stop their baking, and Esther volunteered to take out the cakes and pies already in the ovens. We're running low on oil, so Fannie told her not even to do the washing up, just wait till morning, she said. She's certain the lights will come back on in the morning, so we can pick up with our work. We have so much to do, with Mother Ann's Birthday just day after tomorrow."

"Surely she isn't still planning a big celebration," Rose said. "No one will be able to get here."

"Oh, you'd be surprised," Abigail said. "Snow can melt so quickly, especially late in the winter. Besides, Fannie has asked Mother Ann to intercede—after all, it's her own birthday, and she wouldn't want all this lovely food wasted."

Rose was too tired to suggest that Mother Ann might have

more pressing matters that needed her divine influence. But perhaps Mother would have a few moments to help Hancock through this difficult time. Rose sent a silent prayer of her own for help finding a killer before any more human life was lost.

As Rose reached the dining room, the men began to file out. Fannie must have told them to leave as soon as they had finished eating, rather than wait for the sisters. Sitting around would just waste oil and candles. Rose stood aside and waited as the men walked past her and toward the men's staircase. Each held a light that cast eerie shadows on his face. Rose shivered, remembering the Pullman porter Hezekiah's words about demons roaming the corridors of Hancock Village. These were live men, of course, yet one of them might be a murderer. She watched each face as it went past her.

The spectral images reappeared as she closed her eyes to sleep that night, after a sparse and lonely meal. As each man's face drifted across her eyelids, a corner of her mind observed his demeanor. Aldon appeared first, looking strained and grim. Johnny peered at the level of oil in his lamp, perhaps wondering if he had enough to continue his nighttime inventories. Theodore dragged with exhaustion, and Otis grinned at Rose as he passed—surely pleased at the prospect of extra sleep.

Sleep was overtaking Rose, confusing her inner sight. The next figure to appear had a grotesquely wrinkled face and was dressed for worship. With her last ounce of conscious will, Rose suppressed the image. It was the dried-apple doll come to haunt her dreams, and she would not allow it to do so. For the day ahead, peaceful sleep was her best ally.

TWENTY-THREE

ROSE AWAKENED WITH A START. SHE LAY STILL, STARING into pitch darkness, listening. If a noise had roused her, it was gone now. And so was her urge to sleep. She tried the light beside her bed, but to no avail. She had no idea what time it was, or how long she had slept. So far, Fannie's prayers had not returned the village to normal. Rose sat up in bed, pulling her blanket up to her neck.

More than likely, it was a dream that had awakened her. She had the foggy impression that, once she was deeply asleep, the dried-apple Shaker doll had returned to plague her mind. Perhaps it was trying to bring her a message. She believed, as did other Believers, that long-dead Shakers often spoke during trances or dreams. Though such experiences seemed to elude her, she tried to be open to their appearance. She closed her eyes, conjured up the visual memory of the strange doll, and invited her dream messenger to speak again.

At first, nothing happened. She stared at the doll, revolted by the shriveled face and the hint of horns still visible under the hat. Then the image began to change. The red horns bled slowly down the brother's Sabbathday surcoat and pooled at his feet. Repulsed, Rose opened her eyes and chased the image away. But it returned. This time, she forced herself to pay attention.

Why was her vision only the Shaker brother, not the sister? She hadn't even seen the brother doll. Was it only because she had watched the men file out of the dining room some hours earlier? Or was there some deeper message? She thought back over the faces that had preceded the doll in her half-dreaming imagination. And then she knew. Aldon, Johnny, Theodore, Otis—Sewell had not been among them. Sewell had not come to evening meal.

What if those dolls represented, in some horrible way, intended or potential victims? All along she had thought of Julia and Dulcie as the victims, so she hadn't seen how the dolls might connect with the killer. But if Dulcie had actually tried to kill herself, that left only one female victim. A male doll might then indicate a second victim, this time a man.

Or was her vision telling her that Sewell was indeed the killer she sought? She had pressured him to confess to her. Perhaps he had already escaped from the village, rather than admit how much blood was on his hands.

She tossed aside her blanket and slid off her bed. Her curtains were closed, but a faint square of light hinted at moonlight outside. She stumbled across the room toward the window and pulled the curtains open. Perhaps Fannie had some influence after all—the snow had stopped, and the moon, though weak, was making an effort to shine. At least it outlined the shapes in her retiring room. She located her only set of dry clothing and pulled it on right over her nightgown. Might as well be as warm as possible.

As she reached her retiring room door, her foot kicked something light. She could barely see a small object on the floor. She bent to pick it up. It felt like a wad of fabric. She must have caught the hem of her long dress on something and ripped it. She'd have to darn it back together later. She stuffed the fabric in her apron pocket and left.

A large window at the end of the hallway allowed some moonlight to penetrate, so Rose did not light her lamp. She might need the oil later. She wasn't ready to rouse anyone else. In fact, she wasn't sure whom she could trust. She lifted the phone in the hallway and jiggled the cradle gently. Still dead.

As quietly as possible, she hurried to the side of the dwelling house where the male novitiates lived. If this had been North Homage, Elder Wilhelm would have threatened to have her removed as eldress for such behavior, but this wasn't North Homage, and lives were at stake.

Rose paused and counted doors. Some, she knew, hid empty rooms. Following worldly desires, the men had spread out so they would not have immediate neighbors to snore and disturb their sleep. Sewell should be in the fourth room on the right. She blessed whatever instinct had made her ask, when she had first arrived, who lived in which retiring room.

She tiptoed to Sewell's door and listened for a few moments. She heard no sounds from within. Rather than take the risk of knocking, she eased the door open and peered inside. The curtains had not been drawn, thank goodness, and she could see the tightly made bed. A quick glance along the wall revealed that Sewell's outdoor coat was missing.

The stars had reappeared in the now-clear sky. Rose sent her most fervent thanks to the Holy Father, Holy Mother Wisdom, and especially to Mother Ann. She would have preferred not having to slog through knee-deep snow in the middle of the night, but she left this detail out of her prayers.

Instinct alone sent Rose in the direction of the abandoned Meetinghouse. It was where Sewell always seemed to be. He loved the building, wanted desperately to save it. Her heart told her he might be inside, but whether dead or alive, she couldn't say. She knew only that she must hurry.

She didn't need to light her lamp. The moon, finally and gloriously bright, glimmered on the snow and bathed the vil-

lage in blue-white light. As she crossed the road, Rose easily
made out jumbled tracks in the deep snow, which convinced
her she was heading in the right direction. She stepped in the
tracks as best she could, noting that some seemed farther
apart than her long legs could reach. It was a safe guess that
at least one set was made by a man. Moreover, they were
clear and sharp. Since there was no wind, she concluded the
tracks had been made since the snow ended—not long ago,
she suspected. Whoever made those tracks might still be inside the Meetinghouse.

As she approached the brethren's entrance to the Meetinghouse, she noted that the footprints in the snow led inward only. There were other entrances, of course. She
stepped to the west side of the building. Keeping close to the
wall, she worked her way to a window that was still intact.

With so many windows boarded up, it was difficult to see
inside the dark Meetinghouse. Yet there was no mistaking
what lay no more than a few yards in front of her, illumi-
nated by moonlight. A man lay on his back, deadly still, his
arms stretched straight out from his sides as if nailed to a
cross. Something long and slender stuck up from his chest.

Rose groaned and pulled away from the window. All her
prayers had done no good. She was too late. She forced herself to look again through the window and around the Meetinghouse. She saw no evidence of another person lurking
inside. The fiend had surely left as soon as the deed was
done—and had probably left the village as well.

Rose slogged around to the nearest entrance and pushed
open the door, not caring if she made noise. She ran to
Sewell's still body. Without much hope, she reached for his
wrist. There was no pulse. His skin was cool to the touch.

She lit her lamp and examined Sewell more closely. She
recognized the handle of a screwdriver—perhaps the very
one he had held when she questioned him earlier. It pro-
truded from the left side of his chest. A dark circle stained

the area around the wound. A clean, precise blow by some-one who knew where to aim. Someone able to catch Sewell off guard. Someone he trusted enough to meet in the middle of the night.

She sat back on her heels and looked around. She could see her own damp footprints leading to Sewell's body. The other footprints looked too large to belong to a woman, though she couldn't be sure. The floor was a mess.

Might the unsuspecting Sewell have brought along the weapon that would kill him? It seemed unlikely, since the killing gave the appearance of precise planning. Rose crawled all the way around Sewell's body, looking for any-thing that might help. She had checked the pulse in his left wrist, and now she saw that his right hand was tightened into a fist. The police might be furious with her, but she carefully pried open his fingers. Inside was a small piece of stiff fab-ric, badly crumpled. She pulled it back into shape. It was a tiny blue wide-brimmed, flat-topped hat, just big enough for a doll's head.

As soon as she returned to the Brick Dwelling House, Rose tried the phone again, still with no success. She couldn't expect help from the police anytime soon. It was time to gather a few trusted folks to support her. Gennie wouldn't like it, but the first room Rose visited was Helen Butterfield's. She knocked softly. When no one responded, she opened the door. Helen was not in her room. Her bed hadn't been slept in, and her heavy wool coat was nowhere to be seen. Helen's absence surprised and disturbed Rose. Could she have been wrong about Helen's role?

She gazed out Helen's window at the empty village, des-perately trying to think. Absently, she put her hands in her apron pocket and felt the wad of fabric she'd found on the floor of her retiring room. She thought she could feel some-thing hard inside. Rose lit her lamp and sat at Helen's desk.

The cloth was bunched up tightly, so it felt smaller than it was. She spread it open. Inside, wrapped around one corner of the cloth, was a small, inexpensive ring with a fake ruby. Dulcie's promise ring, given to her by Theodore. This was probably what Helen had found in the hay under Dulcie's unconscious body. And now she'd left it for Rose to decipher.

What did the ring mean? Why would it have come off? Nay, it probably hadn't come off. Dulcie had surely removed it herself. Rose had a sudden image of Dulcie holding the ring to her heart as she jumped. Was Helen trying to tell her that Dulcie had, indeed, attempted to kill herself and her baby? If so, it followed that the folks who'd had alibis for the time of Dulcie's fall were still suspects for the murders of Julia and Sewell.

Rose turned over the piece of cloth. It was calico with red-and-blue checks. The corner that had been pulled through the promise ring was stained with oil. Was Helen also telling her that this was the bit of calico Dulcie had taken from under the hem of Julia's skirt? Did the oil stain implicate Theodore, who used such rags to clean farm implements? Was he, after all, the father of Dulcie's child?

Rose shook her head to clear her jumbled thoughts. Nay, something was wrong with all this. Certainly it made sense that Dulcie had taken the calico to protect Theodore from suspicion, but Helen had not found it in the barn with the ring; Rose would have seen her do so. Helen must have searched Dulcie's room and found the rag there.

How confused and desperate Dulcie must have been. She thought she was protecting her future husband by hiding the oil-stained cloth, and then he cruelly rejected her and her unborn child. No wonder she tried to take her own life.

To preserve oil, Rose extinguished her lamp and sat in the dark, thinking. If Theodore had indeed murdered Julia, wouldn't he have either married Dulcie or killed her to keep her silent? Surely he wouldn't have sent her away. She might have gone straight to the police, or at least to Rose. Theodore could not be the killer.

Rose smoothed the calico over her lap. It was faded, frayed, and looked just like the rags Rose had seen Theodore and Otis using in the barn. Otis? Nay, none of her searching had uncovered a reason why he might kill Julia, and he showed no anxiety about what Dulcie might say when she regained consciousness. The entire village had access to such rags. Rose could only conclude that the oil-stained rag had been placed under Julia's dress on purpose, to implicate Theodore—and perhaps to destroy Dulcie.

Surely only a lover could entice Julia to dress in a dancing gown and meet at night in the Summerhouse. Perhaps he promised her a gift if she would do so. He thought he had covered his tracks, so no one would suspect their relationship. He would have thrown guilt onto others. No doubt he chose the Summerhouse because Julia's body would chill quickly, making it difficult for anyone to establish an alibi. He wanted to create as much confusion as possible.

And then, he prepared the dolls. The horns suggested a spiritual motive, such as the need to cleanse two souls of evil. Yet that implication might be a ruse, too. Rose rubbed her aching forehead and willed herself to think clearly. The killer must have brought the brother doll to his meeting with Sewell and not noticed that the dying man was clutching its tiny hat. So the "gift" that Julia was reaching for was probably the sister doll, which the killer then returned to its hiding place. The dolls must have been messages to his victims. The killer had not meant for them to be seen by anyone else. Rose stood so suddenly the calico rag fell to the floor. She grabbed it up and stuffed it back in her pocket, along with Dulcie's ring. There was no time to lose. She went directly to Gennie's room and entered without knocking.

"Gennie? Wake up, it's Rose."

"Rose? What . . . ? Has something happened?"

"I'm afraid so." She held Gennie by the shoulders. "It's Sewell. He's dead."

"Oh no! Do you mean murdered? Sewell? But then he can't be the killer."

"That's right. Come on, get dressed. I need your help."

With the resilience of youth, Gennie leaped out of bed and shivered into her clothes. "What do you want me to do, track the killer?"

"I want you to stand guard at the front doors."

"Is that all?"

"Gennie, it could be dangerous. I want you to be very alert and careful—and stay out of sight. If anyone goes in or out, come and get me right away, but don't try to stop them. Is that understood? And even more important, I want you to test the phones frequently. If they start working again, call the Pittsfield police at once."

"All right, you can count on me."

"Oh, and one more thing. Helen Butterfield isn't in her room, and her bed hasn't been slept in—"

"She's the killer, isn't she? I *knew* it. I never trusted that woman."

"Gennie, you and I will have a long talk when this is over, but for now—nay, Helen is not the killer. I believe she is a private detective who has been investigating right along with us. If she comes in while you're watching, she's the one person you can show yourself to, and be sure to ask her to find me right away."

"But where will you be?"

"I'm not sure. Just tell her to look everywhere, and the same goes for you. Don't be afraid to call out to me. Something tells me everyone will soon be up and about, anyway."

"Rose? You know who the killer is, don't you?"

"I think so. But I must be certain. Run along now. And keep out of sight."

Rose next visited Honora Stearn's room. She entered

without knocking. The bedclothes were tangled, and her pillow had slid off the bed, as if she had left in a hurry. A dress hung from a peg. Since Honora had been forced by the snowstorm to stay in Hancock, she probably had no change of clothing. One of the sisters would have lent her a nightgown, but there was no sign of it anywhere. Honora could have gone to the washroom, of course, but Rose doubted it.

On her way toward the staircase, Rose tried the phone again. No luck. She went down to the hired men's wing and directly to Theodore's door. Pausing only for a deep breath and a quick prayer, she knocked lightly. She heard movement inside and stepped back, preparing herself for the shock she would see on Theodore's face when he opened the door.

"Be very quiet," she said quickly, as Theodore started to speak. "Something terrible has happened, and I need your help at once."

Theodore shook his head as if he was convinced this was a dream. Then he glanced down at his nightshirt—from which Rose had averted her gaze—and closed the door in her face. She'd give him a minute, she decided, before bursting in on him. To her relief, a fully dressed Theodore opened the door again in short order. Without a word, he followed her down the hallway, carrying his unlit lantern. She next roused a surprised Otis and ordered him to throw on some pants. She led him to the novitiates' floor, where she urged quiet.

"Be prepared," she whispered. "We may be confronting a killer. You two stay back out of sight. Is that understood? Do not interfere unless I am attacked."

"You should let us handle this," Theodore said. "This is a job for a man."

"Do as I say, and don't argue."

"Hush," Otis whispered hoarsely. "I hear something. Upstairs, I think."

Rose silenced the men with a hand gesture. There it was—a faint scraping, interspersed with a low rumbling that might have been a voice. Rose ran toward the stairs, and the men followed. They reached the hired workers' floor without encountering any reason for the noises, so they climbed to the fourth-floor attic. The sounds had become louder. They were just above Rose, who was now halfway to the fifth-floor attic.

She stopped and gestured to Otis and Theodore to stay behind. Theodore scowled his disapproval, but Otis put a restraining hand on his arm. Rose tiptoed up the stairs until she could just see over the landing. One light shone from the alcove to the left of the stairs, where she'd found the mysterious desk and chair. Aldon was bent over the desk with a paintbrush in his hand. The mingled odors of paint and kerosene assailed her nostrils.

"You can see why this is for the best, can't you?" he was saying. "You must understand that you are not like the others, not truly evil. I'll make that clear to God, so you may enter His kingdom without a stain. That's what I'm doing right now." Aldon straightened a bit as if to view his handiwork. "The Father will understand when he sees this. It's you as an angel—a true angel, not the cruel appearance of one. I've always known your soul was pure. That's why your mind could not accept the evil I was tempted into."

Aldon was so engrossed in his task that he never looked up. Rose took a chance and eased up one step so she could look around the attic better. As she expected, she saw Honora to her left, tied to a chair against the side of the stairwell. Her head lolled to the side. Whether she was dead or just unconscious, Rose couldn't tell.

Rose edged up yet another step. Now she had a full view of Aldon's secret corner. Next to his desk was a large pile of rags. She prayed to God she was wrong, but she suspected Aldon meant to burn down the entire dwelling house.

A quick glance back at Aldon assured Rose he was still lost in his project, which looked like a doll. With all the strength she could muster, she charged up the steps. Aldon's head jerked up. He jumped up from his seat and grabbed his lantern.

"You can't stop me. You can't stand in the way of God's will," he said. His voice rang with the power of one who believed he was anointed by God.

"Murder is never God's will," Rose said, matching his power with her own.

"You don't know. You can't understand."

"Perhaps I understand more than you think," Rose said. "You believe that God wants you to destroy evil."

"God has given me the ability to draw evil to me, so that I can identify it and destroy it. That is why He made me as I am."

Rose took two steps toward Aldon. He stretched out his right arm so the lantern swung just over the pile of rags. Rose stepped back.

"Julia was evil, wasn't she?" Rose asked softly.

"Julia was a Jezebel, a Delilah. She threw herself at me and at other men. She couldn't stop, so I had to stop her. But I am not without mercy. I gave her a chance to save her soul. I tried to show her how evil she was, so she could repent with her last breath and be saved."

"You showed her a doll—a Shaker sister, dressed for worship, but painted with horns."

"Yes! I wanted her to understand. It was to save her soul."

"What about Dulcie's soul? And the soul of her unborn child?" She knew she might be goading him into dangerous actions, but she hoped to keep him talking, explaining himself, so she might catch him off guard.

"Dulcie's soul is weak, and she knew it. I didn't have to punish her; she punished herself and kept her bastard from defiling the world."

"Her child was your child. Weren't you angry that she killed it?"

"I was tricked. Julia tricked me. She used to dress Dulcie in pretty clothes and flaunt her in church, all to trap me."

"Julia threatened to tell everyone that you had seduced Dulcie, didn't she? So you killed her."

"Don't you see? It was Julia. She drew on the strength of Satan. She had to be destroyed." As Aldon closed his eyes, frantic to find the words to excuse his behavior, Rose completed her step up and moved closer to him.

"And Sewell? How was he evil?"

Rose caught her breath as Aldon's lantern shook violently over the pile of rags.

"I never wanted to punish Sewell, but he forced me to."

"You loved Sewell, didn't you?" Rose asked, in a gentle voice.

"Yea." Aldon spoke in a whisper.

"Your love was both pure and carnal, and the more you fought the carnal side of it, the stronger it became."

Aldon's face twisted in anguish, and the hand holding the lantern spasmed. Rose heard quiet footsteps behind her and knew that Otis and Theodore were creeping up the stairs. She stretched out her arm behind her back to warn them to keep out of sight.

"Sewell was a gentle soul," Rose said. "He did not deserve to die."

"He fooled you, too. He was more evil than Julia. Julia tempted with her body, but Sewell—he tempted with his heart and his soul. How can a mere mortal fight such powerful evil?"

"Surely you tried with all your might? You are a Shaker novitiate. You knew you must be celibate, and yet you sinned right here in the village, didn't you."

"Satan worked through Sewell to tempt me into horrible evil," Aldon said. "And now the entire village must be purified by fire and by sacrifice."

"Wait," Rose cried, desperate to stop him. "You've already taken care of Julia and of Sewell. Why destroy the entire village? What have they done to deserve such a fate?"

"They are tainted. We are all tainted by the evil we allow to live among us. It is God's will that we all die."

"That is a lie. It was you alone. Did God tell you to try to throw suspicion onto Theodore and Johnny and the others? I think not."

As soon as the words left her mouth, she knew she had pushed too hard. Aldon roared like a wounded lion. "You do not know the mind of God," he cried. "We must all die." Just then, Honora groaned and lifted her head, distracting Aldon for a split second. Rose leaped up the last two steps and dove for his arm. She was too late. He dropped the lantern. Rose fell on the pile of rags, and the lantern landed inches from her face. Oil leaked from the lantern onto the pile of rags, cutting a trail of fire. Rose rolled away and struggled to her feet. Aldon seemed mesmerized by the growing flames, but Rose knew there wasn't much time.

"Warn the others," she cried. "Get everyone out." As Rose turned to go to Honora, Theodore rushed past her, toward Aldon. He pulled Aldon away from the flames. Aldon swung at Theodore's head and missed. Theodore countered with a blow to Aldon's stomach. The struggle took the men away from the alcove and to the side of the stairwell across from Honora and Rose.

Honora was conscious now, and shrieking. "It's all right," Rose shouted. "Stop wiggling so I can untie you and get you out of here. Honora, you've got to keep still and help me."

Honora tried to quiet her trembling. Rose could barely control her own fingers. The rope slipped out of her grasp. The rags had burst into a ball of flames that blocked the entrance to the stairwell. Honora writhed in panic, and her chair tilted sideways. Rose threw her body against it to stop it from falling toward the fire.

After precious moments, Rose was able to steady the

chair and slip the ropes over Honora's head and under her
feet. The delay had been costly. Flames had turned the pile
of rags to ashes and leaped to the dry wood of the desk and
chair. Rose looked over the banister. It protected three sides
of the stairwell. At the landing, the banister twisted into two
hairpin curves that slanted downward to form the railings for
the stairs. There was a space between the upper and lower
sections of railing through which Rose could see to the floor
below. The opening was just big enough for a person to slip
through and fall. Rose could easily jump over both banisters
to land on the stairs, but Honora was so panicked she might
not make it.

In the seconds it took to assess her situation, Rose was
vaguely aware that Otis was nowhere to be seen. Presumably he had gone to warn the residents to flee the dwelling
house. At least, she hoped he hadn't simply fled in terror.

The flames were gaining power. It was now or never.
Honora was a big woman, but Rose found the strength to
drag her to the railing and lift one of her legs over it.

"Honora, I want you to do exactly what I do. We are going
to jump for those stairs just below. They aren't far away, can
you see them?"

"I can't do it."

"You must. Watch what I do." She swung her leg over the
banister, then lifted the other over, so she was sitting precar-
iously on the thin length of wood. "You're already partly
there. Now lift your other leg, like I did. Come on."

Honora was whimpering with terror. Holding tightly to
the railing with one hand, Rose reached over to coax her.

"Rose, get out of the way. Now!"

It was Theodore's voice. She looked across to the other
side of the stairwell. Aldon had one leg over the banister and
was leaning forward. Theodore held his other ankle. Aldon
struggled wildly and slid farther over the railing, pulling
Theodore behind him.

There was no time even for prayer. In one desperate move, Rose shoved Honora back and away from the railing, while she pushed herself forward. She felt her heels hit something thin and hard, and then she crashed against the stairs. The force of her fall rolled her sideways. The opposite railing stopped her from tumbling down an entire flight of stairs.

As she came to a halt, she heard a piercing scream, and then a crash. She looked up to find Aldon hanging from the upper railing, one ankle still in Theodore's grip. Aldon was wriggling to free himself.

"Don't move," said a nearby voice. She obeyed. Otis jumped over her and ran up the stairs two at a time. She pulled herself up so she could see what was happening. Otis held something in front of him that momentarily hid the growing fire—a blanket or a cloak. With a leap, he threw himself on the desk and chair. All three crashed to the floor. Otis crawled and stomped with his hands, shouting a few choice curses.

"Rose, I can't—" Theodore cried.

Rose looked up and saw Aldon falling right toward her. She rolled out of the way just as Aldon crashed on the stairs and crumpled into a ball.

Theodore leaped over the railing and landed a few steps above Rose and Aldon. He bent over Aldon. "He'll be all right, just knocked out. Maybe a broken arm." He sounded disappointed.

Rose limped to the top of the stairs, where Otis wilted against the railing near the quenched fire.

"Sorry to ruin the furniture," Otis said, with a feeble grin.

Honora went to Aldon, knelt over him, and took his head in her lap. She stroked his forehead and murmured endearments between her sobs. "Let me take him," she begged. "I can make him well again."

Rose sat on the step above her and put a comforting hand

on her shoulder. It would be cruel to say what was in her mind, so she did not. Aldon had taken human lives, and he would have taken many more. Honora could no longer help him.

TWENTY-FOUR

THE TRAIN RIDE BACK TO NORTH HOMAGE SEEMED SLOWER
and quieter than the one to Hancock had been. Rose and
Gennie sat side by side, each preoccupied with her own
thoughts, silently watching the countryside gradually turn
from white to brown. Rose spent hours in prayer as she considered her role in the tragedies that had befallen Hancock
Village. Though Fannie had assured her she had saved all
their lives, Rose feared that by pressuring Sewell to confess
to her, she had also triggered Aldon to strike sooner than he
had intended. Sewell must have warned Aldon of his impending confession to Rose. Perhaps he even urged Aldon to
confess, as well.

Dulcie had destroyed her own baby and almost killed herself. Rose felt deeply responsible for Dulcie's tragic and
desperate act. Perhaps she wouldn't have leaped from the
upper floor of the Stone Barn if Rose had not urged her to
talk with Theodore. As a Shaker, Rose should not have forgotten how cruelly the world heaped shame on those who
were different. An unwed mother would be given no mercy.
She should have known.

At least Dulcie had agreed to let the sisters care for her
until she was fully recovered, and she could continue to
work for them. Her future might yet be bright—Otis, the unexpected hero, visited her daily.

Rose had done her best. Now there was nothing left but to pray—and to schedule a good long confession with Agatha once they were back in North Homage.

When she came up for air, Rose sensed that Gennie was confused and unhappy. She had lost her normal sparkle, and she showed no interest in chatting or exploring.

"Are you terribly angry with Grady?" Rose asked.

"Grady? Yes, I am. I told him so the last time we spoke on the telephone. We had a dreadful fight. Imagine hiring Helen Butterfield as some sort of detective and bodyguard, as if I couldn't take care of myself. And that detective he hired to watch me on the train nearly scared the life out of me. I'm glad I didn't know that the man he talked to when he got off the train was yet another detective Grady hired to spy on me. How could he have done such a thing?"

"He was worried something would happen to you. He loves you very much."

"He'd better find a different way of showing it," Gennie said, her pretty mouth puckered in a deep scowl.

"I suspect Grady has begun to realize he made a mistake. If he had asked me ahead of time, I would have warned him off. However, you must admit that Helen proved useful in the end."

Gennie relented with a slight laugh. "Yes, I nearly fainted with surprise when I saw her clumping along on those snow-shoes behind two police officers, after you all had already captured Aldon and saved the village. I thought she'd never catch her breath."

Rose laughed, too, and the atmosphere lightened—but only for a moment.

"Is there more bothering you, Gennie?"

Gennie nibbled her lower lip in silence for a minute, then turned to face Rose. "It's Aldon and Sewell," she said. "Carlotta told me all about it. She said they were . . . well, you know."

"That they fell into the flesh together?"

"I never heard of such a thing before."

"You have not been out in the world for very long, Gennie."

"Carlotta said they were wicked and unnatural and both deserved to die."

"Carlotta is wrong."

"Well, obviously Aldon went completely mad, but Sewell was a dear. He didn't deserve to die, did he?"

"Nay, he did not." Rose sighed. Indeed, celibacy was a blessed state, but so difficult for some people to live. "Gennie, would you like my thoughts on the matter?"

"Yes."

"I believe that the true evil in Hancock—excepting among the Believers, of course—was pride. Wretched, overweening pride. Aldon could not bear for the world to see him as anything but perfect and holy, nor could he bear to think of himself in any other way. The more he fought his impulses, the stronger they became. He needed to believe that he was the pure one, that it was the others who tempted him."

"Did he leave his church because he believed it was full of folks trying to lead him astray?" Gennie asked.

"In part, though I suspect he also feared that exposure was near." Rose thought about Billy, who had finally confided in her his horror at Aldon's attentions to him. He was too embarrassed to talk about it publicly, but someone else might be more willing to expose Aldon.

"So is he truly mad?"

"In the end," Rose said, "he began to see himself as God's instrument for destroying evil. He believed God condoned the killing of anyone Aldon deemed impure. Indeed, he is surely mad."

"But he deliberately planted evidence to incriminate other people," Gennie said. "He even made Sewell bring poor Honora to the village the night he poisoned the buckets in the barn. He knew how she'd act at a worship service. He made his own wife look guilty—along with practically everyone else."

"It's hard to know at what point his cunning veered into madness," Rose said. "Perhaps he began to believe that the others he was incriminating deserved the blame more than he did."

After a moment of quiet, Gennie said, "Now that I think of it, a certain Grady O'Neal has a bit too much pride. He seems to think he knows better than I do what's best for me."

"You're probably right," Rose said. "Will you be able to forgive him?"

Gennie grinned. "Oh, I suspect so—but maybe not until he's had a good long time to think about it."

Rose closed her eyes and finally relaxed. She was heading for home, spring was on the horizon, and little Gennie was all grown up.

DEN OF ANTIQUITY MYSTERIES

by
TAMAR MYERS

LARCENY AND OLD LACE
0-380-78239-1/$5.99 US/$7.99 Can

As owner of the Den of Antiquity, Abigail Timberlake
is accustomed to navigating the cutthroat world of rival
dealers at flea markets and auctions. But she never thought
she'd be putting her expertise in mayhem and detection to
other use—until her aunt was found murdered . . .

GILT BY ASSOCIATION
0-380-78237-5/$6.50 US/$8.50 Can

THE MING AND I
0-380-79255-9/$5.99 US/$7.99 Can

SO FAUX, SO GOOD
0-380-79254-0/$6.50 US/$8.50 Can

BAROQUE AND DESPERATE
0-380-80225-2/$6.50 US/$8.99 Can

ESTATE OF MIND
0-380-80227-9/$6.50 US/$8.99 Can

And coming soon
A PENNY URNED
0-380-81189-8/$6.50 US/$8.50 Can

Murder Is on the Menu
at the Hillside Manor Inn
Bed-and-Breakfast Mysteries by
MARY DAHEIM
featuring Judith McMonigle Flynn

CREEPS SUZETTE	0-380-80079-9/ $6.50 US/ $8.99 Can
BANTAM OF	
THE OPERA	0-380-76934-4/ $6.50 US/ $8.99 Can
JUST DESSERTS	0-380-76295-1/ $6.50 US/ $8.50 Can
FOWL PREY	0-380-76296-X/ $6.50 US/ $8.50 Can
HOLY TERRORS	0-380-76297-8/ $6.50 US/ $8.50 Can
DUNE TO DEATH	0-380-76933-6/ $6.50 US/ $8.50 Can
A FIT OF TEMPERA	0-380-77490-9/ $6.50 US/ $8.99 Can
MAJOR VICES	0-380-77491-7/ $6.50 US/ $8.99 Can
MURDER, MY SUITE	0-380-77877-7/ $6.50 US/ $8.99 Can
AUNTIE MAYHEM	0-380-77878-5/ $6.50 US/ $8.50 Can
NUTTY AS A	
FRUITCAKE	0-380-77879-3/ $6.50 US/ $8.99 Can
SEPTEMBER MOURN	0-380-78518-8/ $6.50 US/ $8.99 Can
WED AND BURIED	0-380-78520-X/ $5.99 US/ $7.99 Can
SNOW PLACE TO DIE	0-380-78521-8/ $6.50 US/ $8.99 Can
LEGS BENEDICT	0-380-80078-0/ $6.50 US/ $8.50 Can

And Coming Soon

A STREETCAR NAMED EXPIRE
0-380-80080-2/ $6.50 US/ $8.99 Can

....